HAWK

New York Times and USA Today Bestselling Author
HEIDI MCLAUGHLIN

THE BOYS OF SUMMER

HAWK

HAWK
THE BOYS OF SUMMER #4
HEIDI MCLAUGHLIN
© 2019

COVER DESIGN: Okay Creations.
EDITING: Ultra Editing Co.
Traci Blackwood
Models: Cody Smith | Madison Rae
Photography: RPLUSMPHOTO

 Created with Vellum

New York Times and *USA Today* bestselling author

HEIDI MCLAUGHLIN

Fall in love one book at a time.

BOSTON RENEGADES

It's another hot day down in Fort Myers. Those of us stuck in Boston aren't jealous at all! Wait, yes, we are. We've seen the sunny Florida photos posted on Instagram and we want it. We want the sun and the warmth. We want the snow to melt and for the wind chill to be non-existent! Come on, summer!

Now that we've complained enough about the weather, let's have some BoRe news!

Pitcher Max Tadashi is day-to-day with a sore shoulder. Rumor has it he hurt himself surfing. We reached out to pitching coach, Cole Fisk, via text message and he replied with "LOL". We're not sure what to make of it but as soon as we learn more, we'll update you.

With the recent acquisition of Damon Lamb, Coach Wilson is giving first basemen, Kayden Cross, a break . . . at least for now. Lamb, a recent graduate of Clemson has moved up the ranks rather quickly after a stint with the Lowell Spinners, the Portland Sea Dogs, and finally Pawtucket. He's expected to split time in the infield during the upcoming season.

GOSSIP WIRE

We're happy to share that this site, your very own *BoRe Blog*, has been listed as the official news source for the Boston Renegades . . . :throws confetti:: We can't thank our readers enough because if it wasn't for you reading, commenting and giving us tips, we wouldn't be the site we are. We also have to give a huge shout-out to GM Ryan Stone for giving us this opportunity.

The family unity is strong this year in Fort Myers. Lots of wives, children, parents, and in-laws have made the trek down.

Newlyweds, Travis Kidd and Saylor Blackwell-Kidd were spotted with their daughter, along with Cooper and Ainsley Bailey and their twins, at Disneyworld the other day. The couples look very happy as do the children.

ONE

HAWK

THE ONLY TIME I enjoy Florida is during spring training. It's not overly hot, muggy, or humid. The temps barely reach the eighties, which is perfect to me. After April, once we're up north and playing ball, coming down here to play is miserable. There's nothing like taking a shower, drying off, and putting on damp clothes or climbing between cool, wet sheets due to the humidity. Sure, the humidity in Boston can be a bitch, but it's nothing like in gator country.

There's a towel around my neck. It's one of those frog towels — in pink — and the guys like to tease me about it. One, I don't care about the color. I'm not ashamed to admit I like pink. Two, it keeps me cool and right now in the training room, I'm sweating like a hog walking toward a fire pit because the air conditioner is on the fritz . . . whatever that's supposed to mean.

The training room is a happening spot, though, with a group of us here for different ailments. Mine is mostly related to age. Not that I'm old, but you couldn't tell from my body. The aches, pains, and bones cracking when I get up each morning is a sure sign that I'm falling apart and that scares me. Pitchers don't have a long shelf life. Over time — and

I'm talking a few years, not decades — the strength in our arm starts to subside, our accuracy isn't as sharp, and we go from being a starter to a reliever, or if we're lucky, a closer. We just move down the line until retirement. Most of us are too pigheaded to hang it up, thinking we still have some gusto if we just train harder. Joke's on us. If our agents can't find us a team, we just wither away into the background. No big send off like teams used to do.

And what really freaks me out is the fact that lately I've been feeling tight. It doesn't matter what I do to loosen up, my body is stiff. My arm is sore, my hips ache, and my fingers feel numb when I wrap my hand around the ball. Probably not the best symptoms to have as we get ready to head into the season and it's the fear that something's wrong that keeps me from saying anything to the trainer. One word and I'm sidelined, added to the injured list, and sent down to the minors for rehab once I'm cleared. I'm not the only one who thinks like this. Most of us do. Right now, my primary catcher, Michael Cashman, has a deep thigh bruise which should keep him from playing. He hasn't said a word and the only reason I know is because we're sharing a hotel room and I've seen him buck naked. Not a sight I wish to see again, that's for sure. The trainers don't know because Cashman won't take his spandex off in the room. If they can't see it, they can't treat it and tell Coach that he needs rest. No one wants to start the season on the injured list.

Once therapy is done, the guys and I head out to the field. School's out for the day which means the fence will be lined with kids looking to meet us. Honestly, it's one of my favorite parts of the job, meeting the young fans. I can only hope that I'm the type of role model they need as they look forward to their future. I do what I can to stay out of the media, keeping my nose clean and my image about as spotless as I can.

Kids holler our name as we walk down the line. Hawk, Ethan, Travis, Cooper, Bryce . . . it's always funny when we have a new teammate, especially when they're a rookie and the young fans haven't learned their names yet. As they approach, the kids go quiet and wait for the rookies to sign. The rookies eat it up though, and encourage the kids to ask them questions. It's all part of the media training the Renegades must go through every year, thanks to likes of Ethan Davenport and Travis Kidd.

Baseballs, posters, and ball caps are held out for us to sign. But it's the kids with their trading card collection that gets most of my attention. I was once that boy, using my allowance to buy pack after pack of Topps Baseball Cards. My mom always scolded me for chewing the pink, chalky stick of gum, saying it was nothing more than paste and sugar and it was going to rot my teeth out, but I didn't care. There's nothing like getting a new pack of cards, sticking a wad of gum in your mouth so big that you could barely chew it, hopping on your bike and speed peddling over to the ballpark to swap with your friends. We never cared about the game until the crowd cheered and then we'd stop what we were doing and do our part as fans. Either hoot and holler because our team got a hit or scored a run or boo the other team for who knows what.

Watching these youngsters, with their notebook of cards, it brings back a lot of memories. I used to keep my cards organized by team and in alphabetical order. Each card slid gently into a sleeve to protect its value. When my mom finally cleaned out my bedroom back home in Montana, she asked me what she should do with the cards. "Keep them," I told her. "Put them someplace safe because someday they're going to be worth money." It's been awhile since I've been back home, and I should probably ask her what she ended up doing with them.

"Wow, my rookie card. I haven't seen one of these in years," I say to the young boy on the other side of the fence.

"I found it at a trade show, only five bucks."

Ouch. Is that all I'm worth — five bucks? I suppose being one of the highest paid pitchers in the majors doesn't equate to jack shit when it comes to a trading card. "Lucky you." I sign my name and hand the card back to him, watching as he meticulously puts the card back into the sleeve. "How much is it worth now?"

He looks at me and shrugs. "I'm not sure, but my dad says I robbed the guy blind when I bought it."

Without a doubt in my mind, I know the grin I'm sporting is wide and beaming. I like this kid's father. He should be my best friend. "Yeah ya did, buddy." I give him a fist bump and move down the line, signing everything that's handed to me. By the time I get to the end, my autograph looks like shit and my hand hurts. I try not to make a scene as I push my thumb into my palm, but it fucking hurts and I know I'm grimacing. I'm thankful my back is to the crowd, because kids or not, they're all on social media and the last thing I need is for someone to post about the pain they think I'm in.

We walk toward the dugout. Some of the guys are horsing around, a few are on the phone or texting, and some — like me — are lost in their own thoughts. I'm past the point of wondering if there's something wrong and on the verge of going to see a doctor. The thing is, I don't know what type of doctor to call and if I ask any of the trainers in the clubhouse . . . well that just can't happen. With Max Tadashi day-to-day, we're already a man down in our rotation. The team can't afford for me to be out, spring training or not.

As soon as I step into the dugout, Cole Fisk is coming toward me. He tosses a ball and thankfully I'm able to catch it. "You're up."

"For what?" I ask, playing stupid. It's not my day to pitch.

"Floyd is throwing like garbage. Wilson wants to change it up."

"Alright." The last thing I want to do is pitch, not with the way I'm feeling right now. Not that one more day of rest is going to change anything; I've felt like this for months, long before training started, and I've ignored it, thinking that whatever it is would go away with time.

I make my way toward the bullpen. The guys are throwing and horsing around. The fake smile is plastered on my face when I step through the gate being held open by Cashman. "Fucker," I mutter because I'm pissed he won't be catching for me tonight.

He laughs and pats me on the back. "I'll be back before the season starts."

"Should've taken care of that shit long before preseason." Who the hell am I to talk? I head over the mound and start my warmup with catcher, Jose Gonzalez. We toss back and forth until my arm starts to warm, and then my throws become harder. Right now, his chest is my target and he barely moves his glove to snag the ball.

"I'm ready," I tell him as he crouches down. We go through my arsenal of pitches. Fastball, cutter, breaking ball, slider, curve and the one that gets me every time I'm up to bat against a National League team: the knuckle ball. It's not my favorite to throw either, and the catcher has to be ready for the possibility of a wild pitch but I have it, just in case. It's something I taught myself while playing catch in the backyard of the ranch I grew up on. My high school coach made me use it primarily because no one could hit it. Made sense at the time and it's probably why we won a few championships. Still doesn't mean I like it.

Gonzalez stands and comes over to me. His mask rests on top of his head. Normally, you can see his dark hair, but today he's wearing a red do rag to keep the sweat from his eyes. "You doing okay?" he asks with his glove covering his mouth. The fact that he suspects anything is wrong and is trying to keep it on the down low says a lot about his character.

"I'm good."

"You sure? Because your fastball seems to be about eighty. Want me to turn on the clock?"

I shake my head. "Nah, just saving the heat for later."

He taps me on the shoulder and jogs back to the plate with his leg guards clanking together. I go through the motions again, this time adding what little strength I have left.

"Better, man." He tosses the ball back.

Right, better. Never mind the pain. I can get through whatever it is I'm battling. I just need to double up on the ibuprofen because it's probably just inflammation, and I know I can treat that.

We're signaled to make our way to the dugout for the start of the game. The stands are filled, and people line the fence in their portable chairs, their buckets of popcorn in their laps. You'd think after years of playing baseball I'd hate the smell of hot dogs and popcorn, but I don't. I love it. It's a sign of spring and summer and a rite of passage for any baseball fan. Any sports fan for that matter. That's how you know the game is about to begin.

The starting line-ups are announced, and the national anthem sung. As I head out to the mound, I tell myself I can do this. And I can. I can be the best. I threw three days ago and was fine. No issues.

After my five warmup pitches, I'm good. I'm loose. I'm feeling great. I step to the rubber after the first batter enters the box. Gonzalez gives me the pitch, fast ball, right corner. I think about shaking him off but know what he's doing. I have to trust him. I start my motion, kick my leg up and cock my arm back, and follow through my pitch, watching Gonzalez barely move his mitt to catch my fastball.

"Strike," the ump hollers, although it sounds more like he's grunting.

Pitch after pitch.

Batter after batter.

My arm is on fire.

And I don't mean the good kind even though we have a three to nothing lead. My shoulder burns, my fingers are numb, but I'm in the zone. In between innings, I sit in the dugout and root on my teammates. I wear my coat, even though it's warm out, and when it's my turn to bat, I approach the plate with confidence.

It's nothing more than a façade. I'm in so much pain, I want to quit.

But I won't.

TWO

BELLAMY

THE STOP SIGN MOCKS ME. I've come to a full and complete stop, and yet I'm still sitting here, waiting to make a right turn into our subdivision. I'm trying to hold it together, to not cry in front of my son, but it's difficult. The move to Montana from Spokane has been hard on my son. He's struggled to fit in, and whether it's been two years or two days, seeing him so sad has made me wonder many times if I made the right choice when I uprooted us and moved here. I thought it would be better for him with my mother being here and all, but the only person to benefit has been me.

My little guy has his head resting against the backseat window. His eyes are puffy and red from the heartache he feels after being told he didn't make the baseball team. I wish I could take his pain away and tell him that everything will be okay, but I don't know that it's true. How do I tell my son to keep trying, to keep working, if all he hears is that he's not good enough? Even I want him to give up and try something different, and I shouldn't feel that way. I should be the one encouraging him to follow his dreams, telling him he can be anything he wants to be, and yet I just want to wrap him in my arms to keep him safe from this big, scary world.

"Hey, bud, I see Brady. Maybe you guys can ride your bikes today."

Chase sighs heavily. "Brady made the team."

Of course, he did.

I finally let my foot off the brake and inch forward. There are so many kids in the neighborhood that I'm always afraid one will dart out in front of me. Kids these days aren't always paying attention to their surroundings, they're more interested in their cellphones or portable gaming devices. After I turn right, I make an immediate left down another road, and then right again until reaching the cul-de-sac where my ranch style home sits back off the road.

"Want to get pizza for dinner?" I ask after shutting the car off. I'm trying to do whatever I can to lift his spirits.

"No, thanks." Chase opens the door and gets out of the car. He all but drags himself to the front door while I stay in the car, watching him. My phone rings and as I pick it up, I see it's Chase's father calling. I'm tempted to send him to voicemail, but he'll call until I answer because he hates leaving messages.

"Hello?"

"Bell, it's Greg." He does this every time, as if my caller ID doesn't tell me who it is or that after knowing him for seventeen years, I've forgotten his voice.

"I'm aware." Since he walked out on Chase and me, I've been less than cordial. It's a slap in the face to think you're happily married to your high school sweetheart and running a very successful business, only to find out that your husband not only had an affair but got his mistress pregnant and has chosen her over his family. Fun times all around.

His lackluster parenting is what really prompted our move to Richfield, Montana. It's hard enough going through a divorce, especially when it takes you by surprise, but when your eight-year-old son (at the time) misses his father and Daddy can't be bothered to spend any time with him, divorce

becomes incredibly messy. Greg didn't balk when I told him
that we were going to move to Montana — he just said he
thought it would be a great idea, and that he had an old
college buddy here that could "help me out" when I needed
something. Now, even though we're hundreds of miles away
from each other, he's constantly in my business. He couldn't
have cared less when we lived in the same city, but now I can't
eat dinner out without Greg knowing.

I don't need anything bad enough from him to deal with
that shit.

Besides, his college buddy is the same man who keeps
cutting my kid from the baseball team. So, once again, Greg
fails his family. So much for him 'helping out'.

"Tryouts ended today?"

I roll my eyes. He already knows. "Yep."

He must adjust a stack of contracts on his desk because I
can hear papers shuffling. Not to mention he's sighing heavily
and muttering under this breath. "Bellamy," he says my name
with such frustration and exaggeration. I imagine he's
pinching the bridge of his nose. "He didn't make the team.
Brett called me right after. He really needs to try harder or
he's never going to amount to anything."

I pull my phone away from my ear and flip it off, wishing
like hell he could see me. "There's more to life than baseball,
Greg."

"He's a boy. Boys play sports."

"And read books, play video games, ride bikes . . . he's
living the life of a ten-year-old, not that you would know."

"Bell . . ."

"Don't *Bell* me. Are you coming for Easter? You're
supposed to."

He sighs. "Priscilla—"

"I don't want to hear your excuses, Greg. I just want an
answer. You need to spend some time with your son. If
you're coming let me know. As far as baseball goes, I don't

know why he didn't make the team; Brett didn't say anything to me so you can ask him yourself if you want to know why. Chase has done everything he can to get better. He's gone to camps. He's done all the workouts with Brett. So, I don't know what else to do, but I do know it's really none of your business."

"He's still my son."

"Ha!"

"Bell, your attitude doesn't help. I'm trying to do my best."

"Right. Anything else?"

He grumbles something unintelligible. "I'll talk to Brett. Maybe Chase can practice with the team."

"And what, not play in the games? Where's the fun in that?"

"It's better than nothing and it gets him out of the house, making friends."

He has friends . . . except he really doesn't. He tags along with a few of the neighborhood kids, but no one ever comes over to the house and asks him to play. I glance at the house, wondering what my son is doing.

"Do you want to talk to Chase?"

"I'm on my way to a meeting. I'll call him later."

That's code for no.

"Whatever, *Dad*." I hang up, not giving him a chance to respond. He calls his son once a week, if that, and only for a few minutes. I squeeze my phone and scream, wishing like hell I could wring Greg's neck. After a few minutes with my temper tantrum, I emerge from my car and head into the house.

When I walk through the door, I know I won't find Chase in the living room or kitchen. He's either in his room or in the backyard, trying to get better at baseball. I knock on his door and hear his tiny voice telling me to come in. His walls are decorated with posters of different sports players. I have no idea who they are, but he talks about them like he's known them all his whole life.

Chase is on his bed, facing the wall. I lay down next to him on his comforter which has every baseball team logo on it. It was a gift from Santa last Christmas. "What's for dinner, bud?"

"Dunno."

"I'm not familiar with that restaurant. Or is it food? Does Grandma know how to make it? Do you know what's in it?"

Silence.

I reach for his hand and he gives it freely. I know there will be a day when holding your mom's hand is uncool, but until then, I'm going to do this until he tells me we have to stop. "I know you work hard, Chase. I wish there was something I could say or do to make things seem fair."

"It's because I'm not friends with Matty and B Mac. They're the cool kids. They decide who's on the team."

"Well I think you're a pretty cool kid." I push his hip a little bit, hoping he laughs, but he doesn't and that makes me want to cry.

"You have to say that because you're my mom."

"Actually, I don't." As much as I hate letting go of his hand, I do it so I can turn and face his back. I run my fingers through his light brown hair and wish things were easier for him. "When I was a little girl, my dad used to tell me that if I wanted to be friends with someone, I just had to walk up to them and tell them."

"That was the olden days. It doesn't work like that anymore, Mom."

Ouch, bud. "Well, how about we have a party for your birthday? We can invite all the kids from your class. We can get one of those jumpy castle things and a pinata."

"I'm not a baby."

"You're *my* baby."

"Kids will make fun of me. They already call me a baby and a loser at school because I'm so short."

There's no holding back my tears no matter how hard I try. I pull him to my chest and weep. His plight breaks my heart. I don't even know what to do to help him, except love him and try to give him every reassurance I can. My words though, fall on deaf ears because of the actions of others. I know my son isn't perfect. I know he has faults and can be a sasshole sometimes, but he's still just a child who should only have to worry about his homework and when to come in for dinner.

We stay like this well into the night, with dinner long forgotten and my ringing cell phone ignored. There isn't a single person that I need to speak to that can't wait until later. At some point, Chase turns to face me.

"How come Dad doesn't come visit me?"

Loaded question. I inhale deeply, giving myself a moment to compose my thoughts. As much as I want to badmouth his father, I won't. With only his nightlight illuminating the room, I smile. "Bud, I wish I had an answer for you, but I don't. Your father is busy at work and your sister is still really little."

"She's not my sister."

"She is, but I understand why you say that. The decision your dad made, it's not her fault. It's not yours either. You're both just caught up in adult drama."

His eyes start to water. "I don't care. I hate him," he says through tears. "I hate him so much."

Me too, bud. I pull him to my chest and hold him while he cries. Anger burns deep inside me . . . at his father, at the Little League coaches, at the kids who just can't be nice. I don't want to be *that* mom, but I can't sit by and watch as my son loses a bit of himself each time he gets knocked down.

When Chase is finally asleep, I slip out of his room. My purse and briefcase are by the door where I left them. There are real estate contracts that need to be signed, scanned, and emailed but those are going to have to wait until later. I pick up my cell phone, scroll through my contacts until I come to Brett Larsen's name and hit the text bubble.

Hi, Brett - it's Bellamy Patrick, Chase's mom. What can I do to help my son? Two years in a row now he hasn't made the team. I've sent him to camps, clinics and have paid you for private work-outs. Is he that bad of a player?

I read and reread the message, hoping I don't sound desperate. If my son needs a different hobby, I need to know. But this coach, Brett, who is friends with my ex-husband, insists Chase has what it takes yet won't give him an opportunity. My stomach growls but I'm not sure I can eat anything, and when I look in the refrigerator, nothing looks appealing.

Brett makes me wait almost an hour before he responds. My finger hovers over the alert, afraid of what his message might say.

Meet me tomorrow and we can discuss.
Where?
My office, lunch time.
I'll be there.
Maybe something positive will come from this meeting.

BOSTON RENEGADES

Hawk Sinclair has been placed on the 10-day injured list. No word yet on what his ailment is, but we do know it has to do with his throwing arm. Sinclair left the game the other night and while most of us thought it was a pitching change, Sinclair was pulled due to injury and sent back to Boston for further evaluation.

When we reached out to pitching coach, Cole Fisk, he gave us a Bill Belichick type response, saying that Hawk flew like a bird! I don't know about you, BoRe fans, but having two smart ass coaches in Boston is way too many for our liking.

With Sinclair out of the rotation, all eyes are on Max Tadashi, waiting to see if he will remain day-to-day.

GOSSIP WIRE

Ethan Davenport's niece, Shea, took a foul ball to the shoulder the other day. The kicker? It was off her uncle's bat. No word on if the two are on speaking terms, but grandmother assured us that Shea is fine and angry that her uncle was too fast on his swing.

With the off-season acquisition of pitcher, Seth West, his girlfriend (Dallas Cowboy cheerleader, Seraphina

Davies) has joined him in Florida and seems to be fitting in with the other WAG's. Welcome to the Renegades, Seth.

THREE

HAWK

BY THE THIRD INNING, I'm garbage. I'm fighting to stay in the game, shaking off any type of fastball Gonzalez is asking for because I can't muster up the strength to get my arm to throw with any velocity. In between innings, he's in my ear, asking me if I'm okay. I give him one-word answers because anything else just won't suffice. I'm waiting for him to go to Fisk or Wilson and tell them that I need to be yanked. But he won't. There's a creed among pitchers and catchers. We have each other's backs, no matter what.

It's the bottom of the fourth. My coat is off, my glove is in my hand and I'm walking to the mound along with Gonzalez. He bends and picks the ball up, holding it in his hand. "Are you sure?"

"Of course," I lie to him.

With visible reluctance he sets the game ball into my glove and walks toward the plate. Once he crouches down, I start my warm-up pitches. My arm protests and I have no doubt in my mind that my face shows every detail of the pain I'm in.

The batter steps into the box. I hide my face behind my glove so only he and Gonzalez can see my eyes. If they saw my face, they'd see me gnawing at my lower lip. I inhale deeply and let the air out of my lungs as slowly as possible. I don't want to do this, not anymore. I need rest, medical attention, and a freaking ice bath. The sign is given, fastball-high-inside. My body goes through the motions. My arm cocks back, my leg kicks out, and I'm grunting. I give it everything I have to get this ball to the plate.

As soon as I release the ball, I double over in pain and scream out. There's commotion all around me but all I see is blurry cleats. Hands are on my back and multiple people are asking me questions that I can't answer because I can't catch my breath.

Wilson crouches down so he can look at me. "What's up, Hawk?" I don't even have to say anything, he knows. "Is it your back? Can you walk?"

"No, I can walk. It's my arm." I straighten and glance into the stands. The nice thing about spring training is that it's intimate, our fans are close. It also means they don't miss anything when something happens to a member of the team. I can see the concerned look on their faces and pray my parents aren't watching this game. If they are, there's no doubt my mom is on the phone, trying to get a hold of anyone who can give her answers. Our GM, Ryan Stone, made the mistake of giving her his cell number years ago and I bet he's regretting that now.

"Let's get you to the trainer."

I don't need help walking but he keeps his hand on my back the entire walk to the dugout. Everyone in the stands is clapping. I raise my arm — my left, not my right — and wave to everyone. Wilson passes me off to Fisk, who walks with me to the training room.

"Pulled a muscle?"

"I don't know, Coach. I can't feel my arm." I happen to look at him when I say those words and wish I hadn't. I don't need to ask him what he's thinking because it's written all over his face — he's deeply concerned. And I know he can see that mine is screaming, "I'm fucking scared."

Inside the training room, a couple of the trainers are setting up the machines we often use: Stim and ultrasound, but something tells me that neither of these are going to work. I've never had an injury that's resulted in scarring, that I'm aware of, so ultrasound really isn't going to do anything for me. And stim . . . well everyone thinks stim fixes everything. I've never been a fan of the deep pulsating action, but what do I know?

Cait, our lead trainer, has me sit on the table. When Stone hired her, the guys were very hesitant about coming to see her. Mostly because she's very pretty. After a few days on the field with her, we realized she's just one of the guys. Doesn't mean we don't try to flirt with her though.

She and Fisk talk for a minute before he turns to leave. He has a group to coach, after all. "So, what happened?" she starts preparing the electrodes. "I turned away right before it all went down."

"Dunno, can't feel my arm."

She pauses for a moment and sets the electrodes down. "At all?"

I shake my head quickly. "If I do, it burns and feels heavy. It's an effort to move it."

"Bad stretch?"

This is where I lie. "Maybe I slept on it wrong?" It's too early to hit the IL and my team needs me. The last couple of years, we've been expected to make a playoff run but we always seem to fuck it up when it counts the most. Whatever is going on with my arm needs to be fixed within ten days, at the most.

"Possible, but unlikely to cause you this much pain. Lie down, please."

I do as she asks. She starts moving my arm in every direction she can, adding pressure in different places. I know the whole time while her hands are trained to feel for any abnormalities, she's trained to watch our faces because try as we might, we can't hide pain forever.

"I don't feel anything pulling and definitely no knots. I'm going to start you on stim and then we'll do massage for a bit. See if that can loosen whatever is going on in there."

She places the electrodes on my arm, turns on the machine and disappears. With my free arm draped over my eyes, I try to visualize the annoying sensation actually doing something to help my arm, but it's hard. Every so often, I jump from the stimulation and when I do, my sore arm throbs so much that the pain brings tears to my eyes.

"Are you okay?"

I hadn't heard her come back. I nod, but I'm sure she knows what's going on under my arm. There's no need for me to make eye contact with her. The last thing I want to show her is that I can't take the pain. Cait removes the electrodes and adds some oil to my skin. From her first touch, I hiss.

"Stop," I tell her.

"It hurts when I touch your arm?"

"It hurts no matter what. I think the stim made it worse."

"I'll be right back. I'm going to go make you an appointment with the physician."

"For what?"

She gives me a sad stare. "I'm not sure."

Over the last couple of days, I have been poked, prodded, and studied as if I'm some medical mystery. I can't explain it. My arm hurts when I lift it, leave it by my side, when it's in a sling, and especially when I bump it against something. I can't drive, at least not with my right arm. Sleeping is almost impossible. Dressing myself is even harder and for the first time in my adult life I wish I had a damn girlfriend or wife, or at least wish my mother was here so someone could help me. Although, asking my mother to pull down my shorts so I can use the bathroom is not high on my priority list. I'm not sure I'd even ask a girlfriend, but a wife — definitely. It's that whole sickness and health vow that I'd take advantage of.

Today, I'm stuffed into a tube for an MRI. The nice tech gave some old-fashioned headphones, the kind we got back in the late eighties/early nineties with our Walkman. She didn't, however, ask me what type of music I'd like to listen to, which I think is a ploy on her part. I can't move, not that I want to anyway because doing so would cause excruciating pain in my arm, and the music she has playing through these headphones is soft jazz or classical. I'm not a music aficionado by any means so I can't be sure what's playing. What I do know is it's putting me to sleep, which is fine. Everyone can use a thirty-minute power nap during the day.

When the table I'm lying on starts to move, my eyes flash open and blink rapidly to adjust to the lighting. I make sure the johnnie I'm wearing is still covering all the important parts and try to sit up without using my arm so much.

"The radiologist will look this over today and give you a call."

"Great, thanks."

She walks me back to the changing room and wishes me a good day. Inside, there's a few men of various ages. I do everything I can to avoid eye contact, but the young one in here knows who I am.

"Hawk Sinclair, right?"

Man, how I want to say no, but my full sleeve of tattoos is a dead giveaway. Plus, my return to Boston without my team has been highly publicized thanks to the *BoRe Blog*. When Stone told us that the BoRe reporter was going to have exclusives, we thought he was joking. We understand ESPN, Fox Sports and our very own NESN getting the exclusives, but a blog? Hard to believe, but I guess things are changing in terms of spreading the news.

What I'm going through isn't news though. It's a damn travesty and should be kept in the clubhouse. I was hoping Wilson wouldn't put me on the IL, that this issue would stay under wraps, but when I wasn't ready three days later, he had no choice. Between him, Stone and Cait, they all thought it best that I return to Boston to seek treatment. The only thing I've done since my return is spend hours in physical therapy and doctor appointments.

"Hey, man. How's it going?"

The fan sticks his hand out to shake mine, leaving me no choice but to keep the smokescreen up that everything's okay. We shake and pain radiates through my arm.

"Think I could get an autograph?"

I look down at what I'm wearing, wondering if my ass is hanging out for all to see. "Uh, sure. Let me change first."

"Oh, okay." He looks dejected. I mean, what am I supposed to do? Just sign while wearing this hospital gown? And what am I signing? He has nothing for me to write on.

Pulling my clothes out of my locker, I turn and find the guy right behind me. I smile and sidestep past him and into a room. Thank God the door locks and I can dress as slow as possible. Not that I'm doing that on purpose; it really does take me a long time to get dressed these days. I'm hoping that by the time I come out, he's gone, and I won't have to worry about forcing my arm into writing my name. It was hard enough when I had to fill out page after page of information on my injury.

When did it happen? I don't know.

On a scale of one to ten, where is your pain level? A million.

Do you feel more pain in the morning or evening? Um, all the time.

Do you feel safe at home? Nope, not at all. Those shadows that lurk in the corners get me every time.

On a scale of one to ten, when you're doing your normal daily activities, how do you feel? Like I want to die!

When I open the door, the guy is standing there, but this time he has a sheet of paper and a pen ready for me. I smile, grab the pen, and scribble my name. It hurts like fucking hell, but I do it.

"Please make it out: 'To Terry, thanks for being my biggest fan, Love Hawk'."

My hand pauses on the paper. Is this guy for real? There's no way I can write that much, not right now. "Sorry, gotta run," I tell him as I set the pen down and book it for the door. There's a time and place for autographs and photos, and the hospital dressing room isn't one of them.

FOUR

BELLAMY

BEING LATE for anything is one of my biggest pet peeves. My clients, who just *had* to see a farmhouse on fifty acres which is forty miles from town at half past ten this morning, were almost an hour late and are taking their sweet time walking through the house. Every time the husband turns and looks at me, I smile sweetly even though I'm wringing their necks in my mind. My meeting with Brett Larsen is soon. Even if I leave now, don't hit any traffic and speed, I'll be late, and that's the last thing I need when I'm trying to do whatever I can to help my son.

After a thorough walk through highlighting all the features of this house, then taking them out onto the back porch to show them the view, I left them to talk it over. And they're still talking. This house has been on the market for over a year. It's not going anywhere. They could easily have the conversation about whether to invest in a massive piece of land at home. Not while I'm pacing back and forth on the front porch, wringing my hands together, and glancing into one of the two large picture windows. To make matters worse the husband seems to know when I'm passing by each time, and just happens to turn his head to smile creepily at me.

There's no doubt in my mind that I'm exaggerating all of this, but the fact remains that they were late, which is making me late for my next appointment. I'm about to go back into the house to see if there's anything else they need, hoping to speed things up because I really need to go, when the door opens, and they walk out. They're holding hands and both are smiling. Instant gratification soars through me as I know they've decided to buy the place. *Finally*. The sellers will be ecstatic now they've moved to the big city and adapted to condo living. Can't say I blame them. One reason I bought my house where I did was because of the HOA. The homeowner's association has a landscaping company that comes in during the spring, summer and fall to maintain our yards and they plow in the winter. For a single mom, these are huge benefits.

"Beautiful home, isn't it?" I direct my question toward the wife. I'm normally spot on with reading people. Mostly when I'm showing a house, I can tell right away if the buyers are remotely interested. It's usually the wife. If she doesn't love the entrance from the second she walks in, all bets are off.

The husband beams while the wife looks pensive. There's something she's unsure of and I sense that it's her husband who wants this house. She needs my attention. I take her by the arm and ask her to follow me and also ask the husband to stay where put. We walk up the stairs and I use buzz words like 'grand' and 'elegant'. When we step into the master bedroom, we keep walking until we are in the bathroom. I move over to the window and sigh. The view from the upstairs is breathtaking and I need to sell her on it.

"The house has been on the market for a while," I remind her. "We can negotiate a better selling price. And when we do, I think you should take the savings and redo this bathroom. Make it your sanctuary: Radiant floor heating so you're never cold. A walk-in closet with built-ins. A stand-up shower in the corner with dual sprayers, and by the window, put in a deep garden tub so you can look out. I can see you soaking, watching the snow fall." I finish with a satisfying sigh and a long pause. "That's what I would do in this room."

"It's so far from the city."

I'm in complete agreement and fight the urge to look at my phone. My meeting with Brett will not happen today and there isn't anything I can do about it. As much as my son comes first, so does work. Without my job, I can't pay the bills, and lord knows his father isn't going to cough up any extra child support.

"There's a lot to be said about living away from the city. It's quiet, the air is cleaner and if you want to walk around in your pajamas all day, who is going to see you?"

"It takes longer for police, fire and ambulances to reach you. People target out of the way homes for crime," she adds.

"The crime rate is so low here, it's not even a statistic, and there's a fire station a mile down the road." I know I've lost the sale. If she's paranoid about safety, there's no way she's going to make an offer on this place. "Let's head back downstairs."

Her husband's sitting on the steps when we walk out. He smiles, but it quickly changes as he takes in his wife's demeanor. He wants the house, probably to hunt and fish on the property, but it's clear he's going to have to convince her this is the right place for them.

"You have my contact details. Let me know what you decide. In the meantime, I'll continue to look through the MLS for anything that might suit you better."

"Thank you, Bellamy, for meeting us today."

"Of course, we'll speak soon." They walk to their car and as eager as I am to get the hell out of here, I wait until they're out of sight before putting the lockbox back together and making sure the door is secured. This isn't the first time I've lost a sale and it's definitely not going to be the last, but it frustrates me, nonetheless. With them being adamant they see the house today and then being late, there was a sliver of hope they'd make an offer.

As soon as I'm in my car and my Bluetooth connects, I ask the AI to text Brett Larsen and wait for her to tell me to start speaking.

I'm so sorry, Brett. I've been with a client all morning. Can we reschedule?

The text sends as I speed down the road and as luck would have it, traffic is stopped. I don't remember seeing any construction signs along the road when I came through so I can only assume the cowboys from the nearby ranch are moving their cattle. If I've caught the tail end of it, I honestly won't mind. That means I'll get to stare longingly at men on horseback, watching them wrangle the steer. If they just started though, I could be here for a bit.

Luckily, I have cell service and Brett texts me back. He tells me he's tied up for the rest of the afternoon and suggests dinner. I look at my calendar and see that I have a PTA meeting tonight and a few showings the next couple of nights. I tell Brett that I'm not free and suggest lunch tomorrow. I don't want to put this off any longer.

Busy until Friday. Dinner work?

Perfect. I think it would be great for Matty and Chase to spend some time together.

No children. Adults only.

Should I touch base with Annie?

No need. She has a book club thing that night.

Oh, book club. Maybe I should talk to her about joining. It would be nice to sit around with other women, discussing the merits of literature while drinking wine. Of course, I'm not up to date on the latest trends when it comes to reading. I still prefer a paperback over an eBook and will listen to audio-books while I'm driving, but most of those are self-help narrations. *How to Be a Better Parent. Single Parents Unite. Parenting with an Absent Partner.* Come to think of it, maybe I should listen to a romance book or two because these parenting books aren't helping at all.

Oh, okay. Where and what time?

Maria's. Eight o'clock. I'll make the reservation.

After the AI reads his reply, I grab my phone and look at the screen. Surely, I heard her wrong because why would he want to meet at the nicest, most expensive restaurant in town? Maybe the other coaches will be there. That would be ideal; then they could give me a list of Chase's weaknesses and what I can do to help him.

See you there!

I feel good about this meeting and I'm confident that Chase will be on the right path to make the little league team. It doesn't even have to be Brett's team, although according to Chase that's the best one. Any team would do for now. He needs the playing experience and the consistent practice. Before traffic starts moving again, I send a text to my mom, asking her if she can watch Chase for a bit. With dinner, the meeting shouldn't take longer than an hour and a half, two, tops. We can talk before and while we're eating to save time.

By the time I make it back to town, I'm starving, in need of coffee and know I should stop by my office to at least make an appearance. We're not required to be there every day as we work solely off commission, but it's nice to touch base with the in-office staff.

The bell on the door chimes as I push it open. My best work friend and office manager for the real estate company, Karter Watson, smiles when she sees me and comes around the oval shaped desk. She's normally in her office so I'm surprised and elated to see her.

"Lunch, let's go," she says as she grabs my arm and takes me back outside. We walk a few doors down and enter Betty's Bakery. Growing up here, Betty's only served breakfast. About five years ago, her daughter took over and expanded to lunch, which has paid off in dividends for their business. They're always busy and sometimes have a line out the door, especially when they start making and serving their pumpkin donuts.

"Why so eager?" I adjust my briefcase and purse as people push by to check in with the hostess or leave.

"Owen has been up my ass all morning," she mutters under her breath.

"Why are you whispering?"

She looks around and before she can answer the hostess calls out her name. "Did you have a reservation?" I ask her.

"Yes, I was eating here no matter what after the shit show this morning."

The hostess shows us to our table, sets the menus down and leaves us. I lean forward. "Tell me what's going on."

"Phoebe had an affair. Owen found out last night."

"What?" Phoebe and Owen were high school sweethearts, like most married couples in town. Affairs aren't unheard of here, just not very common.

Karter nods. "Owen came storming in this morning, slamming things around, and you know how I feel about that stuff. So, I go in there, ask him what his problem is, and he looks at me. Bell, his eyes were menacing. I've never seen him look so angry before. He tells me that he caught Phoebe in action with Eddie Peterson."

I gasp and cover my mouth with my hand. "No!" Eddie and Owen have been best friends since elementary school and inseparable.

"Yeah, can you believe that?"

"No, I can't. Eddie? Really?"

"I said the same thing, like there's no way. Their kids freaking play together, right?"

"Uh huh."

"Right, so me being me, I called Phoebe's sister, Janelle,

and asked what's up because surely Phoebe would've called her sister, right."

I nod, trying to keep up.

"Shocker. Janelle had no idea. She called Phoebe, Phoebe called Owen, who ripped me a new one for butting my nose in where it doesn't belong."

"You're literally the town gossip," I tell her, and she shrugs.

"Owen shouldn't have said anything, but he did. Like, with details that I really didn't need to know."

As tempted as I am to ask, I don't. When the waitress comes by, we look at our menus quickly and place our orders. After she's gone, I make the mistake of telling Karter that I'm going to dinner with Brett and the other coaches.

"Girl, don't. Brett Larsen is evil scum and he probably wants something from you."

"A house? I can't offer him anything else."

She cocks her eyebrow at me and eyes me up and down, but I brush her off. "He's married and will no doubt have heard about Owen and Phoebe. This town can't handle another scandal." Besides, he's a coach and coaches help children get better. That's his job.

FIVE
HAWK

AS A PROFESSIONAL ATHLETE, the last thing you ever want to hear is that you need surgery, especially when it's on the part of your body that makes your money, and the season has already started. I have what's called thoracic outlet syndrome. It's the cause of the numbness in my hand and fingers and explains why my arm has felt tired and hurts to move. Unfortunately, it's becoming more and more common for pitchers to experience this. A few of my peers have opted for physical therapy, while most have gone straight for surgery. That's where I'm at, in recovery.

The MRI showed a pinched nerve in my neck. I thought it would be easy to take care of — massage, stretching and a few trips to the chiropractor and I should be good as new. I was wrong. According to the doctor, the veins and blood vessels in my shoulder and neck were compressed, resulting in the pain and numbness I felt. Removing what is known as the first rib in my shoulder, dissecting the muscles and nerves was the only option.

Telling Wilson, Fisk and Stone was not easy and thankfully I wasn't the one who had to do most of the talking, the doctor was. Still, before I went under the knife to have the uppermost rib removed, I questioned everything. Mostly, my recovery time. I would have full use of my arm in a few days, but the muscles around my shoulder would be weakened from surgery. I would be out a minimum of twelve weeks, almost half the season. That's a hard pill to swallow when your team has high hopes of making the playoffs. It's even harder to look your teammates in the eyes knowing they're battling their own injuries, some that likely also need surgery but they're waiting until the season is over.

There's a machine beside me beeping. And another one. And another one. I can't see the others, but I can hear them and the more I focus on the sounds, the louder they become. I try to lift my arm. It's second nature for me to use my right arm to do everything, but the pain brings tears to my eyes.

"Don't move your arm." Her voice is soft and quiet. I open my eyes and look to see who is speaking but my curtained off space is empty. It's just me and the machine. I watch it for a minute, studying the green line moving in waves, monitoring my heartbeat. My mouth is dry, and it feels like I'm waking up from an all-night bender — something I haven't done since Travis Kidd got married on New Year's Eve. I smack my lips together to try and create some saliva to get rid of the dryness.

"Here, drink this."

Ah, the angel with the prettiest voice is back. I try to do as she instructs, sipping through the straw but it ain't easy. I'm groggy, my fine motor skills are shit right now and my tongue feels like a foreign object.

"Are you in pain?"

What kind of question is that? The surgeon cut into my collar bone and neck, removed a bone, and she wants to know if I'm in pain? Of course, I am . . . or am I? Her question gives me pause. My arm is sore. There's no doubt about that, but I'm not sure if it's because I know it is or if I'm in pain.

I grunt out a half intelligible response but I'm not

convinced she's paying attention because she's focused on my chart and the monitor. She presses some buttons and tells me she'll be back shortly. I think I tell her okay or I nod, I'm not sure which to be honest.

At some point I must've dozed off because when I open my eyes again, things are much clearer and my mom is sitting next to my bed, reading a book. Once again, I try to lift my arm to rub my face, but the pain — which I'm *definitely* feeling now — is too much and I cry out.

"Don't move your arm, Hawk."

"Yeah, I've heard that before."

"Well, maybe you'll start listening." My mom appears by my side, smiling. Even though my hair is short, she brushes it away from my forehead. "How are you feeling?"

"Tired."

"Any pain? Want me to get the nurse?"

I start to shake my head, only to have pain radiate through my entire body.

"You may not want to do that."

"I'd really like to cuss at you," I tell my mom who smiles sweetly at me. She knows I wouldn't, but there are times, like right now, when I'd love to be a smartass and say something sarcastic to her.

"I don't care how old you are, I'll wash that mouth out with soap."

"I don't doubt it," I mumble.

Mom frets with the blankets on my bed, making sure I'm okay, and finally presses the button for the nurse. I sense that she's fighting back her tears. When I called to tell my parents that my season was likely over, my mom cried. My dad did the "macho dad thing" and told me everything would be okay. I'm doing my best to believe him, but I'm not so sure.

Out of the others I know of who have had this done, only one was sidelined a bit longer than expected but he also had

Tommy John surgery beforehand and missed two seasons. Since then, he's been unstoppable in most games.

The nurse comes in, checks my vitals, and tells me that I need to get up and walk every two hours to keep the blood clots from forming. Great, another ailment to worry about. She says my mom can assist me and to feel free to use the hallway to get my exercise. After she leaves, my mom stands next to me expectantly.

"What? Now?"

"Are you waiting for the Renegades to win the pennant?"

"That's a low blow, Ma."

She chuckles and moves my IV stand out of the way so she can reach me easier. "Moving is going to hurt, but I got you."

That she has. For as long as I can remember, my mom has been my rock, my biggest cheerleader, supporter, and best friend. There isn't a doubt in my mind that she has my back and will do what needs to be done to make sure I'm on the path to recovery.

The decision to return to my hometown wasn't made lightly. It was pretty much my mother's doing. She didn't want to leave me while I rehabbed and knowing it could take up to twelve weeks, she said it would be better for me to come home.

Home is such a funny word when you think about it. Not the meaning, but what it entails. For the longest time, I've considered my apartment in Boston my home. Yet, as I step out of my dad's truck and look at the house I grew up in, there's this odd sensation that washes over me, pushing me to the brink of tears. I know my emotions are all out of whack because of my injury but looking at my parents' two-story farmhouse brings back a lot of memories from when I grew up here. On the outside, the house looks like everyone else's right down to the wraparound porch, but behind it is where the life is. It's where I learned to throw a baseball and football, run faster than all get out because a damn bull chased after me, and where my friends and I built our own baseball field after watching Field of Dreams. I think my parents were secretly happy about this because they always knew where I was. The downfall? The field didn't have electricity so once nightfall came, our games were over.

Richfield, Montana isn't a small town, but it's not large by any stretch of the imagination. We don't have the big super-stores, and everything is locally owned. Building the baseball field gave kids a place to play. We used to hold mock tournaments and set up our own little league series. My dad constructed an old-fashioned scoreboard, much like the one at Lowery Field, and the moms would get together and have a concession stand that was really meant to feed us lunch.

It wasn't until I donated money to build a true park, that the kids in Richfield had a real place to play. It was the least I could do after the Renegades drafted me. I wasn't going to be home and I didn't want my parents worrying about the maintenance. The last I knew, my father let the grass take over the old field, which makes me sad now even though I know it was for the best.

Also behind the house is where our livelihood begins. The barns, tack house, bunk houses. At last count, my father has ten men and women working for him as ranch hands and wranglers. This is where I met Brett Larsen, my best friend through middle and high school. His father came to work for my father and brought him along. It was unheard of, a cowboy bringing a child to work, but Brett's mother had died when he was younger and they didn't have much family. It worked out for me because I always had someone to play with and my mother never seemed to mind that Brett hung out in our house.

"Not much has changed." My dad's words are gruff, hard. His skin is weathered from the sun, wind, and harsh winters. My mom wants him to retire but my sisters and I know the day he retires is the day he drops dead on the ranch somewhere.

"Everything's changed." It may not seem like it, but the vibe is different. I already feel like an outsider. "I should never have stayed away."

My dad rests his hand on my shoulder. This is as much affection as I'll receive from him. He's not a mean father, by any means, he just doesn't express himself well when it comes to matters of the heart. "This life wasn't for you. We knew that the minute you picked up a baseball."

"Still, it's my home. I should be here in the off season to help."

"Nah, that's what my sons-in-law are for."

I feel as if the comment is backhanded, almost as if I'm not good enough to work a ranch. I know I am. I also know that growing up, I did my chores as fast as I could so Brett and I, and whoever else rode their bikes over, could do other things.

All around, we are surrounded by grasslands but in the front of the house, my mother has made sure the ranch looks like a home. Flowers of all sorts, wind chimes hanging from the roof of the porch, a couple of rocking chairs so she and my father can look out over their land. This is where it's quiet, where my mom will read a book or play with my nieces and nephew.

"Is Nolan a cowboy?" I ask of my ten-year-old nephew.

Dad shakes his head. "Nope, been trying to make the baseball team."

"What do you mean trying?" I look at my mom, who avoids eye contact. I know something's up and my dad isn't going to tell me, but my mom will later when he's not around.

Dad sighs. "Lots of politics in town. Come on, I think your sister cooked up a feast for your return."

I follow my parents up the stairs to their house and as soon as the screen door shuts, my twin nieces, Ali and Ava, come barreling toward me. They're six and dressed like little cowgirls, complete with hot pink boots.

"Be careful, girls. Uncle Hawk can't use his arm all that much," Mom says.

I crouch down and give them a one-armed hug. "Well, well, well . . . aren't you two the most adorable cowgirls I've ever seen."

"We're so glad you're home," Ava says.

"Yep, now Mama can stop yelling at the TV for a bit. She says you're not playing baseball no more." Hearing those words from Ali really sends my heart into a tailspin. The fact that my sister thinks my career is done adds even more despair to what I'm already feeling.

"Come on now, the Renegades are still playing. I'll do enough yelling for the whole family." I wink at Ali and give her another hug before my mom tells them to run along. She tells my father to take my bags upstairs and pulls me into the kitchen where my sisters are busy baking.

For the longest time, the three of us stare at each other. There's a lot of resentment when it comes to them. They've never been happy with my decision to pursue a career in baseball and felt that my place was on the ranch and nowhere else. Family first. That's the motto on the ranch.

The standoff continues until my mother tells us to knock it off. We finally hug, but the effort on all our parts is weak. I figure I have a few months to win back their affection before I have to return to being public enemy number one.

BOSTON RENEGADES

We are a few days away from the season opener, which if anyone out there is counting, means our beloved Renegades will be back in Boston soon. They will make one pit-stop in Montreal to finish off their pre-season with back-to-back games against the Blue Jays.

Speaking of Montreal. They're still trying to get baseball back in their town and they're doing a fine job promoting the match-up between the BoRe's and the Blue Jays, selling out both games. The problem lies with the Tampa Bay Rays ownership and their desire to split the season between Florida and Montreal. Much of the team and staff have balked, saying they're not going to uproot their families, especially those with school aged children, to play in a different city. If you've ever attended a Rays game, you know they have very little support from the community and most people in attendance are there to see the competitors.

All-Star pitcher, Hawk Sinclair, is out for the majority of the season after undergoing thoracic outlet surgery. This is a fairly new procedure with fewer than fifty pitchers in the majors having done it. While the surgery seems simple, the rehab period is twelve weeks. Manager Wes Wilson confirmed that Sinclair came through surgery as expected and is in his Boston home resting. We reached out to Sinclair, who had this to say: While the pain in my hand, arm and shoulder has subsided, I'm sad to miss the season and hope to be back in the dugout for the wild card race.

GOSSIP WIRE

Former Renegade, Jasper Jacobsen, was involved in a car accident in Toronto. At press time, we have no word on any reported injuries.

We hear there may be a new bundle of joy on the way . . . only we don't know to whom. Saylor Blackwell-Kidd, Daisy Davenport and Ainsley Burke were all spotted at the upscale store *Baby Pod*. When asked who was expecting, the three women who are often together, laughed.

Random note — we also asked Ainsley Burke why she goes by her maiden name, to which she replied: Ainsley Bailey . . . and left her comment at that.

SIX
BELLAMY

MARIA'S on Main has been a staple of Richfield for what seems like eons, having been in the same family for over a hundred years. This is a replica of one in Italy and here you will only find authentic food, which means no fettuccini alfredo or Caesar salads. I don't come here often. It's expensive and you must have the right palate for a place like this. Something Chase doesn't have. If there isn't chicken fingers and fries on the menu, it's not a place for us.

As soon as I step in, I close my eyes and inhale deeply. The scent of tomatoes, anchovies and mushrooms washes over me. My stomach growls, reminding me that I haven't eaten since this morning. After a moment, I open my eyes and scan the restaurant, looking for Brett. Once again, I'm late, thanks to another showing that ran later than planned. Being a single mom, I take as many calls as I can get. If you want to list your house, I'm your gal. Want to buy a house, condo, or some land? Call me, I know just the place you're looking for. I work all day, some nights, and on weekends too. Any other time, besides now, I'd be home with Chase, making him dinner. I *do* put limits on when I'll work. If he has an activity, a game or needs help with a project, I'm there. I refuse to miss anything my son has going on. My mother helps a lot, but it's not the same. It's also not fair that I play the role of both Mom and Dad, but it what it is, and I knew my life would be this way when I decided to move us back to Montana.

After what seems like the longest week of my life, which is over dramatic considering the crap my ex put me through, I'm following the hostess while looking at the couples already seated and wondering if I'm underdressed. Today, I wore what I call my "normal work outfit" — a pencil skirt, blouse, and blazer with fashionable, yet comfortable heels. The women here though, are in cocktail dresses, and it dawns on me that this is where people in town come to get engaged, go on romantic dates, and celebrate milestones. I can't help but glance at the different tables as I pass. Everything here seems far too intimate for a constructive meeting about little league. Couples are holding hands, drinking wine, and showing their affection in various ways.

I smile when I see Brett, but it quickly vanishes when I see he's alone. We're at a table for two, not five or six. He holds his hand out, motioning for me to take a seat. "Are you going to sit?"

I'm standing here with my hand clutching my shoulder straps, looking around. "Where are the rest of the coaches?"

He looks at me oddly and the corner of his mouth lifts in a sly smile. "It's just us."

"Oh." After much hesitation, I finally sit, ignoring the feeling in my gut. Something isn't right. I know Brett has money, but why choose here if it's not a meeting? Surely, the others should be here as well.

Brett hands the menu to me and I open it. I already know what I want: The spaghetti with only a little sauce because I don't want to get my blouse dirty. It's the same thing I've ordered before and I know I can afford it, but I look anyway in case something else jumps out at me. The waitress stops at our table and Brett orders a bottle of wine. A bottle. Not a glass or two. After scanning the menu, I do everything I can to keep my eyes from bugging out. The wine is three hundred dollars a bottle.

Three hundred dollars a bottle.

She returns instantly with two glasses and I tell her that I'm not drinking. I'd like to, but I need to keep my senses about me.

"Of course, she is," Brett says. The waitress listens to him despite what I say, and sets a glass of red in front of me. I'm tempted to down it, to mask the anxiety I'm feeling, but I don't. I smile softly and tell her my order, only to have Brett change it. To say I'm stunned would be an understatement. I repeat my order and hand the menu back to the waitress, who immediately looks to Brett for confirmation. He shakes his head rather quickly, as if he's telling her to ignore me.

"Do you always order for people?"

Brett tilts his head to the side and grins. He lets out a little laugh before leaning forward. "Just those that I like." He reaches for my hand and for a brief moment he's touching me until I realize what the hell is going on.

Not so subtly, I pull my hand away and rest it on my lap. "I'd like to talk about Chase."

"I see," he says. He sighs heavily and straightens in his chair. "I'll cut to the chase," he laughs at his own joke, which I don't find funny. "I like your son. He's a good boy and has what it takes to be a decent ball player."

"But?" I interject, knowing it's coming.

"He needs training."

"Which is why I'm here, Brett. What can I do to help my son? He wants to play baseball and I'm willing to do whatever it takes."

"Anything?"

"Anything," I reiterate.

Once again, he leans toward me. I'm watching his eyes,

trying to figure out what he's doing. As soon as I feel his hand on my leg, I push my chair back, bumping hard into the person behind me. I mumble a weak apology to the man who is likely wearing red sauce due to my actions.

"What do you think you're doing?"

He cocks his eyebrow. "Isn't it obvious?"

"You're married."

"My marriage has nothing to do with this. We both want something from each other. It's a win-win."

My mouth drops open in horror. "You expect me to sleep with you in order for my son to make the baseball team?" I seethe.

"If you don't," he says quietly. "I'll make sure Chase never makes a damn team in this town." He picks up his wine and takes a sip, never taking his eyes off me. I'm disgusted and feel dirty for even sitting here.

Thankfully, my chair is already far enough away from the table that I don't have to move. I throw my napkin on the table and stand with my bag in my hand. "You're a pig, Brett Larsen. You better hope I don't tell Annie about your proposition."

He chuckles, takes another sip and says, "You can try but I doubt she'd believe you. Remember, you're the one who said you'd do anything to help your son." He holds his phone up, shaking it. "Got it right here, in black and white."

"You son of a bitch." His words bring tears to my eyes and I hate that he sees me crying.

"Tsk, tsk. I hold the cards, Bellamy. Remember that."

Without another word, or bothering to stay and fight, I make a hasty exit. I fully expect people to stare but no one does. No one heard or saw him proposition me, and even if I wanted to say something, he has so much clout that no one is going to believe me.

The entire way home, I cry. I sob hard, choking on the words spewing from my mouth as I relive the night, angry at myself for thinking a man like that would be willing to help my son. There was a time when Brett Larsen was nothing more than a washed-up baseball player — the idiot punched a wall and broke his hand in so many places, he had no choice but to give up the game he loved so much and lost his scholarship. He started night school after he and Annie married to become a stockbroker, money manager type. Now he's all high and mighty because he once had a scholarship to play baseball?

I drive around the block a few times until I can control my emotions. Chase will still be up, likely watching television with my mom, and I don't want him to see that I've been crying. He worries about me and since his father left, has become my protector. When I pull into the driveway, I yank the visor down and clean my make-up streaked face.

This was *not* how I expected the night to go.

The notebook I brought to the meeting, that I intended to fill with useful hints and tips, falls out when I pull my bag from the passenger seat. I leave it there, not wanting the reminder of how I've failed Chase. When I get to my front door, I take a few calming breaths, not that they're doing much for me. It's going to take me awhile to get over this. I hate knowing I'll have to plaster a smile on my face when I see Brett downtown or out and about, and I'm not sure whether I should tell Annie what he did. She should know what type of man she's married to, someone propositioning moms who are trying to help their sons. The thought makes me shudder.

I push down on the lock release and step into my house. Chase sees me right off and comes running toward me, talking a mile a minute about the day he had in school. He says nothing about recess or who he ate lunch with, but happily talks about the volcano he has to build for science class.

"I did that too," I tell him.

"Grandma told me. She said she could help."

"No fair. What if I want to help?"

Chase shrugs. "You can, if you have time."

"I do, bud."

"Hey, is something wrong?" he steps closer almost as if he's inspecting my red rimmed eyelids.

"Nah, just really tired. I had a long day."

"Maybe you need to take a long, hot bath."

I run my hand over his dark blond hair and smile. "You're right, bud. That's exactly what Mom needs."

He smiles and runs toward his room just as my mom enters from the kitchen. She's drying her hands on a dish towel and when we make eye contact, she sighs.

"What happened?"

I motion for her to go back into the kitchen with me where I pour myself a glass of wine that I fully intend to finish, and probably refill a few times, so I can put this night out of my mind. My mom and I sit at the small breakfast table. She's drinking coffee and I'm on my way to becoming a wino. Once I start talking, the tears start flowing. My mom doesn't ask any questions, and she holds my hand while I fill her in.

"I'm failing at this parent thing."

She squeezes my hand. "You're not, Bellamy. You're doing everything you can to give Chase the life he deserves."

"Maybe I should move back to Spokane."

"So Chase can watch while Greg plays dad to his sister, but not to him? I think that'll make things worse for Chase. Here, he's the focus of our attention. There, he's subject to the crap his stepmother pulls."

"I know." My voice is weak, and I don't even believe my own words. "I don't know what else to do for him. He just wants to play sports and make friends but those things go hand in hand here, and stupid Brett Larsen is making it impossible."

"We'll figure it out. I'll ask around . . . maybe there's a high schooler who can train with him or take him under his wing."

"Like a big brother or something?"

She nods. "Exactly. Do you remember David Farmer?"

"Mr. Farmer? Yeah, I had him for gym class. He used to coach . . ." My eyes go wide. "Doesn't he run the youth center?"

"Yes, he does. I'll go talk to him tomorrow and see if he has some time to spend with Chase or if he knows of a young man who would be willing to."

"Oh, Mom . . ." I reach across the table and hug her. "Why didn't I think of him earlier?"

"Doesn't matter," she says. "What matters is that we find someone to help Chase and I think David could be the one."

By the time she leaves, I'm full of hope. Brett Larsen can go fly a kite as far as I'm concerned.

SEVEN

HAWK

ALL I NEED out of life is a hot cup of coffee and the view from my parents' back porch. The sun is barely rising over the snowcapped mountain range that seems closer than it really is. There's a fine mist lingering off the ground, making it look like the cattle are missing their legs between their knees and body. When I was younger, my mother used to take pictures from this spot and turn them into greeting cards. She'd sell them down at the local drugstore, which has always been a tourist stop — the place to buy Richfield Montana t-shirts, magnets and hand-painted cows wearing Christmas wreaths around their necks.

The peace and quiet here is a renewed calm. I went from this to the University of Utah, where I played one year of collegiate ball before I signed my major league deal and landed myself in one of the busiest cities in the US. It's surprising I've survived in Boston as long as I have. It's constantly noisy, filled with people always coming and going and the traffic is a bitch, but damn, there's some kind of magic there. The people of Boston love their city, and they love their sports teams. The fans consider us their family. They're not intrusive when they see us on the streets. They care when we're ailing; the sheer number of gifts my manager has sent to my parents' place alone shows me that they're missing me . . . probably not as much as I'm missing them. I'd give anything to be back in Bean Town, wearing layers of clothing, and about to take the mound.

Still, I'm happy to be home. The weather isn't all that much different so I'm still in layers, but now I'm wearing flannel shirts with long john's underneath, and cowboy boots. The door behind me opens and closes. I don't bother to turn around to see who it is. My brother-in-law, Warner, stands next to me with a cup of coffee in his hand.

He sighs heavily. Not once, but twice. There's something on his mind. Thing is, I don't want to know what it is. He and my other brother-in-law, Alan, hold the same grudge against me as my sisters do. They all think I chose wrong, that I should've given up my dream of playing professional baseball and worked the ranch like them. The thing is, working here was never in my blood. I hated doing chores, wrangling horses and chasing cattle through the fields. Being up before the sun never appealed to me and my father saw that early on.

"How's the shoulder?"

"Sore."

"Imagine so."

Warner has taken a spill or two. One time, he and Alan were being stupid and decided to race each other on horse-back. Warner's horse spooked and bucked Warner right into a tree. He couldn't work for three months because of a concussion. According to my sister, that was my fault too because my dad decided to take the afternoon off to watch my game on television. How many grown men need a babysitter? Two . . . and they both happen to be married to my sisters.

"When do you go back?"

Here we go.

I tilt my head from side-to-side, popping my neck. "Twelve weeks, give or take."

"Rehab?"

"Yep."

"Wouldn't it be better if you did that in Boston?"

I set my mug down on the railing and turn toward cowboy Warner. "What's your problem?"

"You," he states so matter-of-factly that for a moment I feel as if I've done something wrong. "Your presence here bothers your sister."

"So, what? She can get over herself. This is our parents' house, not hers."

"It ain't about the house, Hawk. It's your life. It's about Nolan."

"Nolan? What does he have to do with me being here?"

Warner brings his mug to his mouth and takes a long drink as he looks out over the ranch. "Nolan idolizes you."

"I have a clean image, Warner."

"It's not about your image, it's about baseball. He wants to play."

"Let him."

"See that's where your sister and I disagree. We're ranchers."

I have no idea what sound comes from me. It sounds like a laugh, but it's more like complete disgust and disbelief. "No, Warner, *you're* a rancher. Nolan is a ten-year-old boy who wants to run amok, play sports, fish in creeks and kiss a girl behind the barn. No different than you when you were his age."

"I knew this is what I wanted to do."

I shake my head. "Only because at fifteen you were in love with my sister and you figured the only way to win her affection was to come work for my dad. You were just never smart enough to leave." I don't give Warner a chance to respond. I leave him standing on the porch and return to the house. I have therapy later and the drive to Missoula is going to take two damn hours.

In the kitchen, my mom is standing at the sink. I go to her, giving her a kiss on the cheek. "The sunrise was beautiful."

"It always is." She nods toward the porch. "Elizabeth is scared."

"Of what? Nolan not following in his father's bootstraps?" I think my humor is funny, but it seems that my mother does not.

Mom turns the faucet on and holds her hand under the water. I've seen her do this a million times. She's waiting for the water to warm so she can fill the sink with suds to wash the dishes that have already piled in the sink. Warner, and likely Alan, are unable to clean up after themselves.

"It takes a village to run a ranch."

"They should have more kids then."

"Hawk," Ma sighs. "I'm not saying the way she feels is right or wrong."

"What *are* you saying?"

She drops the plug and adds the dish soap. "Watching you pitch brings me so much joy. Watching Nolan would do the same." She turns and looks at me, giving me a mischievous smile. "Don't flaunt it in front of your sister but teach that boy everything you know. Even how to wrangle a horse. It'll make her happy." Ma winks.

After living in Boston for so long, returning to my hometown, Richfield, is a complete cultural shock. In Boston, everything is available. Anything you want. Anytime, day or night. When you're hungry at three in the morning, your favorite Chinese restaurant has no problem delivering. If you feel like doing your own grocery shopping after you win a game, Walmart and Target have you covered. Chain stores, restaurants, and coffee shops exist in multiples. There's a Dunkin' on every street corner, and a Starbucks on every other.

In Richfield, it's mom and pop stores. Here, it's knowing that your dollar is going into the pocket of someone you know. You're putting food on their table, paying their bills, and giving them a life. It's making sure you have a plan if you need something because come dinner time, the stores close, people go home to spend time with their families, eat dinner and load up the car to head to the local high school for football, basketball, wrestling or baseball games. Here, family comes first.

It's what I see as I drive down the road. Moms walking hand-in-hand with their children without a cell phone in sight nor ear buds in their ears. I'm not saying the people of Boston are inattentive to their children, it's just different in rural America.

The speed limit down Main Street is posted at twenty-five, most go ten, maybe fifteen. It's customary to wave at everyone and even stop to say "hi" if an oncoming car is a friend of yours. It's like time slowed down when places like Richfield were created. No one's in a rush, they're stopping in front of shops, chatting with the owners, telling them a story they've probably already heard by now. In small towns, news travels fast. It's not necessarily a bad thing, it's just a fact of life.

The weather is still brisk, unlike the temperatures in Florida right now, yet my window is down, and my elbow is resting on the door of my truck. Even though there's only two cars in front of me, I'm going slow, and taking it all in. It's crazy to me how much the town has changed. I wouldn't say it's evolved over time, but it's definitely not living in the past anymore.

Where there used to be a movie rental store, is now one of those newer massage places where women can go in and get pampered, a facial, and a massage all in one. My married friends tell me it's the to go when they need an emergency present for their wives or mothers.

And then there's Maria's. I've only taken one person to the fanciest restaurant in Richfield and that was Annie Miller. It was our senior year and I had no intention of going until she asked me. Right before the big day, she and my best friend at the time, Brett Larsen, had broken up. He cheated on her. It wasn't the first time he had, but she finally broke things off with him this time. When she asked me to take her to prom, I wanted to say no, respect the bro code and all that, but I couldn't. I had known Annie since kindergarten, and she was devastated. We hung out until college started, things became physical between us but then Brett came back into the picture. Apparently, he was her one true love or something like that, so I stepped aside. That wasn't enough for Brett though. He went all macho, as if he had to prove something, and busted his hand up after trying to hit me. I ducked, and the wall met his knuckles. I can still hear him screaming.

A few people wave and one yells my name. That gets the attention of some others in the area. They stop, look and try to figure out how or where they know me from. Hawk is an unusual name, but unless you grew up here or are a rabid baseball fan, that's all it is . . . a name.

Main Street spans four blocks, and then things start spreading out. There are a few buildings that have been converted into apartments, a grocery store that takes up half a block, and now there's a hardware store that looks massively out of place. I try to recall my parents saying something about a box store moving into town but can't. The store sticks out like a sore thumb though, and yet the parking lot is fairly packed.

On the backside of Main Street is my pride and joy. My heart. I pull into the parking lot, shut the truck off and take in my surroundings. The Sinclair Fields is a facility I developed with multiple baseball and softball fields, press boxes and a concession stand. Light poles, fencing and bleachers are perfectly placed. The scoreboards are dim but will come to life once Little League starts. Having the ballpark built was the first thing I did with my Major League salary. It was my way of giving back to a community that supported me through everything. When I should've been ranching with my dad, he turned a blind eye and allowed me to follow my passion for baseball. Growing up, the places to play were limited, so my dad gave us a small piece of land to play on.

One of the problems with my career . . . no, I take that back . . . the problem with *me* is that I never came home once the season ended. I wanted to rest, relax and rejuvenate, not work and working would be expected, so I stayed away or took my parents on tropical vacations instead. That's probably why my sisters and their husbands aren't very fond of me being home right now. I represent something they don't have: Freedom. They're ranchers, locals. Their lives are here, while I ran as far and as fast as I could without turning back.

Still, having this park built for the youth of Richfield has been one of the best things I've ever done and I'm looking forward to watching my nephew pitch in the next coming weeks. I suppose for that reason, my injury has a silver lining, although the BoRe's may think otherwise.

My phone chimes and I look down at the screen. The alert reminds me that I have an appointment in an hour for physical therapy. Fun times. Nothing like working out an arm that doesn't want to be worked out.

BOSTON RENEGADES

The season is off to a . . . start. Every fan wishes their teams started undefeated, although it's nearly impossible for that to happen. The beginning of the season is temperamental. It's still snowing, raining, and often there are threats of Nor'easters heading toward land. Still, we brave the bitter cold and wind to cheer on our teams.

The BoRe's are sitting with a win/loss record of 6 and 5, and they're being outscored by their opponents 47 to 59. If it wasn't for a few nights of stellar pitching by Cesar Floyd and Max Tadashi, who recently came off the injured list after being day-to-day for a few weeks, our numbers would be vastly different.

Our bats have been stellar, with an amazing on base percentage, and the BoRe's have no trouble scoring . . . it's the defense. Too many misjudged pop-flies, stolen bases and wild throws to first is what gets us into trouble.

The Renegades have a ten game homestand going into this week and then will hit the road to face the White Sox and Baltimore, before taking a one-day break to return home against Seattle, the Rockies and those pesky Astros, and head back on the road to Toronto and Houston. At least, it should be warm in Texas. Maybe the dome will be open at Minute Maid Park.

GOSSIP WIRE

Try as we might, we haven't uncovered who in the BoRe family is expecting. How fun would it be for all the wives to be pregnant at the same time? We ran into Steve Bainbridge at Tasty Burger and asked him what he thought. He said, "if that's the case, they need to pay close attention to the schedule. We can't have most of our players gone on the same day." Something tells me no one in the BoRe organization would appreciate this.

Our favorite designated hitter, Branch Singleton, may not be so single. Rumors are rampant that he eloped during a winter trip to Las Vegas. We've reached out to his teammates, but you can imagine their responses. This story is developing.

EIGHT

BELLAMY

EVEN THE BEST laid plans tend to change when it comes to my life, it's the nature of the beast. My mom manages the local bank and normally can set her schedule the way she sees fit until there's a crisis like there is this morning. It's definitely a perk of living in a small town. Their printers aren't working, and no one can log into the network. It's not the end of the world having to talk to David Farmer alone, except that I'm anxious and eager to help my son, so I find myself mulling over and over again what I'm going to say to my former gym teacher. I'm trying to remember if I had a good relationship with him. Did I show up to class on time? Was I wearing the appropriate physical education clothes? Did I run the mile in the time he allotted? Sadly, I have no answer for any of my questions. I *think* I was a decent student for him, and hopefully respectful, because I'm about to ask him for a giant favor.

The youth center is quiet when I walk in, only the bell ringing against the glass door breaks the silence. The front desk is empty, but I can smell freshly brewed coffee. "Hello?" I call out from the hallway. "Anyone here?"

"We're closed until three," a gruff voice hollers from

behind a wall somewhere. I peer into the office, looking for whomever is here and find no one.

"Excuse me," I say as I step into the office and start toward the open door behind the desk. "I'm looking for Mr. Farmer."

As if on cue, he steps into the doorway. "We're closed. Come back at three."

"But you're here." I point out the obvious. "I only need a minute of your time, Mr. Farmer." I step closer and take a good look at my former teacher. He's dressed like you'd expect, in jeans and a t-shirt. He's got a round belly and seems to be growing his winter beard. If he keeps it up, he could easily play Santa in our winter festival. "I don't know if you remember me, but I'm Bellamy Patrick. I mean Carlisle. Bellamy Carlisle now Patrick. I had you as a teacher." By the time he retired, I was long gone and living in Washington.

He laughs, although not in a humorous sort of way. "I've taught a lot of students over the years, Mrs. Patrick."

Ms. But I don't want to correct him. "I imagine, too bad my son won't have you as a teacher, which is why I'm here . . . for my son, not the teaching part." I'm flustered and losing my train of thought.

He sighs heavily. "We really are closed until three. I only came in to do some paperwork since my secretary is on vacation. If you come back—"

"What I have to say will only take a minute, I promise." I hate interrupting him, but I'm desperate, and I don't wait for him to brush me off again before I tell him what I need. "My son, he's having trouble fitting in since we moved here. It's been almost two years and I am at a complete loss on how to help him. You see, I'm recently divorced, and his father is hardly in the picture. It was my mother's suggestion that I come down here and see if you have a big brother type program."

"Who's your mother again?"

"Rebecca Carlisle. Maybe you remember my father, Herb?"

"Yeah, Herb I remember. What's he been gone now, ten years?"

I nod, not willing to talk about my father passing away. The old man studies me for what, I'm not sure, but his eyes are piercing and boring holes into my psyche. I don't understand the animalistic machismo that flows through this town. Why can't men be normal, caring, and understanding instead of this heavy-handed shit?

"Anyway, back to my son."

"How old?"

"He's ten."

"You should get him into sports."

"I've tried, Mr. Farmer. He's tried out for Little League, football and basketball. He's been to camps, clinics and the open gyms offered. It's a popularity contest here and he's not popular."

Farmer motions for me to sit down in the chair across the desk. As I do, he pulls out the squeaky, rickety chair his assistant uses. "You're not the first one to complain about the sports in this area being a popularity contest." He picks up a pen and taps on the desk. "Youth sports is hard. The coaching is volunteer based. There are rules to follow, such as holding try-outs and creating equal teams. For the most part, this happens. However, when it doesn't, I often find my hands are tied because if I come down too hard on the coaches, they won't volunteer. If I don't have any volunteers, the kids can't play."

"And I understand that. What I *don't* understand is how kids are singled out. My son wants to play. I want him to play. I want him to make friends! And when he's constantly not chosen, it's heartbreaking. I'm not saying he's the best or most talented. All I'm saying is that he wants to play baseball, and it seems like if this is something parents are paying for, he should have an opportunity."

"Oh, he absolutely should. What I'm saying is . . ." his words are cut short by the ringing of the phone. Even though he claims to be closed, he answers anyway.

"Richfield Youth Center. Oh hey, Brett. Yeah, let me pull up the schedule."

My stomach drops when I hear him say Brett. I can only suspect it's the same asshole that is making it so my son can't play. Of course, if I were to accept his advances, I'm sure my son would become the next star of Richfield. I love my boy, but not at the cost of my dignity.

"Field schedule is online. Nope, not making any changes. You can swap with the other coaches if you want, but it stands." Farmer slams the phone down and again, sighs heavily. Something tells me that Brett might be the cause of this old man's gray hair.

I clear my throat. He slowly looks up. It's a long minute, maybe two, of silence before he opens his mouth. "I'll ask the coaches how many kids were cut and see if they can find a spot for him on one of the teams."

It's my turn to sigh and offer up a weak smile. His efforts will be futile, I know this, but it's something. Maybe if Brett knows I've gone to see David Farmer, who basically runs the program, something will change. I stand and offer my hand. He stands with me and shakes it. "Thank you. I look forward to hearing from you. Chase, my son . . . he's eager to start playing with his classmates."

"Yeah," is all he says. I show myself out and when I'm in my car, I'm hoping to feel this unsurmountable relief, yet the only thing that comes is tears. Nothing's going to change. In fact, I fear that I've made everything worse.

I'm not halfway to my office when my phone rings. Brett's name flashes on my screen. I picture him on the other end gritting his teeth and maybe tugging on his hair in frustration.

Either that or he's laughing hysterically at my failed attempt. Chase loses no matter what happens. He'll forever be known as the kid whose mom had to complain to get him on a team.

"What have I done?" I mutter. Nothing but regret washes over me. I know I've made the biggest mistake of my life going to see Farmer. Instead of going to my office, I go to the bank. Inside, I rush to my mom's office, bypassing her assistant and opening her office door. Once I see her, I collapse into a heap on her couch and bury my face.

"What happened?"

Shaking my head, I inhale deeply, but feel like I've taken in no air. My lungs are constricting, my throat is tightening up, and my heart is breaking. "I went to the youth center and Brett called while I was there asking about the schedule. It seems as though I'm not the only one who has complained."

"That's good."

"Farmer gave me this song and dance about coaches being volunteers and without them the kids can't play. He said he'd talk to the coaches and see how many kids were cut and try to find a spot for Chase."

"Again, good."

I finally look at my mom and shake my head. She's wearing her reading glasses, her hair is in a bun, and she's dressed smartly in a pinstriped suit. Our town may be small but being the only bank in town and being the manager, she's important. "Brett called after I left. I don't think I was five minutes away when his named popped up on the screen."

"What did he say?"

Looking down at my phone, I tap the screen to bring it to life and type in my passcode. The text, mail and phone icons all have numbers telling me how many messages are waiting. I press the phone button and then the voicemail one to start Brett's message.

"Bellamy, I believe I was crystal clear last night. You know what you have to do to get your son on a team. Don't fuck with me."

Mom gasps. My finger hovers over the delete button but I don't press it. I'm tempted to call him back and ask him to explain himself but I don't want to know what he has to say. Something in my gut tells me he knows I went to Farmer. My gut is also telling me either Farmer called him after I left, one of Brett's cronies saw me or he's following me. I need to save this message, not that I expect it'll do me any good. I send it to my email and then put my phone down. "So . . . now what?"

My mom sits back in her chair. She picks up a pen and starts tapping it on her desk. The longer she ponders her thoughts, the closer I come to blurting out that Chase and I are going to move. Maybe down south where it's warmer and the people tend to be nicer.

"We'll figure something out," she says, shrugging.

"Even if we do, the damage is done. Chase will be bullied by those kids on the team because Brett Larsen is a petty asshole."

"I could freeze his assets." She starts typing on her computer.

"Don't do anything illegal, Mom. It's not worth losing your job over. If he's this upset over something as trivial as baseball, I can't imagine what he'd do if his money went missing."

"My grandson's happiness is worth a lot of things."

I agree with her. "Maybe just slow down his next loan request or something."

"That I can do." Oddly enough this makes her happy. I give her a kiss before leaving and decide to walk to my office. It's only two blocks away, the sun is shining, and I need the fresh air.

As soon as I step in, my boss, Owen, is hollering for me to come to his office. He waits for me to enter before shutting his office door behind me. Karter must've spent a long time in here after Owen's rampage the other day because the place looks tidy as can be. He passes back and forth behind his desk, muttering to himself.

"Owen . . ."

He holds his hand up and then immediately runs it through his hair. "What in the hell did you do to piss off Brett Larsen?"

Everything I felt in my mother's office comes back tenfold, except this time my heart is racing so fast that I fully expect a heart attack to follow. This was how my dad died, a heart attack.

"I don't know." My voice cracks as tears come rushing forward. Owen is standing in front of me within seconds with his hands on my shoulders. "I just want Chase to have a chance. He's cut him from everything he's tried out for, so I went to the youth center to talk to David Farmer. He's just a ten-year-old boy who wants a chance, Owen. Why is Brett so hell bent on making our lives so difficult?"

"Because you have something he wants, and I suspect you know what it is."

"So, what? I'm supposed to sleep with him?"

He shakes his head. "No, but unfortunately he intends to make your life a living hell until you do."

I step out of Owens grasp and do my own pacing. "What did he say when he called you?"

"He wants me to fire you," he sighs. "I told him no, that you're an asset, but . . ."

I turn and look Owen in his eyes. "But for the company to keep peace, it's the right thing to do?"

Owen straightens up. "I don't cower to bullies and neither should you. There's a plot of land for sale next to his hardware store. They've been using it for storage without permission." He goes to this desk and hands me a file. "Adverse possession applies. Take a surveyor out, mark the lines, take an inventory of what's on the property. The owner wants to sell. And be sure to put a damn for sale sign up so big it blinds that asshole."

"Won't that create a bigger problem?"

My boss smiles. "Sure will, but it will also tie up some of his stock in a legal battle." He claps his hands and rubs them together. "If he wants to pick on someone, he can come after me."

I stand there for a minute, trying to comprehend everything and imagining what my future will hold because of this. Owen is willing to stand up to the monster, but will anyone else? Not likely, and that makes moving more appealing. With the file in my hand, I go to one of the free desks in the office and get to work. I keep telling myself that I'm only doing what my boss is telling me to do, but part of me feels like we're poking a grizzly bear out of hibernation.

NINE

HAWK

MY PHYSICAL THERAPIST is the spawn of the Satan. She's an unruly woman named Emma with crooked teeth, a wart on her nose, and her skin is green. She hides her horns with two the buns she has on top of her head, but I know they're there.

Okay, I may be over exaggerating. She's not the spawn of Satan, but some other evil being who disguises itself as a beautiful woman meant to cause pain in the form of torture to unsuspecting men. "You're being a baby," the young, brunette spitfire says without making eye contact. "How do you expect to be back on the mound if you're unwilling to rotate your shoulder."

"Is this a trick question?" I lean slightly, hoping to make her smile but my wit and charming good looks mean nothing to her.

"It's my job to make sure you're healing."

"I'm healed."

Finally, she smiles. "Good, then lift your arm above your head and bend your elbow."

I do as she says, thinking I'm cool as shit, until she starts pushing on my arm. I scream out and the sadist laughs. "I think I hate you."

"You're not the first athlete to tell me that."

"Do you enjoy hurting people?"

"Not all at. I enjoy helping them recover so they can get back to what they love."

"You're mean," I tell her, proving how childish I am.

She giggles. "And oddly enough, I'm okay with that. Treadmill time, let's go."

She walks away, leaving me on the table. I'm slightly confused as to why I need to get on the treadmill and remain seated until she hollers for me. I walk to the other side of the room and stand in the doorway, looking at every piece of gym equipment you can think of. This facility is a trainer's heaven. Sure, we have state of the art equipment in Boston, but this place is a mecca of machines for exercise and rehab. When I told the BoRe's that I was going to come back to Montana, the training staff there went to work to find me the best physical therapist possible. The only downfall is it's an hour away from my parents and I have to be here three days a week.

"In case you've forgotten, I had surgery on my arm." I make my way over to the treadmills where she's standing, poised to press the buttons that will project me into the depths of hell. I hate running. I loathe it. I will always find a way to get out of it if I can.

Emma smiles softly. "Tell you what . . . how about you don't question my job and I won't question why you waited months to tell your trainer that you were experiencing numbness in your fingertips?"

I glare at her. She shrugs.

"Had you said something earlier, there's a chance you could've avoided surgery."

"Doubt it. There's nerve damage."

"There are new ways, new procedures."

"I don't like new age medicine." I step onto the treadmill and sure enough, she presses some buttons to get the belt moving. Thankfully, I'm only walking, but know she's going to press that button so many times it'll soon be like I'm competing for the Boston Marathon . . . all by myself.

"It's not new age. What I'm talking about has been around for centuries." She presses the button, increasing my speed. "Does your arm hurt?"

"No," I tell her as I jog along.

"Anyway, we send a lot of our patients to a chiropractor who specializes on your vertebrae with the torque release technique."

"Arm hurts and I don't need my back cracked."

Emma decreases the speed but doesn't allow me to stop. "This technique allows for the chiropractor to correct subluxation or spinal misalignments in a non-invasive way. What I'm saying is, had you mentioned the numbness right away, a chiropractor practicing TRT might have been able to help. Honestly, I'm surprised you don't have a chiro on staff doing this for you."

Ignoring her seems like the best option for me right now. I have to focus on this half jog, half speed walk thing I'm doing and I'm trying not to move my arm so much. The last thing I want to do is tear a ligament, pull a muscle or damage the tissue. Let alone, move my arm in a direction that might cause my incision to open.

"When can I start throwing?"

"You have an x-ray in a couple of days, that'll tell us how things are looking in your shoulder." Emma decreases the speed slowly until it's back at zero. "That wasn't so bad, was it?"

"I hate running."

She laughs. "Follow me, Hawk. Let's go work that arm."

The sadist works my arm until it feels like jelly. It hangs limp at my side as I follow her back to her torture chamber. She has me lie back on the table and tells me to remove my shirt. I'm too tired to come back with some smart-ass comment and wish like hell that Travis Kidd were here to say something crass for me. I do as she says, lying back on the thin paper that covers the table.

Emma squirts a thick, clear substance up and down my arm and puts some into the palm of her hand. She starts massaging my fingers, gently pulling, twisting and rubbing the cream into them. The more she works up my arm, the warmer it becomes and the less pain I feel. The sensation feels so incredibly good, I find myself falling asleep.

"Why did you come to Montana for therapy?" she asks.

"I'm from Richfield. My parents own a cattle ranch there and my mom thought it would be best that I come home so she could keep her eye on me."

Emma chuckles. "She sounds like my mom. I have to video chat with her every day, no matter what."

"Most moms are like that."

"How does your arm feel?"

I open my eyes and see a satisfied smile on her face. "It feels really good." But something tells me she already knew this.

"I'll see you the day after tomorrow, Hawk. Have a good day."

Before I can ask her what she used, she's out the door and greeting her next patient. I put my shirt on and slip my arm back into the sling. If anything, I'd like to get rid of this by the end of the week.

On the way back to Richfield, I stop for lunch, hitting McDonald's. When I pull up to the drive thru window, the young clerk recognizes me right away.

"Dude, no freaking way."

How does one answer a statement like that? What would be the appropriate thing to say? "Dude, yes way"?

I smile, nod and hand him my twenty.

"You're Hawk Sinclair."

Um . . . duh?

"Hey, man," I say because what else can I say to something like that?

"You're my favorite player *ever*. What are you doing in Montana?"

I do my best not to grimace. If I'm his favorite, surely, he knows what I'm doing here. "Just checking out the sights."

"Right on. Mind if I get a selfie?"

Before I even agree, the kid is turning around in the window, has his thumb up and takes what must be the worst selfie ever because I'm barely in it. If I were truly his favorite, I'd consider getting out of the truck so we can take a proper photo.

He finally gives me my change and my food. I take my foot off the brake and speed off before he can say another thing. There's a park not far down the road where I pull over to eat. I long for the days when I can multitask, wishing I could read what's going on in the world of baseball. The BoRe reporter has been kind enough to keep me updated, as if I would miss a single thing about the Renegades.

With the last bite of my burger in my mouth, I put my truck into reverse and head toward Richfield. The less than half hour drive to town goes by rather quickly. I'm not exactly eager to go back to the ranch so I take another tour of Main Street, only to find it busier than I've seen in a long time and decide that since I'm back in town, I should probably check in with the director of the youth center. After I had the field built, I left it to the youth center to manage. It was easier that way since I spend all of baseball season in Boston — there was no way I could do both.

The parking lot is empty except for another truck. I pull up next to it, park and make my way to the front. The bell hanging from the door clanks back and forth against the glass, announcing my arrival.

"For Pete's sake, we're closed until three." I chuckle at the old gruff sound of my former coach. I turn into the office and find him hunkered over a desk. On the wall are pictures of all the teams that play at the field and in the center is a large picture of me digging the first hole for the fields and another of me cutting the ribbon for the grand opening. The rest of the area is filing cabinets, house plants, and a watering station.

"I thought you had an assistant."

David Farmer looks up from the paperwork and a slow smile starts to form on his face. "Well I'll be a son of a bitch. If it isn't Hawk Sinclair! How the hell are you, son?" We meet halfway and hug awkwardly. My arm really prevents much contact. "How's the arm?"

"Healing. I'm just coming from therapy."

"I thought I heard your old man say something about you coming back to rehab here, but then I thought there's no way in hell he'd leave Boston for this run of the mill town."

"It's home and my mom pretty much forced me." I laugh.

"Sounds just like Rhonda. Tell me, what brings you by?" He goes to the desk and sits down while I take the seat in front of him.

"Thought I'd stop in and see how things are going. My business manager keeps me up to date on maintenance and things, but that only tells me so much about the fields. Everything good?"

He nods, opens his mouth and quickly closes it. He leans back in the chair and I fear he's about to fall over, but somehow manages to stay upright.

"What is it?" I ask.

"How long are you here for?"

"Rehab is technically twelve weeks. It'll depend on how that goes."

"Wanna coach a Little League team?"

I start to laugh and shut my mouth quickly when I realize he isn't joking. "Oh, um . . . not really. I can't use my arm yet so I wouldn't be much use to a team."

"I could help."

"If you could help, why not just coach?"

"The bylaws preclude me from doing so. I can help out but can't helm a team and we are in desperate need of another coach." Farmer fills me in on a few of the details from around town and I'm surprised to hear that Brett Larsen is limiting the number of kids per team.

"Hold up," I say. "You mean to tell me that Brett is running things in town?"

"It's like a bad mafia movie. People fear him. He's pretty much put Nelson's Hardware out of business. And he's taken over the Little League. By the time I realized what was happening, things were too far gone. If I remove him, his friends go too, and they make up the league in these parts."

"It's Little League, Dave. Everyone should be able to play."

He nods. "Brett only wants the best. Just today, I had a mom in here asking for help because her son wants to play. I mentioned it to Brett, and he told me to mind my own business."

In my life, I deal with shady people all the time. Uncouth business dealings, opportunities that aren't on the up and up, and people trying to take advantage, but never have I come across or been told about someone who's determined to hurt children. I don't care who you are, that shit doesn't fly in my world.

David and I continue to talk for a bit. He suggests I come back during practice and see how things are going. He assures me that Brett will be none too happy to see me, so to prepare myself.

Can't fucking wait.

TEN

BELLAMY

THERE HAVE BEEN many times since my return to Richfield that I've second-guessed working for Owen — this
adventure I'm currently on being one of them. I love being in
real estate. Seeing homes, bringing joy to first time buyers,
and marketing a product that you believe in is a rewarding
job. I also love walking large pieces of land and taking
pictures of the majestic views during the summer, showing
interested parties what they'd see if they built their home
facing east versus west, and vice versa. What I take issue with
is heaving my body through the remaining snow, melting into
deep mud bogs, slipping on patches of ice that have not yet
thawed from the warmer days in galoshes that barely cover
my calves. Thankfully, I had the keen sense of mind to wear
pants today and not my normal skirt so at least my legs are
covered from the dirt splatter, but I'm totally kicking myself
for not buying those incredibly cute and fashionable knee-
high boots everyone is wearing right now because I'm certain
there's mud between my toes.

Yet, here I am, walking the land with clipboard in hand
and camera around my neck, following the surveyor as he
reads a map from the town clerk's office while directing his

associate as to where to place these tiny little flags that are meant to withstand every weather element possible. To be honest, I'm not sure why I need to be here, but Owen insisted. I think he's trying to send a message to Larsen, which Brett probably doesn't give two shits about.

I decide to walk ahead of the survey crew. I don't know exactly where I'm going and tell myself I won't walk too far from them. The last thing I want is to get lost out here. With them not in my line of sight, I take a few photos to use when I list the land and right now, the way the sun rays are bouncing off the few patches of snow, it's giving me the perfect backdrop.

"You're not really dressed for the outdoors."

I jump, my heart beating rapidly. I slowly turn toward the voice that came from behind me and find a horse standing at a fence I hadn't noticed earlier, and because I'm nervous it takes my eyes the longest time to finally look up at the rider. He doesn't wear the usual cowboy hat that most of the men around here wear when they're riding, but a baseball cap. His right arm is in a sling and his left hand holds the reins. For some odd reason, I look at the stirrups, expecting to find a pair of worn out sneakers, but instead he's wearing cowboy boots.

"You make an odd-looking cowboy." My hand covers my mouth and my eyes go wide as a result of my verbal vomit.

"I wasn't aware cowboys had a look these days."

"I'm so sorry," I tell him. "That was incredibly rude of me."

"No offense taken." He slides off his horse and for a man with one arm, makes it look so easy. Even though I grew up in Montana, I never mastered the art of riding. Sure, as a young girl, I wanted to be a barrel racer, bull rider, and saddle bronc rider. In essence, I wanted to be a cowgirl competing in the men's division, mostly because of cousins. My father, God rest his soul, put his foot down and was adamant that I compete in the female division. The only problem — I couldn't stay on a horse. If it went fast, I slipped right off. If it bucked, I went ass over tea kettle. One too many bumps and a bruise too many, my parents had enough and put in me ballet. I didn't fare much better there either.

This guy, who may or may not be a cowboy, drops the reins and comes toward the fence. He rests his good hand on the thick round post and his foot on the bottom wire, giving me a good look at him. He wears a long-sleeved shirt, but I can tell his arms are muscular, the kind you want wrapped around you when you're cold, and his eyes are crystal blue, reminding me of the sky on a beautiful summer day. And he looks like he hasn't shaved for days. The scruff along his jawline and chin is turning into a beard.

"What are you doing this far from town?" He smiles, but it's not a full on cheesy one. The corner of his mouth lifts, almost as if he's going to tell a joke.

It takes me longer than it should to answer him. Can he tell that I'm checking him out? "It's not that far." I turn toward the direction of the town, or at least I think I do, and realize that I'm not sure which direction I am supposed to go. I also strain to hear the men I came here with and can't. My worse fear is coming true. I'm lost.

"It's that way," he points behind me, laughing.

"It's not funny."

"It kind of is. What're you doing around here?"

"We're surveying the land. The owners are going to list the property."

"Is that so?"

I nod and the horse neighs. "I think he's ready to leave."

"She," he says as he rubs her nose. "Are they selling for development?"

"Not sure, but I can let you know if you're interested in buying it." I dig in my pocket for a pen, and hand it to him along with my clipboard. He scribbles quickly and hands it back to me. "Hawk? Is that really your name or are you just busting my chops?"

He laughs. "Hawk Sinclair. My family owns this side of the fence." He extends his left hand to shake mine. It's awkward but pleasant.

"Bellamy Patrick, local real estate agent and poorly dressed for the outdoors. Wait, Sinclair?"

"Let me guess, you know my sisters?"

"Elizabeth, right? I think we went to school together."

He nods. "She's five years older than I am. Our youngest sister is Avery."

"That's right. You, though . . . I don't recall seeing you around town much."

"I live in Boston." He eyes me oddly.

"Huh, well that makes sense. Listen, I should get back. I'm supposed to be with the surveyors and . . . oh, there they are." I wave my arm frantically to get their attention. If Hawk already had to point out where town is, I'd best stay with them so I don't get lost. "Anyway, it was nice meeting you, Mr. Sinclair—"

"Hawk," he corrects.

"Right . . . Hawk." I can't help the smile that's spreading across my face. In fact, I'm fairly certain I'm blushing. "I'll call you when I know more about the property."

"I'd appreciate that." He tips his hat, which looks funny considering he's wearing a baseball cap. It still has the same affect, though, and I find myself staring at him longer than I should. The surveyor yells my name, but I'm too busy watching Hawk climb back onto his horse with one hand, once again, making everything look so effortless. He's watching me too and once again tips his hat before he instructs his horse to trot away. I continue to focus on him, imagining what it would be like to sit in that saddle with him.

"Ms. Patrick!"

"Huh, what?" I turn to the left and right, and finally around. "Hi, are you done?"

"Only with a quarter of the land or so. After further research, this land is at least a hundred acres. We're going to have to go back and get our ATVs to survey the rest."

"Perfect. You won't need me though, will you?"

The two men look at each other. One shrugs, while the other says, "No, there's no need for you to be out here."

"Let's head back to town."

The guys head in the direction that we need to go, and while I should follow them, I glance behind me, wondering where this "not really a cowboy" disappeared too, and secretly hoping he'd come back.

The entire trek back to my car I'm thinking about his sister, Elizabeth. We were acquaintances in high school and hung out with the same crowd, but I rarely see her around town anymore. In fact, I can't recall the last time I saw her, which is odd. Richfield isn't big enough to go missing.

I drive the survey crew back to their office. They tell me they'll have the flags laid out by tomorrow and that if they need anything, they'll call. When I get back to the office, I tell Owen that this trip was completely useless and that the land is much bigger than he led me to believe. Except it wasn't all that useless because I met Hawk Sinclair, who could be a potential buyer.

"It was for your own good," he tells me. "Brett Larsen told me he was coming in this morning and I didn't want you to walk in and see him."

"What did he want?" I swear every time I hear this man's name, my blood boils.

"To reiterate his stance on your employment."

"And what did you tell him?" I'm trying to be strong, but my resolve is wavering. I wish I had recorded our conversation at dinner because it would give me some ammunition to go after him. What he's doing now is harassing me, not that any of the old boys club in town would believe me.

Owen clears his throat and I know this is it. He's going to fire me. "I told Larsen that he needs to mind his own business, that who I employ is none of his concern and that he's more than welcome to take his real estate business elsewhere. He stormed out of here and I promptly sent an email to my listserv, warning all my colleagues about him."

My eyes go wide as he tells me this. "You didn't." Even though I know he did because he looks rather proud of himself.

"I did. Larsen was nothing more than a bully when we were in high school and he still is. People need to put that jackass in his place."

"Well, easier said than done, that's for sure."

Owen gives me a reassuring smile. "You work hard, Bellamy. I'd be a fool to let you go." He returns to his office, which I'm thankful for, because I don't need him to see the giddiness I feel after his compliment.

I'm not seated at my desk for more than a few minutes when Karter plops herself down in front of it. "That hurt."

"The chairs aren't that padded. What's up?"

"How was your hike?"

"Stupid, until it wasn't. Do you know Hawk Sinclair?"

Her eyebrows shoot up and her mouth drops open. "Hawk Sinclair? Are you seriously asking me this question?"

"Yeah, why? What am I missing?"

Karter, being ever so dramatic, fans herself. "Only the hottest guy to ever come out of Richfield."

"Yes, I found him very good looking when I met him, but clearly there's more to this story."

She laughs. "Do you ever sit down with Chase and watch baseball?"

I shake my head. "Honestly, no. I find it boring."

"Girl turn on your TV. Well, don't do it right now because

Hawk isn't playing. From what I heard from Phoebe, who had lunch with his sister, Avery, Hawk is back in town because he had surgery."

"Okay . . ." I let the word drag out while I try to comprehend what the heck she's trying to say to me.

Karter rolls her eyes. "Hawk Sinclair is one of the starting pitchers for the Boston Renegades."

Still nothing.

"The Major League baseball club out of Boston! He's a damn baseball player, Bell! Professional at that!"

"Oh . . . I have a feeling your last sentence was filled with exclamation points."

"It was, only because I couldn't thump you in the head for being so dense. So, you met Hawk?"

I tell her about our encounter and how he might be interested in buying the land. She stands up and does some dance when I inform her that I have his number and she insists that I call him — not to talk about the property, but to pretend that I lost something and to hint that I'll be going back up there. I have no intentions of doing such a thing.

"He's single," she says.

"How do you know?"

Karter shows me her phone. "Player profile."

"Well, I guess it's too bad you're in a committed relationship." I point out.

She laughs. "You're not."

Any response I thought about mustering was cut off by the phone ringing. I glare at her, throwing daggers as she walks out of my office. I'm in no position to date or pursue anyone, not with Brett Larsen trying to ruin my life here.

ELEVEN

HAWK

AFTER A NIGHT of tossing and turning, mostly due to the throbbing in my arm, I decided to get up and take my mom's mare, Cadbury, who was named after the candy because of her rich brown coat, for a ride. It had been quite some time since I found myself on top of a saddle and yet after about twenty minutes, it all came back to me. And so did the muscle strain I knew I'd feel later in the afternoon. Still, being out in the open on a crisp spring morning felt good, but it wasn't until I came across Bellamy Patrick standing near our property line, that my morning changed. My intent was to ask her if she were lost, but one look at her and the way she was dressed for her nature walk and I knew I had to stay and chat. There was an innocence about her that I found intriguing, and I loved her sense of humor. Someone who can joke with you and at themselves is hard to find these days. Most importantly, she had no idea who I was even after I gave her my name. That rarely happens. Usually once I tell a woman who I am, they turn their flirting up to about a hundred and I hate that.

By most standards, it's still early when I get back to the barn. By rancher standards, it's time for a snack because they've been up since before the sun. The ranch is bustling though, under the mid-morning sun. Elizabeth is working with a horse and will teach barrel racing later and Avery runs a 4H program from the ranch after school. Their husbands are likely herding cattle or having a macho tree climbing race, while the other hands are doing their respective chores. Any which way I look, someone is doing something for my parents.

After dismounting Cadbury, I lead her back to her stall and make sure she has fresh water and hay. "Missed you at breakfast this morning."

Mom walks toward me with her pants tucked into her muck boots. When she reaches Cadbury's stall, her horse neighs and comes over to her. They nuzzle, much like people do with their dogs and cats. "How was she?"

"Perfect. I had a little trouble mounting her because of my arm, but she didn't seem to mind."

"She's such a good mare. The twins learned to ride on her. So did Nolan. Speaking of, have you spoken to your nephew?"

"I haven't had a chance. I thought they'd be at dinner last night."

"Me too, but I think Elizabeth and Warner are worried."

"He's just a kid. They should let him explore. What do Ali and Ava do for fun?"

Mom sighs. "Everything. 4H, ice skating. Ava wants to be a logger, so Alan takes her to competitions and is teaching her how to climb. Ali wants to be everything: Princess, hair-dresser, lawyer. She tells your father someday she's going to be a lawyer during the day and a stylist at night all while married to Prince George."

"Do I know this Prince George's family?"

My mom laughs so hard, she has to bend over. "Oh, Hawk. I've missed having you at home. And no, not personally. His great-grandmother is the currently Queen of England."

"Ah," I say, even though I'm utterly lost. "I'll spend some time with Nolan. Maybe take him down to the fields after school."

"Check with your sister first. Don't just kidnap her boy." She laughs, but it's only because she knows that's exactly what I planned to do. I give my mom a kiss on her cheek and head toward the arena where my sister is either training or wrangling a horse. I'm not sure which. When I come to the white, stockade fence, I rest against the top slat and watch my sister. When we were younger, she was one of the fastest barrel racers, competing in Wyoming most of the time and then taking her talents down to Texas. I don't know why she stopped and took up teaching. I suppose it had something to do with Warner and the birth of Nolan.

Elizabeth finishes her run and brings her Quarter horse stallion to a trot. They come toward the fence and I hold out a hay cube for him. "I see you took Cadbury out this morning."

"Yeah, figured she'd be easier than one of the stallions."

"Probably true. How's the arm?" Elizabeth dismounts and drops the reins. Her horse takes this as an open invitation to go roll in the mud. My sister mutters a string of curse words that would rival any sailor.

"I'll hold the hose." It's my offer to help wash him later.

She shakes her head, rolling her eyes as she does. "He's ridiculous. Loves being dirty."

"Anyway, the arm's okay. A bit sore after yesterday. My therapist is a sadist."

My sister snorts and covers her mouth. "Sorry about that," she says as she continues to laugh. "You never were one for pain."

"Nope, it's why I like pitching so much. I rarely have to bat, run bases, and I get every three to four days off to rest."

"Lazy is what you are."

I bat my eyes at my older sister, and she pushes my good shoulder with her gloved hand. "Ma sent you out here to talk to me, didn't she?"

"More or less."

"I know he wants to play, and he should get the opportunity to be a little boy, but Warner . . ."

"Look, I can't give you advice on how to manage your household, but as Nolan's really cool and famous uncle, let the boy hang out with me while I'm here. It's twelve weeks, Lizzy. A ranch hand can take over his chores for the time being. I'll make sure he does his homework, we'll go riding, and we'll spend some time down at the baseball fields."

She smiles and then looks over my shoulder. I turn and find Warner standing in the doorway. I wave, but the gesture isn't returned. "He won't like it."

"Yeah well, like I said, I'm only here for a short time. I want to hang out with my nephew."

"Are you going to hang out with the twins?"

I blanch at her question. "Um . . . have you seen those girls? They're freaky! They're identical in every aspect. Voice, hair, eyes, smile… it's like they belong on some horror story reality thing. It's creepy." Elizabeth laughs but finally admits she agrees with me and goes on to say that I need to spend time with my nieces as well to keep the peace with our younger sister. I know she's right, but like I said, the twins are . . . odd.

When Nolan gets off the bus, I'm there to meet him. He runs up to me and just when I think he's going to jump into my arms, he skids to a stop and gives me a high five. "What, no hug for your uncle?" He turns and watches the bus amble down the road. That's when I get it, he doesn't want his friends to tease him. I put my hand on his shoulder in hopes that he knows I understand. "Come on, let's go."

"Where?"

"I don't know, downtown. Maybe stop by the field and see what's going on there. We could get some ice cream if you promise not to tell your grandma."

"I promise," he says with a smile.

All the way into town, Nolan tells me about school, his teachers and his favorite subject, P.E. I honestly believe it's every boy's favorite class because it's the only time, aside from recess, where we can burn energy. He asks about baseball and if I'm sad that I'm missing most of my season. I'm honest with him and tell him that it hurts to watch the sport I love so much while feeling like I should be there supporting my team-mates. But I know that if I were there, I'd probably be working too hard at recovery, which would likely set me back. I also tell him that I'm happy to be back in Montana to spend some time with him and that we need to convince his parents to let him fly out to Boston during his summer vacation. Nolan, of course, is in full agreement.

"Grandma tells me you want to play baseball," I say as we pull into the almost packed parking lot of the stadium. Through the closed windows I can hear kids yelling and that brings a smile to my face.

He nods and goes to this backpack. He unzips it and pulls out his glove. "It used to be yours. Grandpa found it in the barn and said I could have it." He hands my old mitt to me. I want to slide my hand inside of it but the strain on my shoulder would be too much. Instead, I hold it and turn it over a few times. This glove has seen a lot of wear and tear. I'm honored that he's using it, but he really should have a new one. It would be something I'd buy for him, because I don't expect his father to do it and I've gathered that Elizabeth doesn't say much to disagree with her husband.

"Wow, I haven't seen this ol' thing since I started high school."

"Yeah, Grandpa found it in the rafters one day. It's okay if I keep it, right?"

"Of course, until Cooperstown comes asking for it. Never know, maybe I'll be in the Hall of Fame after I retire."

Nolan shrugs. "You're already an all-star. They'd be dumb not to put you in the Hall of Fame."

I reach over and ruffle his hair. "I need to win a few championships and throw a lot more shut-outs before they'll even consider me . . . and I can't really do that while I'm injured, now, can I?"

"Nope, but you'll be stronger when you return."

My nephew makes me smile. "You know what, kid? You need to be a motivational speaker when you get older. You're wise beyond your years."

He looks down at his lap and fiddles with the worn-out leather on his mitt. "I want to be like you."

"Yeah? Well, let's go see who's out there playing and see if we can't find you someone to throw with. Unfortunately, your uncle is out of commission for another few weeks, but I can coach you."

We meet at the front of my truck and walk into the park together. Every field is bustling with activity and the first thing I notice is that it's all boys, no girls. The second thing I notice is the group of boys standing off to the side, watching but not participating.

"Do you know those boys?" I ask Nolan.

He nods and points, even though it's not polite to do so. "That's Nick, Blake, Gavin, Chase, and Ben. The boy on the very end is Sebastian but we call him Bash because he likes to hit things."

"Does he hit you?"

Nolan looks up. "No, just the walls and stuff. He's really nice but doesn't have any friends."

"Are you nice to him?"

My nephew shrugs. "Sometimes, but kids like Brady, Ryker and Tate tell us who we can and can't like."

"That's not cool."

"Nope," he says, shrugging again and sighing. "That's school for you, though." I don't remember school being like that, at least not until I had college offers coming in and the guy I thought was my best friend started acting like a jerk.

Nolan and I make our way deeper into the park. There are fields on both sides, filled with kids batting, pitching, tossing the ball back and forth, and running the bases. It feels like I'm back in spring training with all the activity.

Walking toward us is the former best friend. I'd know his ugly mug anywhere. He smiles and I know it's that fake as fuck shit he used to do when we were younger.

"I heard you were back in town but couldn't believe it until I saw you with my own two eyes. How the hell are you, Hawk?"

If my arm wasn't in a sling, I'd probably hug him. Actually, I'd probably punch him in the face just for being a douche all those years ago. Instead we shake hands, and he clasps my one good one with both of his, as tightly as he can. I hold back the laughter bubbling deep down because he's trying to hurt me and he's not even fazing me.

"Yep, came home to recuperate and see how things are going here."

Brett turns left and then right. "As you can see, things are good. Very active. The community really uses the Sinclair Fields."

The way he says it leaves me feeling sour, almost as if he's bitter. He spent years playing in my parent's makeshift baseball field. You would think he'd be happy with a state-of-the-art facility to coach in. It seems that the name on the front is what bothers him the most.

"How are things? You and Annie good?"

"Yeah, yeah," he says. "Annie's great. Business is booming. What about you, married?"

Shaking my head slowly. "Nah, no time for that right now. What is it that you do?"

"Invested in corporate capital. I own the construction store at the end of Main Street."

"You own that monstrosity?" Somehow that doesn't surprise me, and he's taken great offense for me saying as such by the look he's given me. He opens his mouth to retort, likely with something crass, but closes it rather quickly when someone calls out, "Dad". Brett turns around and his shoulders stiffen. Coming toward us is one of the players, dressed in full uniform.

"Little early for uniforms, isn't it?"

Brett glares.

"Hi, I'm Matty." To my complete shock the young woman sticks her hand out to shake mine. I would've never guessed Brett Larsen would let a girl on his baseball team, but apparently, I was wrong.

"Hey, Matty. Nice to meet ya, I'm Hawk Sinclair."

"I know. I watch you all the time. Sorry about your shoulder."

"Me too."

"Hey, Nolan."

He waves. "Hi, Matty."

While she and Nolan make small talk about some class project, I'm ignoring Brett and everything around me to focus on Matty. She looks familiar, but more so *seems* familiar. It's like I've met her before or know her from somewhere.

"We have to go," Brett says as he pulls his daughter away from us. He doesn't go back to the dugout but leaves the park, tugging her along.

"Do you know that guy, Uncle Hawk?"

I sigh. "Unfortunately, I do."

"He's not very nice."

"No, he's definitely not nice."

Nolan and I find a spot to throw near the kids who are lurking around. I ask them if they want to join, and they all do, except for Bash. Only a few of the kids know who I am, so Nolan takes it upon himself to do introductions and give them my stats for last year. Suddenly, I'm a hero or the coolest guy in Richfield. I'll take it. I do my best to instruct them on form and stance, but with one arm, it's limited. I'm not a coach by any means, but I think it's safe to say my nephew is going to make one hell of a pitcher.

TWELVE

BELLAMY

I'M knee deep in my flower bed, pulling dead, wilted clumps of weeds, leaves, and whatever else accumulated over the winter, when I hear "Mom" being yelled from down the street. Leaning back, I place my hand on my forehead to shield the sun so I can see what's going on. Chase, along with a few other boys, are pedaling down the road, racing each other. I stand and start heading toward my son, out of sheer fear that he's going to get hurt. I hate that my first reaction is that someone is trying or going to hurt my son. I can't help but think this way, especially after the last few days. When Chase said he was riding over to the baseball fields, I wanted to stop him, to tell him no, but I couldn't. I was surprised he wanted to go over there, given everything that's been going on, yet so proud of him for trying to stand up for himself. I'm halfway down the driveway when I stop abruptly. I hear laughter.

Chase is laughing.

He's laughing, right along with the other boys. No one is chasing him or calling him names. They're all riding next to each other with their baseball gloves hanging from their handlebars and one boy is tossing a ball in the air. I think that he must be the cool kid of this little posse, riding with one hand, seemingly without a care in the world. I turn my focus back to Chase and for the first time in a long time, my son seems happy and I'm thankful that my sunglasses can hide the fact that I have tears in my eyes because I wouldn't want him to see me like this.

The boys come to a skidding halt in my driveway and all five of them drop their bikes and come rushing toward me. I hear "Mom", "Ms. Patrick", and "baseball" all at once and have to put my hand up in a silent request for them to all stop talking.

"One at a time, boys." I haven't had to say something like that before and realize I love it. Never, in the past couple of years, did I suspect I'd be standing here like this, telling a group of boys who look happy and excited to be standing next to my son, to not all talk at once so I can understand each of them. I could easily get used to this.

"Mom, you'll never guess what we just did!"

"Tell me!" I beg.

"We. Played. Baseball!" Chase holds his arms out and punctuates each word with a jab in the air. My mouth drops open, not only in surprise but in shock as well. Could Brett have changed his mind? Was it David Farmer putting his foot down or did Brett realize he had made a mistake?

"And Ms. Patrick, it was amazing!" says the boy next to Chase.

"What's your name?" I ask him and the rest of the group.

"Mom, this is Ben, Blake, Nick and Gavin."

"It's nice to meet you," I tell them. "Okay, now fill me." I crouch down so that I have to look up at them. I want to see the excitement in their eyes when they share their amazing day.

"Ms. P . . . it's okay that I call you that, right?" Gavin asks. *Son, you can call me anything you'd like at this point as long as you never hurt my son.*

"Absolutely!"

"Great, okay. So, we're at the ballpark, right?" I nod along with him. "And we're just watching because none of us made the team and this guy comes up to us with his kid—"

"No, that was his nephew. Nolan's in my class," Blake adds. The two boys argue back and forth until I tell them it's fine either way and to continue with the story because I'm on the edge of my seat with anticipation.

"Okay," Gavin says, sighing heavily. "This guy tells us he wants to teach us how to throw. I mean I already know how, but this guy is Hawk Sinclair! You know who that is, right Ms. P? He's a pro at baseball and stuff. Pitches like a hundred miles an hour!"

Hawk Sinclair, the cowboy stranger from this morning.

"Mr. Larsen didn't ask you boys to play?"

"Pfft, my mom says Mr. Larsen is a . . ." I give Ben a stern look. I'm sure I agree with his mother, but he doesn't need to say it in front of the other boys.

I clap my hands together and stand. "It sounds like you boys had a great afternoon."

"We did, Mom. It was the best. Tomorrow, Mr. Sinclair said that if we come down to the park, he'll teach us how to throw a knuckle ball."

"That's great, although I don't exactly know what that is."

Gavin takes a baseball out of his glove and shows me what a knuckle ball looks like. I have to say, it doesn't look very comfortable, especially when you have the tiny hands of a ten-year-old.

"Wow, that's amazing, Gavin!"

"I'm going to be a pitcher like Hawk."

"Me, too" and "so am I" are echoed among the group. I tell Chase he has a little more time on his bike in case he and the boys want to ride around or go tell their moms about their exciting day and remind him to be home in time for dinner. He doesn't give me a hug but does yell, "bye, Mom!" as he hops on his bike and peddles toward the street. I don't know how long I stand there, watching as they ride away, but it's long after they've disappeared around the corner. I can still hear them laughing and wonder what could be so funny. With boys, you never know. What I *do* know is that seeing him smile makes my heart happy. My son had a great day, but I'm worried about what tomorrow may bring.

Returning to the task at hand, I attempt to focus on the winter clean-up that must happen. My mind is elsewhere though, thinking about the man I met earlier and how he changed my son's day. Of course, I hear Karter's voice inside my head, telling me that he's single, and that I should call him . . . which I absolutely shouldn't do. However, I want to thank him for what he did.

I finally give up on the overgrown weeds and head into my house to clean up and make dinner. The options are limited and the longer I stand in my kitchen with the refrigerator door open, the more I realize that I need to spend some serious time walking the aisles of the grocery store to restock everything.

"Dinner out it is," I say to myself. I think tonight calls for pizza. Downtown has a great place called The Depot. It's family friendly and Chase loves their pizza because it's not heavy on the sauce. I prefer their white pizza with pesto, chicken and broccoli, which I know Chase won't touch. The Depot always has an arcade, all you can eat soft serve, and a great salad bar. It's the perfect way to end the night.

When I hear Chase in the garage, I open the door and greet him. He's still smiling and it's the best sight ever. "Good day?"

"Great day," he replies as he comes into the kitchen. He sets his glove down on the table and sighs happily. "I made friends today."

"You certainly did, bud. Why don't you go wash up and we'll go out for pizza?" He nods in agreement and takes off down the hall. I will never understand why life has to be so hard. The boys he was with earlier are in his class, in our neighborhood. They see each other every day in school and on the playground. But, it's people like Brett Larsen who put this divide between the kids and the adults, who makes it seem like if you don't follow his path, you don't belong.

I *want* to belong.

I want *my son* to belong.

I'm ready to go when Chase comes out of the bedroom with clean clothes on. The dirt smudges on his face were cute, but I'm happy he washed them off. All the way into town, he prattles on about Hawk and how cool he is and how he can't wait to see him again tomorrow. Technically, I could see him to tomorrow too, or at least talk to him if I find out the asking price on the land. Surprisingly, the thought of speaking to him elates me, and I know it's because I want to thank him for spending time with my son.

Once we're parked, Chase is leading the way into the restaurant. He tells the hostess that we need a table for two and follows behind her to our seats. The confidence he's showing is new, and I like it a lot.

"Hey, Mr. Sinclair!" Chase yells out as we're making our way to our table. My steps falter as Hawk's eyes meet mine. He smiles and my lady bits jump for freaking joy. I try to smile back, but by the look on his face, I guess I must be more grimacing than smiling because he looks embarrassed.

"Hi, Chase. It's good to see you again."

"This is my mom," my son says, pointing toward me.

"Chase, I met Mr. Sinclair this morning. He was riding a horse." *He was riding a horse* . . . What the hell is wrong with me? Did I suddenly turn into Baby from *Dirty Dancing* with her whole, "I carried a watermelon" line?

"You ride horses?" Hawk laughs and for the life me, I hope he's laughing at my son's excitement of the fact that his idol can not only pitch but also ride a horse, and not my ridiculous commentary.

"Yeah, I do. Have you ever been on one?"

Chase shakes his head so fast I fear he's jarring his teeth loose. "Mom, can I ride a horse?"

"Sure, bud. Someday."

The hostess taps her foot, getting my attention. She holds up the menus and then places them on the table, a few away from where Hawk is sitting. "Bud, our seats are over there."

"You can join me if you want," Hawk says and once again we're making eye contact and my palms are sweating, my mouth is incredibly parched, and the devilish side of my conscious is saying things that aren't acceptable for others to hear in public.

"Um . . ."

"My nephew is with me if that helps you make a decision."

"Oh, you have a nephew?" I cringe. Of course, he does, and I know this. If the black hole of mortification could swallow me up, I'd appreciate the help in ending my awkwardness. It seems that's the only way I know how to be around this man. "I'm sorry, I don't know . . ."

He laughs but doesn't miss a beat when he stands, comes over to the side where I'm standing, and pulls out the chair. "Nolan and I would really like it if you and Chase joined us for dinner."

"We don't want to intrude."

"Hey, Chase!"

I follow the voice saying my son's name. This kid is smiling as he comes toward Chase and when he calls his friend "Nolan" in response, I know there's no way in hell I'm going anywhere. I find myself, once again, staring at the man beside me. He's dressed differently from before. Gone are the long sleeves, replaced by short ones which show off the muscles I suspected he had, along with full arm of tattoos. I try not to gawk, but there's no use in denying that I think Hawk is sexy.

"Looks like you're about to join us for dinner," he says so only I can hear him.

"Looks that way." I take the seat being offered and set my purse down on the floor. Hawk introduces me to his nephew before handing the boys a cup of tokens and telling them to scram.

"How much do I owe you for those tokens?"

"Not a single thing," he says as he leans back in his chair.

"Okay, then. How much do I owe you for putting a smile on my son's face?"

Hawk's demeanor changes and he leans forward. "About that . . . what can you tell me about the Little League program?"

I swallow hard and try not to think about the possible ramifications of what I'm about to say. He helped my son and that tells me Hawk is one of the good guys.

THIRTEEN

HAWK

ALMOST EVERYTHING about today has left a bad taste in my mouth. I know I shouldn't get involved in town politics because I don't live here. I shouldn't care that some big box store is putting the little guy out of business. Nor should it matter how the parents run the Little League program, but that's not who I am. It never has been. Back in high school, I ran for school president when I was a freshman, which was unheard of. Most underclassmen only run for their class. Not me. I wanted the top prize. I lost by one vote and that was the last time I lost. It's in my nature to care, to butt in when my opinion isn't asked for, and to make sure my stance on any and everything is heard loud and clear. So, I intend to figure out what's going on around here because seeing those boys standing there, longing to be on the field with their friends, was *wrong*. They should've been playing. All of this was evident when I asked them if they'd like to play catch and their faces lit up like it was Christmas morning.

The entire time I worked with them, Brett was lurking in the shadows. I was half tempted to call him out, ask him to join us, but the thought of having to spend another minute with him turned my stomach. I can't quite figure him out and

I'm not sure I should try. Our friendship came to blows many years ago and some things are better left where they died.

My nephew, though, *man* can he pitch! The kid is already trying to master the knuckle ball and suggested I teach the other boys, which was pretty hard to do with my left hand, but a few of them got it. The whole group of them was eager to learn, which again, put me on edge because they should be out there playing. That's why I had the fields built — to give the youth a chance to be kids and not have to act so grown up all the time.

Once the other boys left and the park started clearing out, Nolan and I hung out a little longer. He wanted to practice his batting stance and after rummaging through the shed, I found a bucket of balls. I dumped them out on home plate, flipped the bucket over so I could sit on it and tossed balls to my nephew until the sun went down. Afterward, because he knows me so well, he suggested we get pizza.

Which is how we've ended up at The Depot, and now the pretty real estate lady is being led to a table by the hostess and her son, Chase. What a character Chase is. That little guy is so eager to learn that he soaked up everything I taught him today and asked if we could do it again tomorrow. Of course, I said yes, which delighted Nolan.

I watch Chase and his mom as they come closer, wondering if I should say something or if she will. Earlier this morning, I was a bit tongue-tied when speaking to her. I wasn't expecting to find someone out in the middle of nowhere, let alone a beautiful woman. I can't even remember what I said to her, I just know I gave her my phone number, hoping she'd call.

She hasn't.

It's like they're walking in slow motion, knowing that I'm contemplating my next move and purposely giving me time to figure out a way to get their attention. I could stand up, wave my one good arm and cause a scene. Or I could sit here and wait for Nolan to come back from the bathroom and pay my nephew to go talk to them for me. The latter sounds like the best plan.

"Hey, Mr. Sinclair." I look up from the menu when I hear my name and try not to smile. I love this kid. He did exactly what I couldn't do. The best part about this situation? His mother stops right behind him. The worst part? I look at her, really study her, and find the prim and proper lady from this morning is gone, and in her place is someone that I'm extremely attracted to although I don't know why. I know nothing about her, yet I feel like she's been part of my life for as long as I can remember. It's odd, I've never felt this way before and I find myself glancing back and forth between her and her ring finger. Nothing, not even a faint line. I want to invite them to sit down and give the boys my wallet, so they'll leave us alone, because every part of me wants to know everything there is to know about this woman.

She smiles and I realize I'm staring like a crazy ass stalker. I turn away and mumble, "Hi, Chase. It's good to see you again."

"This is my Mom." He points to the blonde bombshell standing behind him, who is wearing an old college sweatshirt with her hair in a bun and barely any make-up on.

"Chase, I met Mr. Sinclair this morning. He was riding a horse," she says as her face morphs into pure mortification. I laugh. I can't help it. It's such a random thing to say, but I love that she blurted it out.

"You ride horses?" Chase is overly excited about this fact, which I find odd since he lives in Montana and most people out here ride horses.

"Yeah, I do. Have you ever been on one?"

Chase's head goes back and forth so fast, my eyes are having a hard time keeping up with him. "Mom, can I ride a horse?" he turns to her.

"Sure, bud. Someday," she says endearingly to him. I

know in this moment it's going to happen because I'm going to make sure Chase has the opportunity. "Bud, our seats are over there."

"You can join me if you want?" I try to make my voice as even as possible, without a hint of desperation, but it rises at the end like a prepubescent boy getting excited.

"Um . . ."

"My nephew is with me if that helps you make a decision."

"Oh, you have a nephew?" She immediately covers her face. Damn, she's cute when she's blushing, which is often considering how awkward our encounters have been. "I'm sorry, I don't know . . ."

I can't contain my laughter and I don't want to torture her anymore. I stand, move behind her, and pull out her chair. "Nolan and I would really like it if you and Chase joined us for dinner."

"We don't want to intrude."

"Hey, Chase!" Saved by my nephew. Although, he's only a temporary distraction. Being this close to her, I can smell her perfume. The sweet scent sends my thoughts into overdrive and makes my mouth water with anticipation of a goodnight kiss at her car door when we leave, which is not going to happen. Something tells me that Bellamy isn't a kiss and run kind of gal. I clear my mind of all the thoughts I have about her and try to pay attention to the boys. This lasts for about ten seconds when I turn slightly to see if she's going to sit down. She's staring, boring holes into me. Not out of anger, but attraction. I can see the desire in her eyes and start to think that maybe a kiss later isn't out of the question.

"Looks like you're about to join us for dinner." My words come out too softly and I fear that she's going to tell me no, but she doesn't.

"Looks that way."

She sits down and I go back to my seat, jamming my thigh

into the corner of the table. It fucking hurts and if I were anywhere else, I'd let everyone around me know. I bite the inside of my cheek and grunt through the pain.

"Bellamy, this is my nephew, Nolan."

"It's nice to meet you, ma'am," he says.

"You too, Nolan."

"Here." I hand the boys a cup of tokens. "I'll come get you when the pizza arrives. Stay together, buddy system and all that." Nolan and Chase walk side-by-side, bumping shoulders. I want to ask his mom if he has trouble in school, with making friends, but don't want to seem like I'm nosey. The boy gives off a vibe that he's lonely.

"How much do I owe you for those tokens?"

"Not a single thing." I lean back in the chair and stretch my legs out under the table. I probably look like a fool. I definitely feel like one. I can't imagine what she's thinking right now with me kicked back, my arm in a sling, looking like some roughed up gangster.

"Okay, then." She smiles. "How much do I owe you for putting a smile on my son's face?"

I know my features change when she says this. It's my opening and I'm going to take it. I lean forward. "About that . . . what can you tell me about the Little League program?"

My question has caught her off guard, which wasn't my plan. Bellamy Patrick is easy to read. There's definitely something going on here and it involves her son.

"I grew up here," she starts off. "Left after high school, went to college in Washington, fell in love, got married, had a kid and subsequently fell out of love."

"I'm sorry."

"Actually, I should be. I'm sorry, you asked about Little League and here I am giving you a recap of my life story."

"I've enjoyed it so far," I tell her. "Please continue."

"Right," she says, smiling. "Where was I? Oh, after my divorce, I thought raising Chase here would be a good thing.

We moved shortly after the baseball season started last year. Obviously, we missed try-outs, but Brett said Chase had potential and that I should send him to these camps and clinics. Plus, Brett holds these open practices or whatever and the kids can go work out with him. Whatever Chase asked to do, I did. We were both confident that he'd make the team this year."

"And he didn't?"

She shakes her head. "Nope and when I ask Brett . . ." she pauses, looks down at the table and sighs. "Anyway, Brett says he needs to work harder."

The waitress arrives at our table, poised to take our order. "Do you know what you want?" I ask Bellamy. She nods and tells me. "Okay, we'll have a large cheese, large white and a family salad."

"And to drink?"

I glance at Bellamy. "Chase can drink soda if Nolan can."

"Four sodas," I tell the waitress. Once she's gone, my attention is back on the beautiful woman across from me. "When I had those fields built, it was so kids had a place to play. When I was growing up, we played at my parent's ranch. My dad cleared a space, we put some bleachers in which were no more than 4 x 10's or whatever they were, sitting on stumps. But we lined the field and played until dark. My mom would even run this makeshift concession stand. After I went to college, my dad let the grass grow over it, which was fine because once I signed my deal, I had those fields done up.

"Anyway, my point is, Chase should be playing, and I don't understand why there are kids without a team right now."

Bellamy looks around, her facing growing grim. I reach my hand across the table and give hers a squeeze. "I've probably said too much as it is."

"You haven't said anything other than your son didn't make the team, which I think is bullshit since I've seen him play. He's smart, a total sponge when it came to soaking up what I taught him today and is more than eager to play. That's exactly what coaches want in a player. So, my question was and still is, what do you know about the program?"

"It's corrupt. It's a popularity game. Most of the kids on the team are bullies and I think that's because of the mentality Brett Larsen has. He's a creep and trying to ruin my career, which means he'll probably try to ruin yours as well."

I laugh hard. "He can try. What's he going to do, call the media and tell them I'm having dinner with a beautiful woman and her son?"

She blushes and I find myself wanting to run my fingers over the pink of her cheeks. "I don't know," she says quietly. She adjusts in her chair and tries to smile.

"What did he do?"

"Do you know David Farmer?"

"I do, he was my high school baseball coach."

She nods. "I went and saw him the other day, asking for help. Mostly, I wanted to get a mentor or something like a big brother for Chase. I told Mr. Farmer about the tryouts and all that, but I never got to the big brother part because Brett called, and I just panicked and left. Next thing I know, Brett's texting me, calling my boss, and basically making my life hell. Which is why you found me out in the field this morning . . . down on the main road, this land abuts Larsen's property for that stupid store he built, and he's been stockpiling his over-stock on the property. My boss wants to stick it to Brett and is working with the owner to sell the property because adverse possession rules apply."

"I'm interested in the property, but more concerned with Brett. I saw him earlier and the vibe I got . . . it's off."

She nods and do I.

"Farmer asked me to coach a team, but I can't. Not with

my shoulder. I don't mind helping if someone else has the time."

"But not many people are willing to piss Brett Larsen off."

I frown, not liking the way things are around town. "How much is the property?" I wasn't interested in that piece of land until now. I had every intention earlier of telling my dad about it so he could expand, but now I think I'm going to make the purchase.

"I'm hoping to have the price tomorrow."

"You'll be sure to call me right away, right?"

"Yes, of course," she says.

"Good." I lean back in the chair but am still uncertain about what's actually going on. I want to ask her more, but I also want to get to know her. I don't want her to think the only reason I asked her to sit with us is because of this. I need to change the subject, something light and fun.

"So, do you watch baseball?" I ask, wiggling my eyebrows at her.

Again, she blushes. "Sorry, no. Chase does, and I have a feeling that tonight he's going to tell me all about you. Oh, plus one of my closest friends does. In fact, I think you're somewhat of a local hero around these parts."

"And yet, you had no idea who I was this morning."

"Did that bother you?"

I shake my head slowly. "Not in the slightest. It was nice being able to have a conversation with someone without them falling at my feet, professing their insta love for me."

She leans forward and I do the same. "Hawk Sinclair, I can promise you that I won't go gaga over you every time you enter the room."

"What about if we're in private, Bellamy?"

FOURTEEN
BELLAMY

HIS QUESTION LEAVES ME STUNNED. There isn't a doubt in my mind that I look like a gaping fish, seeking water to keep me alive, but I can't help it. I want to say something . . . anything, yet nothing comes to mind. He can't be serious, can he? We just met and I don't do the hook-up thing. I have a son to think about and can't be entertaining men on the fly.

Hawk adjusts in his seat and starts to chuckle. I don't know what he finds so funny unless I'm misunderstanding the situation, but I'm pretty certain he propositioned me. Or maybe I propositioned him. *Oh, God.* Did I?

Suddenly, I'm flushed and in desperate need of something to drink. I'm about to stand when the waitress stops at our table with a tray of glasses. Eight in fact, four of them filled with water and the other four are empty so we can go to the soda machine ourselves.

"Thank you," I say to her as she sets a glass down in front of me. I don't care if it's rude or not, I pick it up and put that straw in my mouth so damn fast and start . . . Nope, can't do it. I decide to drink directly from the cup itself because I don't need Hawk getting any more ideas. After she leaves, he reaches forward for my glass, taking it away from me.

"I'm afraid I've offended you."

My head twitches in a half-assed attempt to say no. "N - not at all," I stammer.

"I did and that wasn't my intent. I was simply making a joke because, like I said, you're not like most women and I don't know . . . I'm not even sure why I said that. I'm sorry. Sometimes my mouth gets the better of me."

"Apology accepted." Except now there seems to be nothing but awkward silence between us. He's focused on his glass of water and I'm fiddling with my fingers. Every so often, we look up at each other and make an attempt at a smile, but nothing more.

"This is stupid," I say.

"What, dinner?"

"No, this . . ." I motion between the two of us. "This weird pregnant pause we have going on. I get that women probably throw themselves at you, and they should . . . you're gorgeous." Instantly I feel my cheeks heat up. "And part of me wants too, because of what you did for my son today."

Hawk leans his good arm on the table. "Let me get this straight. You're somewhat attracted to me . . ." I start to talk, but he holds his hand up, silently asking me to let him finish. "Because of what I did for your son?"

I let his words sink in while I gnaw the ever-loving crap out of my inner lip. "Chase's dad is absent. He has a new family and didn't really say much when I told him I wanted to move back to Montana. I think . . ." I sigh, taking a deep breath. "My decision was easier for him, too, because it's what his new wife wanted — all of the attention to be on her and their daughter — Chase was just in the way. Anyway, what I'm trying to say is, as a single mom, knowing that a man took time out of his day to make my son happy makes him the most attractive man to me."

He seems to ponder what I'm telling him. I didn't say

those things about Chase's dad to make Hawk feel bad, but to let him know where I'm coming from.

"I don't know if it was just playing catch with him or if it's something you said, but when my son came home from the park today, he was riding his bike with some boys who've never come around before and he was laughing. He was so *happy*." I pause and inhale deeply to calm my emotions. When I glance at Hawk, he's staring at me intently. I clear my throat and lean closer so my voice doesn't carry to the other tables. "I don't remember the last time Chase laughed so much, and now he's off with Nolan like they've been best friends forever."

Hawk looks over his shoulder toward the arcade room and then back at me. "I'm going to have to let what you've told me sink in before I respond. I have a real hard time understanding how children can be so mean to each other."

"Me too, but around here parents are extremely divided."

"I've gathered."

The waitress comes back with our pizzas and salad and after she sets them down, without any warning, Hawk whistles so loudly I fear my eardrums are bleeding.

"What the hell?"

"Watch," he says, cocking his head toward the arcade. Within seconds, Nolan and Chase are walking back to the table.

"Mom, I'm going to go wash my hands. Come on, Nolan." And just like that both boys are running toward the bathroom.

"How did you do that?" I ask in amazement.

He shrugs. "My dad taught me how to whistle when I was younger than Nolan. Living on the ranch, there's all these hidden threats and while my dad didn't mind my sisters and I roaming, if a ranch hand saw something, they or my dad would whistle. If we didn't whistle back right away or appear quickly, they'd mount up and come look for us. Now, you tell me how you got my nephew to wash his hands so easily."

"I'm a germaphobe, which means I need to go wash mine as well."

I stand and take a step to leave but Hawk's hand clamps down on my wrist. "Are you talking like OCD levels?"

"No, just the level that a restaurant is never truly clean." He sighs, almost as if he's relieved that I'm not extreme. In the bathroom, I take care of business, wash my hands and check what little make-up I have on to make sure my eyeliner isn't running. The door opens and normally I ignore whoever is walking in, but something tells me that I need to see who it is.

Annie Larsen is standing there, staring.

"Hi, Annie," I say, smiling.

"My husband told me that you propositioned him. That you're willing to sleep with him in order to get your son onto the team."

I turn to face her and really study the woman in front of me. Her clothes are loose fitting, like she's lost some weight, and there are bags under her eyes. She doesn't look like the refined and posh version of her normal self.

"Annie . . ." I pause and gather my thoughts. "I had dinner with Brett, at his suggestion. I thought it would be all of us, including Matty, but he insisted it be only us. I know you don't want to believe me, but I have the text messages to prove it. My phone is at the table I'm sitting at if you'd like to come read them."

She drops her head in defeat. "He's cheating. Weirdly enough, I had hoped it was you because it would make sense. I find receipts all the time, and his calendar is filled with the initials BP so when my sister saw you at dinner the other night, I figured it was you and I asked him."

"Annie, I'm so sorry . . . but I can promise you I'm not that type of woman."

She nods and walks toward one of the stalls. "How is he?"

"Brett? I wouldn't know I—"

"No, Hawk. How is he?"

"Oh . . . um, fine I guess."

"Don't hurt him, okay?"

Before I can respond, she steps behind the wooden door and locks it. I don't want to leave her but staying in the bathroom to wait seems like an odd thing to do at this point. "Ann, if you need to talk, call me," I say out loud. "I know what it's like to be married to an adulterer." With that said, I walk out and back to the table, bumping into Hawk on the way.

My eyes scan the restaurant for any sign of Brett. If Ann is here, surely, he is as well. The restaurant is packed, and the lighting isn't the best so it's hard to see.

"Who are you looking for?" Hawk asks.

"Brett," I tell him. "Ann came into the bathroom, accused me of having an affair with her piece of crap husband."

"Annie's here?"

My steps falter and Hawk turns. "What's wrong?" he asks.

"Nothing, just . . ." I sigh. "She told me not to hurt you."

"We were good friends growing up, but she's always been in love with Brett. I took her to senior prom after he cheated on her. I guess some things never change." He reaches for my hand and pulls me alongside of him.

When we get to the table, the boys are already stuffing their faces and I'm pleasantly surprised to find Chase with some salad on his plate. For some reason, I find myself making Hawk's plate. He doesn't say anything but smiles so big that I assume he appreciates my odd and overly friendly gesture. Still, while we're eating, I can't get Ann off my mind. More so, that Hawk seems happy she would make a comment like she had. As much as I hate thinking this, I'm going to have to ask Karter for the lowdown on them. They're younger than me and were in high school long after I left Richfield.

Every so often, I look around the restaurant and tune out what the boys are talking about to see if I can see or hear anything. Mostly, I'm looking for Brett. I want to be prepared if he decides to interrupt us or plan what I'd say to him if he stopped by our table. Every time I scan the area, Hawk's watching me. He probably thinks I'm paranoid or looking for an escape route to get away from him. Truth is, this is the best night I've had in many, many years. I don't even care that we're in a busy restaurant with rambunctious children all around. I'm fairly sure I like the man sitting across from me, even if it's not something I'm ready to admit to anyone but myself.

The boys polish off a large pizza by themselves and both claim to be in a food coma and say they're having food babies. Hawk suggests they go back to the arcade until we're ready to leave and hands Nolan some money.

"Let me pay for this round of tokens," I say, as I dig through my purse for my wallet. By the time I have a twenty out, the boys are gone. I glare at Hawk. "You can't pay for everything."

"Why not?" he asks, shrugging.

"Because, I'm not someone who takes advantage."

"I never said you were."

"Well, I don't want you to think I expect it because of who you are, either, so you'll just have to let me treat you to dinner or lunch sometime."

Hawk smiles and damn it if it doesn't twist my insides. "Do you cook?"

"Yes."

"Do you have a grill?"

"I do."

"Tell you what, I'll bring the steaks and use your grill. You do everything else and we'll have dinner at your place tomorrow."

"Um . . ."

"Too forward?" he asks. "I think you bring it out in me. Normally, I'm a really mellow kind of guy."

Take a risk, my inner voice says. "Dinner will be perfect. But first, you need to tell me about yourself."

Our waitress is back with the check, but Hawk tells her we're not done and wants to see the dessert menu. I glance at my watch and see we've been here for almost two hours. It's getting late and the boys have school tomorrow. I'm about to tell him this when he starts talking.

"I'm the middle child. I have two sisters. My oldest, Elizabeth who you went to school with, she's married to her high school sweetheart, Warner, who loathes me. He's probably sitting on my parent's porch with a shotgun, waiting for Nolan to come home, but that's a story for another day. My sister Avery has twins, they freak me out."

I can't help but laugh when he shudders. "Why?"

"I don't know. They're identical in every way. The way they walk, talk, look. They have a freaky twin language and they scare me. I love them, but they give me the heebie-jeebies. Anyway, my parents are still married. My mom takes care of the ranch hands, does some photography, is my biggest fan, and does some crafting on top of being the best grandma in the world. I know this because she has the coffee mug to prove it. My dad is a hardworking rancher who inherited the ranch from my grandfather. And then there's me — the semi-disappointment, but not really — son."

"What do you mean?"

He clears his throat and takes a drink of soda. "My dad wanted me to be a rancher. My mom, she's the dreamer. There's no doubt in my mind that she wears the pants, but my dad can be a real hard ass sometimes. He was never fond of me playing baseball, which I get, but supported me, nonetheless. I was awarded a full-ride to the University of Utah and by my junior year I had been drafted by the Renegades."

"In Boston?" I clarify.

"Yep. Finished my first semester of my senior year, went to spring training, spent a few months in AAA and then I was called up." He stops and looks at me. "AAA is one level below where I'm playing now."

"Which is the top of league . . . yes?"

"Yeah, exactly. Anyway, that's my life. I love my family, love my teammates. I'm doing what I love in a great city. . . "

"But something's missing?"

His eyes dart up, meeting mine. "How did you know?"

I shrug. "Women's intuition and all that. I feel the same way sometimes. I love my career, I love my son, but there are times when I'm sitting there with this gaping hole and I don't know what I should do to fill it."

"I didn't feel it until I came back here."

"You don't come home often, I take it?"

Hawk picks up a discarded straw wrapper and starts rolling it between his fingers. "It's hard with my dad, brothers-in-law and the ranch. There's a lot of guilt. I take my parents on vacation to spend time with them and avoid coming home . . . well, mostly my mom because my dad doesn't want to leave. When I had surgery, they were both there though. My mom made me come back here to rehab."

"Would you rather be in Boston right now?"

"No, I'm perfectly content sitting right across from you at this very moment, Bellamy."

It's the way he says my name that sends shivers down my spine. I'm waiting for him to laugh or tell me he's just kidding, but he doesn't. He studies me. For what, I don't know, but his intense gaze is penetrating, digging deep for whatever he's seeking. I think I'm seeking the same thing.

FIFTEEN

HAWK

THIS BEING up before the sun stuff has to stop. I've never been a fan of taking pills, especially something that could cause an addiction, and the only form of pain relief I'm taking now is ibuprofen and aspirin. However, I'd like to sleep at least one night without tossing and turning, without thoughts weighing heavily on my mind, and without wondering if I'm going to have a spot on the Renegades when I return from rehab. Sure, I have a contract, but those are easily pushed aside for the newer, stronger, *healthier* pitchers coming up the ranks. My agent says I have nothing to worry about, but it's his job to say those things. I have *everything* to worry about.

Of course, after last night's dinner date, I was worried about something completely unrelated and spent hours surfing social media for anything I can find on Bellamy Patrick. When I met her yesterday, I was intrigued. Mostly because she was traipsing through a mud pit and had no idea where she was. It was never my intention to scare her, but I was honestly afraid she was going to walk right into the barbed wire fence and hurt herself. And last night . . . well that couldn't have worked out any better for me. From the moment I saw her and her son, I knew I would've done anything to have them join us for dinner.

I finally give up on sleep and walk across my room to look out the window, which faces our backyard. There were so many times while growing up that I'd climb out and sit on the roof of the porch. This was where I practiced what I was going to say to my dad when I decided to pursue baseball in college and not something that would benefit the ranch. Although, in a way, my career has actually done so. Over the years, I've gifted my parents with payments on taxes, new vehicles, or the latest and best farm equipment. I may not be working the fields, herding the cattle, or wrangling horses but I'm definitely contributing.

When my teen years hit and girls became my second priority, I'd bring them up here at night to star gaze. Back then, I thought I was smooth and was deemed a player because I was never serious about anyone in particular. I'd wait for girls to ask me out, mostly because there wasn't one particular girl who held all my attention — or as one of my sisters would say, it was because I had to play the *entire* field. It was, and still is, their lame attempt at a pun.

The sky is as black as can be and the only illumination is coming from the barn. If I strain, I can see shadows moving around, and I can definitely hear muffled voices. Around here, work starts before the sun rises and ends after sunset. The days are long, often cold, and can drag on during the summer. Some of the people that work here have done so for years. My parents do their best to keep their employees happy but working on a ranch is hard work and not for the faint of heart.

As I did the day before, I decide to take Cadbury out for another ride. It's not always the wisest to ride off under the cloak of darkness, but it's really the only time I can clear my head. After I dress, I head downstairs and find my mother sitting at the kitchen table.

"Morning," I say as I enter the room. On the table is a breakfast spread of sausage, eggs, biscuits, and gravy. Instead of eating, I pour myself the last cup of coffee in the pot and proceed to change and fill the filter with new grounds and the reservoir with water. I'm not about to have my dad or anyone else yell at me for taking the last cup.

I look over at my mom, she's tired. "Are you feeling okay?" I don't know why that's the first thing I ask my mom. My parents work hard, my father harder than anyone I know, and I know they're getting older, which scares me. I've suggested retirement but know my father would rather ride off into the sunset than stop working, and my mom will do whatever her husband suggests.

She smiles softly, picks up her mug and takes a sip of her coffee. After she sets it back down, she rests her hands on the table. "I'm feeling fine and so is your father. I just worry, sometimes."

"About what?" I place my hand on top of hers. If they're in financial trouble, I want to help.

"About my children. My grandchildren. The ranch. Your father."

"What's there to worry about?"

She doesn't answer but gets up from her place at the table and walks around me to pick up a plate. She starts loading it with food and finally sets it down in front of me. "Eat."

"I'm not hungry."

"I don't care, Hawk. You didn't eat yesterday, minus whatever fast food place you stopped at on your way to therapy, not to mention the pizza you had last night with your nephew, which you can't survive off despite what you may think."

"Hey, I've spent a great many years eating pizza. Look at me, I'm fit." I use my left hand to tap my abs, which I'm afraid to admit could use some work.

Her coffee cup is back in her hand and she eyes me before

taking another drink. "According to Elizabeth, Nolan declared yesterday to be the best day of his life."

"That's a little sad considering we didn't do much other than toss the ball around and go out to dinner. Really, Ma. They have to let him be a boy before time passes him by."

"I've said as much to your sister. I should warn you though, she fully intends to ask you what you're doing with Bellamy Patrick."

My eyebrow raises and I ask my mom, "Why? Is there something wrong with Bellamy?"

She chuckles. "Not that I'm aware of. According to Elizabeth, Nolan talked non-stop about the four of you having dinner and your sister being your sister is probably reading into things."

"Probably, is an understatement." I dig into my food and take a few bites before putting my fork down. "I met her yesterday and ran into her again at dinner. Not much more to tell." I can't look my mom in the eyes when I say there isn't more to tell because tonight, I have dinner plans with Bellamy and I'm very much looking forward to seeing her.

I eat rather fast so I can get outside and away from the heavy gaze of my mother. She's watching me, waiting for me to spill my guts, and I will — just not right now. I wash and stack my plate, kiss her on the cheek and tell her that I'll be around but not home for dinner.

"Tell Bellamy I said 'hi'," she says as I step outside. I turn to find my mother smiling. She gives me a little finger wave and starts to giggle. In the barn, a couple of the ranch hands are busy working, mucking out the stalls.

"Morning, Mr. Sinclair."

"Morning, guys. I'm going to take Cadbury out for a bit."

One of them drops his shovel and walks over to her stall and is kind enough to saddle her up for me. I did it yesterday, but it was hard with one hand, even if I did cheat a little bit. I know I need to let my shoulder rest, but it's against my nature to be idle.

"Have a good ride, sir."

"Thanks," I say as I mount the mare. One little tap of my heels into her sides and we're trotting our way out of the barn. She neighs as we walk past one of the stallions, causing me to laugh. "Cadbury, are you flirting?" I give her a good pat and direct her to where I want her to go.

I'm about to push Cadbury into a full gallop when Warner calls my name. He trots up next to me, "Where ya headed?"

"Nowhere in particular. Do you need something?" Not that I can do much for him and if he only wants to complain about his son, I don't want to listen.

"I'll ride with you."

Lovely.

We start off in silence, which I'm fine with. Warner may have been around a lot when I was growing up, but we were never friends. I always saw him as the clinger who chased after my sister. He's good to Elizabeth though, so I can't complain too much about him.

"Nolan had a great time yesterday."

"Good, I'm glad." I wait for him to add something sarcastic.

"I'd let him play—"

"But?" I interject.

Warner sighs. "But there's a lot of politics in town and I don't want Nolan part of that."

"What do you mean?"

"Look, your sister has wanted to tell you, but I've told her to keep you out of it."

"Out of what, Warner?"

"You know I'm not a sports guy and I've made it clear that I want Nolan working on the ranch, but I'm not a piece of crap father either. Elizabeth signed Nolan up for try-outs twice. We never got a call telling us when to go along. Next thing we know, teams are set and he's not on any of them."

I have a very sick feeling in my stomach as he tells me this. First, David hints that the Little League program isn't on the up and up and begs me to coach, then last night, Bellamy glosses over the drama that's going on, and now my brother-in-law tells me this. Thing is, I shouldn't care. I shouldn't worry about how the program is run, whether it's fair or not. But I do, and the more and more I think about it, the more pissed off I become at Brett Larsen.

"What the hell is going on in this town?"

"Corruption," he states so matter-of-factly that I know he's not lying. "New mayor. He's young, wants to see corporations coming in to bring in jobs. He runs some scam, although no one can prove it yet. Buys up property for himself and then within a year or two, the buildings are destroyed by fire. He collects the insurance money and sells the lot for cheap and always to some city corporation. By the end of the year, we'll have a new pharmacy, restaurant and gas station — all national chains — right along Main Street."

"That's not what Richfield stands for."

"Nope, it's not, but the Richfield you remember doesn't exist. Hell, the people we went to school with aren't even friends with us anymore because we don't play their silly little games. Maybe we should because it messes with Nolan . . . the kids are bullies and their parents don't care because they're bullies themselves."

"Nolan not getting a call for try-outs doesn't make sense."

"Sure, it does," he says. "You screwed Annie Miller and her husband has never forgiven you."

"They weren't together." I remind him.

"To him, I don't think that matters." He sighs heavily. If Brett Larsen is still holding a grudge, he needs to take it up with me, not my family. It's that simple.

We ride for a bit and I tell him about the land that's going up for sale. It abuts my father's property, giving him the ability to expand, but Warner isn't so sure. I'm certain it's a money issue, which means I'll write a check. If my father never does anything with the land, so be it, but I'd rather him own it then have some superstore go in and contaminate the land.

Warner and I don't say much on the way back. He talks some more about my sister and how much he loves her, but that she drives him crazy sometimes. I agree with him. She's a handful. But, when we get back, she's there waiting for him, just as she's always been. I leave the love birds and return Cadbury back to the ranch hand to take care of for me. I need to shower and head into town. There's a little political game being played, and I want to get to the bottom of it. Besides, it's a good way to avoid any questions from my sister about Bellamy.

SIXTEEN
BELLAMY

"WHOA, HOT DATE LATER?" Karter greets me at the door with a cup of coffee and what I'm taking as a compliment.

"I don't know what you're talking about." She's hot on my heels, following me to my desk. I drop my bags and take a seat in my chair. "You're staring."

"You did your hair."

I roll my eyes. "I do my hair every morning."

She eyes me suspiciously and grins. "Could this have anything to do with you having dinner with a very eligible bachelor last night?" The second she asks this, I start to blush and turn away, pretending to be interested in something on my desk, but I know she's already caught on. I do have a date . . . sort of. If you call said bachelor coming over later with steaks to grill a date. Sadly, I'm so behind on today's trends, I don't know what to call it other than dinner . . . at my place . . . to which he invited himself. I couldn't have said no if I tried. He's mesmerizing, intriguing, and he took an interest in my son before he even knew me.

"How'd you hear about last night?" I ask her.

"You're the talk of the town. I swear, that's all I've heard about since I stood in line for coffee this morning."

"Okay, but what exactly did you hear?" The only person I told was my mother. Unless it was Annie, although I don't see her being a blabber mouth.

"That you and Hawk, the Hottie, we're having an intimate dinner together."

"At the Depot . . ." I point out. There isn't a single romantic vibe to a family pizza parlor. "Besides, Chase and Hawk's nephew were there. Not sure how intimate dinner can be over pizza and salad with two kids around."

Instead of sitting across from me, Karter sits on the edge of my desk. I want to ignore her and pretend she's being ridiculous, but I also want to tell her everything. How we spent hours just talking, and how I can't wait to see him again tonight.

"Don't," she says, out of the blue.

"Don't what?"

"Fall in love."

I wave her off. "Seriously, Karter? We had pizza with the boys."

"Yes, but I see that dreamy look you have in your eyes. I get it, Hawk's good-looking. He's kind, sweet, and very generous. But he lives in Boston and rarely returns to Montana. In fact, my mom says the only reason he's here is because of his shoulder injury."

"His mother insisted he come home," I interject. "I know this, Karter. He told me."

"Oh." Which is probably the least she's ever said in her entire life. "Before I forget, an Adrienne Hubbard called here looking for you."

Adrienne Hubbard and I used to be best friends until I divorced Greg. Her husband, Robbie, is best friends with my ex and when a divorce happens, it tends to divide friendships, too. I cried harder over losing her than I did my ex. "Did she leave a number?"

Karter shakes her head. "Sorry, said she'd call back. New client?"

"No, old friend."

My phone chimes with an email alert. Instead of reading it on the tiny screen, I boot up my laptop. It's my plan to work in the office today, to follow up on leads, check in with some clients who haven't made decisions yet and prepare a couple of listings. Honestly, I want to stay in here and avoid running into Hawk. There's no reason he'd need to come in, even if I do have a price for him on that piece of land.

Karter goes back to her office after she asks if I want to make plans for lunch. I tell her I do and get to work. Once my email is open, I'm on the phone with the landowner, discussing his options. He keeps saying he wants to "stick it to Larsen" and while I couldn't agree more, there are certain steps that have to be taken.

"Mr. Longwood, are you positive you didn't give Surge, LLC or Brett Larsen permission to store on your land?" It doesn't matter what he says, I will have to go and do some research in the clerk's office for a possible filing pertaining to this issue. To prove adverse possession can be difficult and I have a feeling because it involves Brett Larsen, it's going to be an uphill battle.

"I've done no such thing. That man keeps piling his product on my property."

"I know, sir. He's been doing it for years and the law may be on his side."

"It's not," he tells me. "Six months ago, I went to court and they issued an injunction."

A big smile spreads across my face. This is perfect. Of course, Larsen thought he was above a court order. "Well this is very good news. So, Mr. Longwood, how much would you like to sell the property for?"

He gives me very strict stipulations, most of them involve

Larsen and how if he's interested, he needs to make an offer, which I'm not to accept. This is a dangerous game, but Mr. Longwood is adamant that Surge, LLC — or anyone who has anything to do with Brett Larsen — do not buy his land. Challenging, but doable, especially if I can get Hawk to buy it.

As soon as I hang up, Karter rings my phone to tell me I have a call on line one. I don't bother asking her who it is because there's a good chance she didn't ask. It's not her job to screen our calls, but the front desk gal seems to be on an extended leave.

"Bellamy Patrick."

"Bellamy, it's Gregory." *Gregory*. Back when we were together, he was Greg. Fun loving, chill Greg. Now he introduces himself as Gregory and expects everyone to refer to him as such. It makes me want to puke.

I want to groan loudly, be rude, and hang up on him. I don't, but I don't say anything either because I really don't feel like speaking to him.

"Hello, are you there?"

"Yep."

"I expected you to call me after you had dinner with Brett."

I roll my eyes. "I expect you to visit your son, pay child support on time, and be a parent. Seems neither of us are having our expectations met these days."

"Bell, I don't have time to get into this with you. When is Chase's first game?"

"Why? Are you actually going to come to Richfield to watch or do you expect me to have some sort of live video stream going so you can say you were present?"

Greg sighs heavily. "Why is everything an issue with you?"

"I don't know, Greg. You tell me."

"I'm trying here."

"Try harder," I tell him. "Get in the car and come here on the weekends. Make arrangements to see your son. Respect his wishes and keep the new wife and daughter at home. He wants to spend time with this dad, not your new family." I'm worked up, angry. My teeth are clenching so hard that I'm giving myself a headache.

"That's not fair—"

"You don't get to talk about what's fair, Greg," I seethe into the receiver. "You left your son without looking back. I don't care about what you did to me and our marriage, but your son . . . you walked away from him without a second thought. He has every right to ask that you visit him and not bring your family. The longer you stay away, the worse off your relationship is going to be with him."

There's a long pause where Greg and I are both just breathing into the receivers. He finally clears his throat. "I'd like to see Chase. Can we meet halfway?"

As much as it pains me to agree, I do, because it'll make my son happy. "Yes, we can do that. When?"

"What's his schedule like?"

I inhale deeply, unprepared for this end of the conversation. "Chase isn't playing baseball, Greg. Your *friend* . . ." I choke on the word before finishing my thought. Greg and Brett are alike in a lot of ways, I should've seen that earlier. I contemplate what I should say next. If I tell my ex the truth, he won't believe me or find some way to twist it around, and it's just not worth it. So, I lie. "There wasn't any room on the team, but Chase has been working out with a coach so next year things will be different."

"Who's the coach? Do I know him?"

"Nope," I say, shaking my head even though he can't see me. "Local guy who used to play in college. He's helping out." Just as those words come out of my mouth, the door chimes and Hawk walks in. Our office is open concept, except for Karter's office, so he sees me right off and smiles bashfully. He's dressed similarly to yesterday with jeans, white t-shirt, his long-sleeved flannel half-way unbuttoned, and a baseball cap.

He saunters toward me, keeping the same expression on his face, and when gets to my desk, he tips his hat toward me.

"Hello, Bellamy?" Greg yells into the phone. I catch myself staring and turn away.

"Uh, what?"

"Saturday works for you, right?"

I bring my laptop to life and pull up my calendar. "Yeah, that's fine. What time and where?" He decides we'll meet at the mall that's about halfway between both of us so I can shop while he spends time with Chase. The line goes dead. I hold the phone at my ear until I hear the dial tone before slamming it down onto the cradle.

"Do you need me to come back?"

For a moment, I forgot Hawk was there, and now I realize he's seeing my mini hissy fit. *Great.* I take a couple of deep, calming breaths and turn back toward him. He's sitting. When did I miss that he sat down?

"Sorry, that was my ex."

"Ah," he says, as if he knows everything.

"Yeah . . . " I'm tempted to tell Hawk everything, which is really unlike me or maybe it's exactly who I am. I'm not really sure anymore. It's not like I spend copious amounts of time with men and last night was the first real "non-date" I've been on since Greg walked out on me, so I definitely lack experience. Still, I remind myself that Hawk is a stranger, regardless of the way my mind thinks, and body feels, when I'm in his presence.

"Do you want to talk about it? My mom says I'm a good listener."

He makes me smile. It's a good feeling. "I'm afraid the drama with my ex would probably scare . . . " I catch myself before I say something completely stupid. "Thanks for the offer, but I think I'll be okay." I straighten a few things on my desk, doing whatever I can to avoid eye contact with him. "I'm assuming you're here about that piece of land?"

"Actually, I came in to see you."

My eyes dart up to find Hawk leaning toward my desk. If I were bold, I'd grab him by his shirt and pull him toward me because I'd be a liar if I said I hadn't thought about kissing him. He invaded my dreams last night and is the reason I took extra time doing my hair this morning. Karter was right in a roundabout way. I don't have a date, but I hoped I'd see him before tonight.

"What are you thinking so hard about?" he asks. His voice is quiet, husky and tinged with desire. I try to clear away the thoughts I'm having about him and me, our limbs tangled together with a sheen of sweat covering our skin.

"You're blushing." He reaches across my desk and softly trails his fingers down my cheek. I want to hold his hand there, to feel the warmth of his palm pressed against my heated skin, but I'm afraid. I was rejected by the one man who vowed to love me until the end, tossed aside for a new model, and this man sitting across from me, making me feel emotions I haven't felt in years, is leaving town. He's not staying, no matter what I can offer him.

I push my chair back, excuse myself and rush down the hall into the bathroom. The cold water I douse myself with does nothing to curb the pooling of desire in my belly. Could I be someone who indulges in a gorgeous man just for fun? Could I keep my heart out of it?

My head rises and I look at myself in the mirror. My cheeks are red, my neck flushed, and my eyes — they seem dark with determination. I don't want to trick Hawk into anything. I just want to take him to bed. And if I'm reading his body language right, he wants that as well.

SEVENTEEN

HAWK

I'VE NEVER BEEN what my friends call smooth when it comes to women. Sometimes I fumble over my words, get lost in my thoughts when I'm trying to figure out what to say, or as I've proven a few times now with Bellamy, say something completely inappropriate that clearly scares her enough to leave me alone. It's times like now when I miss my friends the most. They get me, they understand my awkwardness. Hell, they even mock me for it, and I let them because it's what bros do. Sure, I give back, but I mostly defer to Travis Kidd for his one-liners and follow what he says. Maybe that's my issue: I'm a follower, and without my team here to support me, I'm lost in translation.

When I see Bellamy walking down the hall, I stand up and try to convey how sorry I am for being a cad. She probably gets hit on all the time, and honestly, I'm surprised she's single. "I'm sorry," I say to her as she approaches her desk. "Sometimes, my filter doesn't work so well."

"Hawk, you didn't say anything inappropriate, I . . ." she pauses and looks directly at me. The force of her gaze is like nothing else I've ever experienced. It's like the room is closing in on us, blocking us from the outside word. My tongue feels thick and my breathing is labored, yet I feel like I could run a mile without breaking a sweat . . . but only if she's running alongside of me. I want to reach out and pull her toward me so I can feel what it's like to have her pressed against my body, to know what it's like to feel her skin against mine. Touching her face earlier was nothing more than a tease. I need the full experience.

"Are we still on for dinner?" I ask and she nods.

"I'll text you my address." *Yes*, she remembers that I gave her my number.

"I'll see you later, Bellamy." The urge to kiss her goodbye is too great and I back up before I do something I shouldn't. I should kiss her, at least on her cheek, to see how she'd react. This way, I'd know whether my instincts are right. But not right now. I continue to walk backward until I bump into the door and the chime rings outs. I wave, as if I'm in fifth grade again and Tamara Williams has just invited me to her birthday party. Damn, I remember that day clearly. She walked toward my desk with her crooked smile. When I saw the pink envelope, I knew. I didn't care if the other boys teased me, I was going to her party — and I did. She was my first kiss, out back behind her big pine tree. Man, I thought I was hot shit back then. Our romance lasted until the end of the school year, although by today's standards, it wasn't much of a romance. I chased her around the playground, she and her friends would giggle when my friends and I would walk by, and we'd sit together when we went to the library or for an assembly. The one kiss we shared on her birthday never had a follow-up though, and once baseball season started, I had forgotten all about her.

I don't know what's gotten into me. I've never been that guy, the one smitten by a pretty lady, and yet, here I am thinking about kissing a woman I've known for only twenty-four hours. It's a damn good thing the guys aren't here to witness any of this.

Speaking of my teammates — my phone dings with an alert from Travis Kidd. I tap the screen and pull up a video of him along with most of the guys. "Bro, we're missing you big time. Hope your recovery is going well because we need you. Do you hear me, Hawk? We need you! Call you soon, man. Oh, and don't be surprised if some of us show up after our West Coast swing." I replay it a few more times, laughing and feeling a bit more homesick each time it plays. I miss the guys, the team, and the camaraderie. Don't get me wrong, I love being home with my parents, but there's something about spending all your time with a group of people who love the same sport you do and who all have the same goal in mind — winning. My mother gets it, but as far as the rest of my family — they just don't understand.

I open the group chat I have going with the guys and start to type out a message, except I don't know what to say. Telling them I miss them seems cheesy, but it would be the truth. Instead, I forget about texting and opt to return the video message. I point the camera toward Main Street. "Alright, guys. I thought I'd show you what my small town looks like. As you can see, it's a don't blink or you'll miss it type of place, but it's still home." I press the small icon on the screen and flip the camera around. "And as you can also see, I'm still a one-armed bandit, but hopefully I'll finally be able to fully use my arm next week. I can't wait to get back to throwing. Talk soon!" I don't say anything about them coming to visit because if they can swing it, I know they will. Our manager, Wes Wilson, is all about family and if the team has a couple days off, he'll encourage them to come visit.

"Hawk?"

I press send and turn to find Annie Miller — I mean Larsen — standing behind me, looking nervous. She's clutching the strap to her purse and her eyes are darting every which way but in my direction. "Hey, Annie." I go to hug her, but she takes a step back.

She gives me a smile that's weak at best. "We need to talk, Hawk."

"Okay?"

"Not here." She's looking around nervously, fidgeting with the strap slung over her shoulder and biting her lower lip, doing everything she can to avoid eye contact with me.

"My truck's right there if you want to go somewhere." I point behind me, but she shakes her head.

"Do you remember where my grandparents lived?" I nod. "Okay, there's a dirt road out by the property, meet me there." Her eyes are still downcast. This is not the Annie I remember.

"Okay." I watch her walk away, her head still on a swivel, looking for something. I'm going to go out on a limb here and say she's looking for Brett, but why? It's not like he doesn't know we're friends. As luck would have it, I'm still standing in front of the real estate office and when I glance inside, I swear Bellamy has me under surveillance. That's an exaggeration, but every which way I look right now, people are staring. *Great.*

I hop into my truck and head toward the end of town. The Millers used to run a successful cattle ranch back in the day and owned most of the land that surrounded Richfield. Old man Miller liked to gamble and lost everything they owned. He started selling off chunks of land, some even to my family, but once that ran out and their herd was gone, there wasn't anything left. The bank took their house and the Millers moved in with Annie's parents. It was our sophomore or junior year when all of this went down and the Millers passed away within months of this all happening. Annie's family was embarrassed, to say the least. They were the talk of the town for a long time and I often thought that was why Annie stayed with Brett throughout high school. She needed him, not only for comfort but for status. The Larsens are well to do and with Annie dating Brett, it gave her family hope.

Her grandparents also used to have the biggest barn in the area and now, as I drive toward it, I see it's dilapidated with most of its roof missing, the doors are gone, and it has this eerie haunted look to it. The house doesn't look much better, with broken windows and moss growing on the roof. "Damn," I mutter as I pass by.

The dirt road Annie wants to meet on leads into a thicket of woods. The road is bumpy as hell and by the time I approach to her car, my arm is killing me from being rocked back and forth so roughly. I park and get out, walk past Annie's car to find her standing a few feet away with her back facing me.

"Want to tell me what's going on and why we're meeting out in the middle of the woods?"

She turns. Her arms are crossed over her chest. I can tell she's been crying, but she also looks angry. "You need to leave."

"I'm sorry?" She just invited me here.

"Hawk, listen to me. You need to go back to Boston and just forget about Richfield." She steps toward me and that's when I see a cut above her eye.

"What happened to your eye?"

Annie shies away. "Nothing."

"Annie, what's going on? I haven't seen you in years and you're acting weird as hell. Can we go sit in my truck . . . or your car . . . and talk?"

"It's not safe."

"What's not safe? Me? Jesus, Annie, I'm not going to try anything if that's what you think. You're married."

She scoffs.

Okay, that's enough to tell me she's definitely not living in Paradise.

"Look, as much as I'd love to sit on your tailgate with a can of beer, I can't. Brett . . ."

Ah, it's all making sense now. The off the beaten path

meeting place, the standoffish approach with wandering eyes. I take a few steps away and lean against one of the trees. Annie sighs loudly, clearly frustrated with me.

"What are you doing?" she asks.

"Resting and waiting for you to start talking."

"I don't have anything to say, Hawk."

"I beg to differ."

"You would."

I don't know how long we stand there with me holding the tree up and her hugging herself, but it was long enough for her to sigh multiple times, for me to laugh, and for her to give me death looks.

"You ready to talk yet?" I go to her and pull her into my arms. She doesn't move her arms but does rest her head on my chest.

"You're trouble. You always have been."

I chuckle. "I'm the farthest thing from trouble."

"I should've gone with you, followed you to school."

I step back and look at her. "And what, not marry the love of your life?"

A single tear falls from her eye.

"Annie, tell me what's going on."

She moves away and goes back to hugging herself. "I'm serious when I say you need to leave. Brett . . . he's not the same as he was in high school. In many ways, he's worse. And you being here is bringing out a side of him I haven't seen in ten years. He blames you for a lot."

"It's not my fault he punched the wall and busted up his hand."

"Isn't it?" she asks. "The things we did?"

"You'd been broken up for months, Annie. You were allowed to move on. Hell, how many times did he cheat on you in high school and you kept going back?"

She shakes her head, either unwilling to answer or she lost count of his many times other girls would come to her and tell her about their night with Brett. He would deny it all, even though everyone knew it was true.

"If you ever cared about me, you'll leave, Hawk."

"Is he hurting you because I'm here?"

"Doesn't matter." She looks at me, stone faced. "Since you came back, he hasn't been himself. He is constantly muttering your name, he's angry and coming home later and later, drunk as a skunk. Matty and I are walking on eggshells and it would just be easier if you left."

I go to her. "Annie, I *do* care about you so if he's hurting you or your daughter, you need to tell me so I can help you."

"Just leave," she pleads.

"I can't. I won't." I contemplate telling her that I plan to be in Brett's face every chance I get, but I don't. "I'm sorry, Annie."

I leave her standing there and head toward my truck. As much as I'd love to appease her, I'm not running out of town because her husband is throwing a hissy fit.

EIGHTEEN
BELLAMY

TODAY IS TURNING out to be a total wash thanks to Mr. Longwood and his ever changing mind. He was willing to sell his property earlier this morning but can't seem to give me a solid answer on how much he wants to list his land for. He keeps going on and on about having multiple assessments done, perk tests, and thinks he might want to subdivide, which is well within his rights, but I can't help thinking that someone is chirping in his ear right now. Of course, I'm the bad guy when I tell him he'll need to put a buffer between a residential lot and the business lot, which angers him. After an hour of back and forth, I finally hand him over to Owen and suggest he finish the deal because I get the sense that Mr. Longwood doesn't like taking advice from a woman. It's fine, I'm used to the old boy's club mentality this town has. Add all this to the fact that earlier, Mr. Hawk Sinclair, the stupidly sexy baseball player who is hell bent on making me fall for his wily charms, stood out front of my office and chatted with Annie Larsen, the woman who accused me of having an affair with her husband. *Ugh!*

I know I'm reading into everything. The way he talks and looks at me . . . I'm certain that's his personality, and the only reason he came in this morning is to ask about the land and to remind me that he invited himself over to my house for dinner. I should've told him tonight wouldn't work, but nope, I volunteered to text him my address because he has my mind swirling in a million different directions. When he's around me, I need to figure out how to keep my wits about myself and not get involved emotionally with him.

As reluctant as I am to text Hawk, I do it. I don't want to come off as someone who doesn't keep their word. Although, I do type out a few sentences explaining why tonight or any night hereafter won't work for me, only to erase everything and not only give him my address but provide directions as well. Then I finally do the right thing and toss my phone in my bag because looking at the screen, waiting to see if he's responding or is the type to have his read receipts on is a form of desperate I don't want to be right now. I decide I desperately need to walk away and get some coffee so I head over to our kitchen area, running into Karter on my way.

"You knew he was coming in to see you today, didn't you?"

"No."

"Lies," she says, laughing and bumping her shoulder with mine. "He's a cutie. Always has been."

"It's funny that I don't really remember him."

"That's because you're so much older than he is. Hopefully he likes older women."

"Oh, my God, will you stop?!" I push her gently, in a teasing way. "Five years isn't anything these days."

She laughs. "You're right. These days, men Hawk's age date teens and older men date women our age. I don't get it . . . or maybe I do."

"Are you and Zach having problems?"

Karter looks at me in complete shock and surprise. "What? No." She waves me off, but something doesn't feel right. I'm about to prod, to push for a little more but the office phone rings and she goes to answer it while I make a fresh pot of coffee.

"It's for you," she says when she comes back into the room. "Adrienne Hubbard."

Shit. I forgot to call her back yesterday.

"When this is done, let me know?" I point toward the coffee maker.

"I'll bring you a cup because we are *not* done talking about Mr. Hottie."

I roll my eyes and shake my head at her as I pass by. It's times like now when I wish I had a designated office so I could close the door and have this conversation in private. I sit down and take a deep breath before picking up the phone.

"Hi, Adrienne, sorry I didn't call you back yesterday. I'm a little surprised you're calling me at work. What's up?"

"Geez, ramble much?"

Only when I'm nervous. "I've been a terrible friend, lately. I'm sorry. How are you? How's Robbie?"

"We're good, missing Montana. Arizona is dry, brown and hot. I miss the snow."

"Ha, you say that now, but it's almost May and we still have mounds of it trying to melt."

"Better than watching the exterminator spray your house for scorpions."

"Yep, you win. Are you and Robbie looking to move back? Is that why you called me at work?"

"I wish, but no. I called you at work because I was hoping you wouldn't be in and I wouldn't have to have this conversation with you."

Color me confused. "Okay . . . "

She sighs heavily. "We've always been close, at least we were until we moved away, but you're still my best friend and it pains me to ask you this because it's so out of character—"

"And you accuse *me* of rambling. Just spit it out, Adrienne." I'm annoyed with this beat around the bush tactic.

Clearly, something is bothering her, and I have a feeling it's Brett Larsen.

"Why are you propositioning Brett for sex, Bellamy?"

My mouth drops open and I swear my head is about to explode. "Wh-what?"

"I'm torn here, Bell. You're my friend, but so is Annie. Brett tells Robbie everything and Annie, she calls here crying. I am a sitting duck here."

"Um . . ." it takes me a very long minute or two to compose my thoughts. When I picture Brett sitting across from me at dinner, I'm murderous. He's a scumbag and now he's dragging my name through the mud. "Adrienne, I'm only going to say this once and it's your choice on whether to believe me or not. Brett Larsen told me that if I slept with him, he'd put Chase on his baseball team, and when I refused, he said I'd pay for it. This was literally a few days ago and just yesterday he tried to have me fired from my job because I went to the youth center to try and find some way to help Chase play baseball as that's all my son wants to do." I pause and fight back the threatening tears. "I know your husband is close to Brett, but the fact that you've even called to ask, thinking that I would stoop so slow as to sell my body in such a way . . . I thought you knew me better."

"It's just—"

"It's just nothing, Adrienne. You know me and you know I'm not that type of person. My husband cheated on me, destroyed my marriage and hurt my son. Do you really think I would do that to another woman? To another child?"

"No, but—"

"There are no 'buts' here. Like I said, you believe whatever you want. But if it helps you sleep a little better tonight, you can tell your husband that I wouldn't save Brett Larsen if he were on fire and I had the only water in town. He's a pig and, frankly, you might want to think about what kind of guy Robbie is spending his time with when he and Brett are off on their golf trips. Don't call me again unless you're going to apologize." I hang up the phone and cover my face with my hands. My tears are hot, fast and steaming down my face.

"Oh, Bell. Everything is going to be okay," Karter says as she pulls me into her arms. I don't know how much she's heard or how long she's been standing there, but I need the comfort from her. "He'll get what's coming to him soon enough."

"Some stupid land sale isn't going to hurt Brett Larsen." I'm a blubbering mess and I know my words sound like I'm speaking through a bubble.

"Nope, but karma is a bitch and I believe in her. He'll get his."

"Before or after my demise?"

Karter pulls me from my chair and into the bathroom. She doesn't allow me to look in the mirror, for which I thankful, but she helps me clean up my face and does so with a genuine smile. "No pity parties allowed. You're about to have dinner with a very handsome man, who by all accounts is interested in you. And even if you don't feel the same way about him, ride this wave my friend. Let him dote on you until he has to leave."

"I'm not going to lead him on or use him."

"That's not what I'm saying. Get to know Hawk, be his friend. Enjoy his company. Don't jump into bed with him or drop down on your knees to give him a blowie." Karter laughs.

"Oh, God."

"I'm serious."

"I assure you; I won't be on my knees nor getting horizontal with him."

"Okay, but if you do, I need all the details."

I know she's serious, but regardless she's made me smile and that was her plan the whole time. She helps me clean up and fixes my make-up, so I don't look like a zombie.

"There, now tell me the truth. Did you put in a little extra time because you knew you were seeing Hawk today?" she asks from behind me as she fixes my hair.

I look at her through the mirror and sigh. "Yes, but I know deep down this doesn't turn out good for me so I'm going to proceed with caution. Be his friend and all that."

Karter smiles knowingly. "Just as long as you proceed."

With that statement, she ushers me out of the bathroom and pretty much out of the office. She stands in the doorway, waving as if she's my mother and I'm off to follow my dreams instead of going home to have dinner with a man I barely know.

I arrive home just as Chase's bus pulls up. He's smiling when he gets off and turns to wave goodbye to his new friends. "Hey, Mom."

"Hey, bud. How was school?"

Normally, I brace myself for bad, but I have a feeling today was a good day for him. "It was so cool. Nolan and I played catch during recess and we sat together at lunch."

Deep down, I know Hawk had something to do with this. "That's great! You know, Hawk's coming for dinner. I didn't know if you wanted to stay or go to Grandma's?" Hawk and I never discussed where Chase would be, and I think that's because Hawk expects Chase to be here.

"I think I'll stay, but when it's time for you to get cozy, I'll go to my room."

I stop midway through the garage and stare at my son. He opens the door to the kitchen and looks at me. "What? Nolan said his uncle likes you and I can see it too." He shrugs and walks inside. "Come on, Mom," he yells. "We're not heating the outside."

I'm stunned by what Chase has said, but then again, maybe I shouldn't be. He's clearly taken to Hawk, likely because he paid attention to him when his own father couldn't be bothered. Ugh, that reminds me I have to tell

Chase that we're going for a long, stupid drive this weekend. That can wait until tomorrow. Tonight, I'm going to let my son have fun with his new favorite person.

While Chase works on his homework, I open a bottle of wine to give me a little bit of confidence. This newfound courage has me sending Hawk a text, telling him that if he's in the neighborhood to feel free to stop by early. I do this because I know Chase wants to spend some time with him and I want to see my son happy.

No sooner do I start wrapping the potatoes to put into the oven, our doorbell rings. Chase is out of his seat and to the front door before I can even suggest he wait for me. I don't want to seem eager, so I continue my task, close the oven door and wipe my hands off on the towel. I don't straighten my hair or clothes and when I turn to leave my kitchen, Hawk is standing there, leaning against the wall with a bouquet of flowers in his hand, my son next to him with a beaming smile across his face. Any thoughts I had about not letting this guy in are slowly washing away. One day . . . that's all it's taken for me to easily see myself falling for this man, knowing full well that he's leaving and we lead two vastly different lives.

NINETEEN

HAWK

COOKING HAS ALWAYS BEEN my thing. When any of the guys have get togethers, the girlfriends and wives usually gather in the kitchen while the men hang out by the grill, and for whatever reason I always find myself with a set of tongs in my hand, making sure the meat is grilled to everyone's liking. But this dinner with Bellamy and Chase is different. It feels special and somehow more important that these steaks are cooked perfectly. Sort of how this night is going so far, effortlessly, in my opinion.

When Bellamy texted and said I could come over early, I took advantage of the offer, mostly because I wanted to spend time with her in her own setting, to see if my desire to get to know her is real or if I was caught up with the idea of meeting someone new. One look at her tonight, walking out of her kitchen, and I knew. She's someone I want to spend as much time with as possible.

Even though the outside temperature isn't ideal for grilling, Bellamy left the sliding glass door open and I want to think it's because she's trying to include me in what's going on inside the dining room. Chase is laughing and each time he does, Bellamy lights up like it's the best sound in the world.

My mother has always said there's no greater joy in the world than your own children, and while I can't agree because I don't have any, I can see the happiness that Chase brings his mother.

He walks over to the door and smiles at me. "Mom wants to know if you need anything." I glance at the small window where I can see his mother's shadow and wonder why she didn't come ask me herself and chuckle. Bellamy's trying to play hard to get and it's cute. Not that I'm trying to get her into bed or anything, but I *do* want to get to know her a lot better. Her son too. As I open my mouth to tell Chase what I want, his mother appears behind him and dammit if my heart doesn't skip a beat or two when she smiles at me.

"I took the potatoes out. I normally slice ours open, throw a chunk of butter in there and wrap them back up for a minute."

"A chunk?"

She shrugs. "I might overdo it a little bit on the butter."

"It sounds perfect."

Bellamy and I maintain eye contact, at least until I wink at her, which causes her to blush. Who knew flirting could be so fun? Chase interrupts my gawking when he comes and stands next to me. On instinct, I put my hand in front of Chase to keep him from the grill.

"Can I help?"

"You can if you promise to be careful. The grill is very hot, and you could get burnt if you're not paying attention."

"I promise." I don't want to tell him I don't need his help because he seems excited to be out here, but I'm also one-handed and if his hand were to slip, he'd likely hurt himself. I hand him the tongs anyway and move closer to him in case I need to intervene. Chase grips the metal with both hands and places the tongs around one of the steaks.

"Be gentle but you have to grip firmly," I tell him. He

does as I say, his tiny muscles straining in his arms as he flips the slab of meat over.

I crouch down so we're eye level and tell him, "Perfect."

"My dad never cooked," he says, never breaking eye contact. "He never did anything with me except yell and tell me I have to try harder."

"I'm sure he was stressed from work." I don't know what else to say. All I know is that he's an absent father and Bellamy is doing her best to fill both roles. However, even as I make this excuse for a man I don't know, I somehow feel like I'm lying to this boy that I've only known for a day.

"I hate him," Chase whispers. He throws the tongs down and runs off into the yard. I don't know if I should follow, but something tells me I should. I take the steaks off the grill, hoping they've cooked through enough, set them on the plate and shut everything down. Inside, I place the platter on the table and without saying another word, I'm back outside and wandering through the Patrick's backyard, struggling to see due to the setting sun. Thankfully, the wooden planks nailed into the tree gives me a good starting spot to seek him out. Of course, being limited to one arm makes it near impossible for me to climb up.

Pressing my back up against the tree, I start talking, hoping like hell he can hear me and that he's actually up there. "When I was your age, my dad wanted me herding cattle and mucking stalls in my spare time and the only thing I wanted to do was throw a baseball. I don't remember when I decided I wanted to be a pitcher but I remember the day clearly when my father whooped my butt for painting a strike zone on the back of the barn. He wasn't mad because I painted the barn but because I was throwing my baseball at it and scaring the horses. After that, he helped me build a field in one of our pastures and my friends and I used to play there all the time. We even had a mini scoreboard and my mom would make snacks for everyone. But still, my dad wanted me to be a rancher because it was all he knew. My grandfather and great grandfather were ranchers so it's in our blood, at least it's supposed to be." I pause and look up at the treehouse. Man, I would've loved to have a treehouse when I was his age. A place to escape and pretend nothing else matters in the world. I suppose I had that with my field, but it wasn't private.

"I guess what I'm trying to say is that dads aren't always what we want . . . or need . . . them to be. I love my dad but know deep down he wishes I lived here and worked on the ranch, and sometimes that hurts. Living in Boston is lonely at times and I wish my parents were there. I also know that being a dad can be hard when your kids don't live with you. My friend, Branch, has a son that he doesn't get to see all the time, while my friend, Cooper, has twins and he carries them both in his arms. Not sure how he does that though. I'm sorry your dad isn't around, Chase. I really am. I know I'm only here for a short time, but I'd really like it if I could teach you everything I know about baseball." I have no idea where the last line comes from but since seeing Coach Farmer, witnessing the way things are being run with the Little League program, and playing with the boys yesterday, apparently my subconscious is telling me I need to coach or at least get the band of misfits together to have some fun.

I'm about to give up and go back inside to admit defeat when I hear rustling above me. Chase climbs down and I pretend like I can't hear him. I'm staring off into the settling darkness when he bumps into my side. "My dad has a new family."

"Yeah," I say. "Your mom told me."

"It sucks."

"I bet. I know I'm not your dad, but I'd love to be your friend."

"But you're leaving soon."

I sigh and nod. "I am, gotta job to do, ya know. The

Renegades want to win the pennant but that doesn't mean we can't be friends. You can call me when I'm in Boston and even come visit if your mom allows it. Maybe you could come with Nolan when he comes to see me over the summer."

That puts a smile on his face. "That would be so cool! Could we go on the field?"

"Of course. You can even run the bases, take batting practice, do whatever you want."

"Hey," Bellamy's voice cuts us off.

"Hey," I say back. She's standing a few feet away from us. I didn't even hear her approach and I don't know if that's a good or bad thing. "We were just having a man to man talk."

"Oh," she sounds surprised. "Well, dinner is ready and it's getting cold."

"What do you say we go in and have dinner with your mom?" I ask Chase as I set my hand on his shoulder.

"Yeah, I think she'd like that."

Me too.

After dinner, which was filled with so much laughter the three of us snorted more than once, and after Chase has showered and gone to bed, Bellamy and I find ourselves sitting on the couch. She's drinking wine and I'm . . . well, I'm holding the glass wondering how the hell I'm going to drink this politely without it being obvious how much of a non-wine drinker I am?

"You know," she says. "You told me to make sure I had wine here."

"Look, I'm going to be honest with you, I don't date much, and figured wine was the right thing to say . . . but I've never really drank wine. I'm more of a beer or liquor type guy."

"I have some beer; do you want one?"

"Yes, please." I don't mean to sound eager, but I hand her my wine glass so fast the liquid sloshes dangerously around the sides, threatening to spill. She laughs as she takes the glass and is back in a flash with a bottle of beer for me.

"It's a local IPA."

"Perfect, thank you."

She sits back down and curls her legs under her. "I want to thank you for what you said to Chase earlier. I didn't mean to eavesdrop on your conversation. I couldn't find either of you and when I heard you out there talking, I stopped and listened."

"I like your son a lot. He's a good boy."

"Thank you."

I like his mom, too.

"The day before we met, I was at the fields. They were empty because all the kids were in school, but I stood there and imagined the sound of the ball hitting the bat, the parents cheering, and a line of siblings at the concession stand. I couldn't wait to show up at a practice or game. But then, I went and saw David Farmer, my vision changed, and was later crushed when I took my nephew back to the ballpark. David wants me to coach and believe me, as much as I love the game of baseball, coaching little kids is not something I ever thought I'd do. After meeting Chase and the other boys and finding out that Nolan wasn't even allowed to try-out because of me, I can't stand by and let this happen — not on the fields that I built for kids like your son."

"What are you saying, Hawk?"

"I'm going to coach, or at least get them started. I'll need to find an assistant, but I'm not going to let those boys stand at the fence and watch anymore."

"My boss will do it. I'll make him."

Our eyes meet and I have every intention of telling her thank you, but she launches herself into my arms. I grimace with pain when she crashes into my arm. There's a look of pure horror on her face when she realizes what she's done.

"Oh, God. I'm so sorry." She rights herself and I immediately wish she were still pressed against me, despite the burning sensation in my shoulder. "Are you hurt? Do you need anything? I can't believe I did that. I was just so excited that my emotions took over because I've tried, I've tried so hard to be a good mom to Chase and do what's right. The camps, clinics and extra practices with Brett, they've all been for nothing and you have no idea how happy you're going to make Chase."

"What about you? Are you happy? Are you ready to be a baseball mom?"

She nods frantically. "I want that more than anything. To see my son out there having fun. I want to cheer until my throat is raw and clap until my hands hurt. I don't care if you guys win a game, being part of a team is all he wants, and you're going to give that to him. I could just kiss . . ." she stops talking and darts her eyes toward the floor. She opens her mouth to say something, but I cut her off.

"Do you believe in love at first sight?" I never have until I met her.

Bellamy shakes her head slowly.

"Well damn, guess I have some work to do there as well." I wink, lean forward and kiss her cheek. "Thanks for dinner. I'll call you tomorrow with the practice schedule." I'm up and out of her house before she can say anything. I don't want to ruin the night by making a pass that she may not be ready for and leaving her on the high she's feeling will make her anticipation for my call even better.

Mother nature has not been our friend and many in the division feel as though the League should schedule the mid to east coast teams to start down south where the climate is a bit friendlier. There have been many rain delays, including for snow, across the AL and NL Central and East, prompting schedule changes and doubleheaders. It only makes sense for the League to investigate further. As much as we enjoy baseball in April, we also prefer to keep our snowsuits packed away until November.

However, despite the inclement weather through the month of April, the Renegades haven't done too shabby as they close out May and head into June. We've avoided any major injuries and our bats are on fire with the Renegades outscoring their opponents 247 to 184 with a win/loss record of 28 and 18. The normal suspects stand out: Kayden Cross, Travis Kidd, Branch Singleton and Ethan Davenport, all batting in the high 200's.

It's looking like All-Star pitcher, Hawk Sinclair, will be back in Boston after the All-Star break. According to reports, he's back to pitching and has decided to use his off time to coach a Little League team in his hometown, aptly named the *Mini Renegades*. The fans are eager for him to return to the line-up and many have left him comments on our blog. We can assure you he's receiving them.

GOSSIP WIRE

PREGNANCY ALERT!

Cooper Bailey and Ainsley Burke are . . . *not* pregnant. Do you like what we did there? But do you know who is? Travis Kidd and Saylor Blackwell-Kidd are expecting. There's no news on when the Kidds' arrival will be here, but by the shirt Lucy Kidd wore to the game the other day, the soon to be big sister is really excited! And so is the staff at the BoRe Blog!

Congratulations, Travis, Saylor and Lucy!

Still trying to unravel the Las Vegas mystery surrounding Branch Singleton. Is he married or not? No one seems to know and Branch isn't talking.

TWENTY

BELLAMY

I AM head over heels in lust . . . not love . . . with Hawk Sinclair. That man knows how to push, pull, and twist every single button I have, and I have a feeling he knows this by the sexy little smirks he gives me to go along with the kisses on my cheeks and the winks. This man loves to wink. What does a wink even mean? Is he joking? Sincere? Does he want to meet behind the dugout for a "cop and feel"? Whenever we're together, which is more often than my hormones can take at the moment, I'm on edge, waiting for him to kiss me. He makes me feel like I'm back in middle school and the rumors are flying that Kent Loftin is going to kiss me on the playground. The anticipation is killing me. Every time we're alone, he leans in and gently runs his fingers along my cheek, his breath fans over me, making my heart race and then bam! He heads for my cheek . . . I think he now realizes how frustrated I am because I swear I can hear him chuckle as he walks away afterward. When we're not alone, his hand is always touching me somewhere: My back, hip, arm. We're in constant contact and secretly, I love it, finding ways to touch him back so he knows that I'm into him. Karter says he's waiting for me to kiss him, to make the first move, and maybe she's right. I think I can be bold and assertive and show him that I like him.

It's not all about the subtle touches or the way he makes me feel, some of my attraction to him is how Hawk is with Chase. I know Hawk is a role model, that being good to kids comes with his job, but the way he is with Chase — it's different. I get the sense he wants to spend time with my son, more so than his own father does. In the past few weeks, Hawk has gone from the guy who played a little baseball with the boys that didn't make the team to a friend, coach, and somewhat of a father figure to my son. The latter scares me deeply though. Hawk is leaving. His job, which is his life, is in Boston and as soon as he's given the green light, he's on a plane and heading back. I know this. Chase knows this. Yet, I can't seem to put the brakes on their relationship because seeing my son smile, hearing him laugh, and seeing him and Hawk together is a feeling unlike any other.

I've spoken to Chase about what happens when Hawk must go back, when this fairytale we're experiencing comes to an end and he tells me he's okay with it, that he understands. I want to believe my son, but even I dread the day when Hawk leaves. He came into our lives when we both needed a ray of sunshine. Right now, he's that ray. That beaming, beautiful sun making our lives brighter.

For the first time in my life I'm a baseball mom, and I love it. I never thought being stressed about getting Chase to practice on time, the carpool schedule, snack schedules, and upcoming games could be so fun, but it is. I love sitting in the stands with my mitten covered hands wrapped around my travel mug full of coffee, screaming my head off for each boy on our team, even though it's only practice. I can't imagine what I'll be like when we play our first game. I love the chaos, the Little League rat race, the snide looks I get from the elitist parents because a professional baseball player is coaching my son. Those sneers are the best. Once word spread that Hawk was putting together a team, albeit a few weeks after the season had started, you would've thought a war was breaking out. Brett Larsen and his cronies are doing everything they can to stop the creation of the Mini Renegades. He's filed a complaint with the Montana Little League committee, who stated they were excited that someone like Hawk was donating their time. He contacted the Renegades themselves, who laughed and said they were expecting his call and that they knew all about Hawk's plans. And tomorrow, Brett and Hawk will go in front of the town council because Brett seems to think they can stop Hawk from participating. The meeting scares me though, because it won't be only Brett standing up against Hawk, it'll be every parent who's wrapped around Brett's little finger. There are a few who tried to jump ship, to come over to Hawk's team of misfits — as they've been dubbed — but he won't take them. He's dedicated to the boys he has.

My phone dings and a smile spreads across my face. I close out of my computer, turn off my desk lamp and head toward Owen's office. His door is open, and he, too, is smiling when he looks at me. I swear, volunteering Owen to help Hawk was the best thing I could've ever done for my boss. He needs the distraction, especially since he's in the process of filing for divorce from his wife. He's thanked me repeatedly for the opportunity. Plus, I think he secretly likes sticking it too Larsen . . . as the rest of us do.

"Don't forget, my house, six sharp!" Tonight, everyone is gathering at my house for a pasta party and Hawk will hand out jerseys. The boys don't know it yet and think they're coming over to hang out and do some team bonding thing, which Hawk and Owen have been pushing from the second he asked the boys to play for them.

"As if I'd forget. Hawk called earlier; the club sent some extra gear."

"Oh good, extra balls and bats will be great," I say, but Owen shakes his head while laughing. "What?"

"Gear, as in things for parents to wear."

"Oh," I reply.

He's still chuckling. "Believe me, you'll want to wear it all."

Since this is my first time with any of this, I take his word for it. Owen closes his laptop and comes toward me, motioning for me to go ahead. Karter is already gone for the day, leaving only Owen and me in the office. He fully expected the wrath of Larsen to come tumbling down upon him once he accepted Hawk's offer, but so far, nothing. It's been business as usual for the agency, for which I'm very thankful.

As soon as I'm in my car, my phone rings and the screen on my center console shows it's Greg calling. I groan loudly, not wanting to speak to him even though I have to. "Hello, Greg." I pull out onto the street and head home.

"Hello, Bellamy. It's Gregory."

"Duh," I say in response as I roll my eyes. "You do realize I have caller ID, right? That my phone tells me you're calling."

"I like to be efficient."

"Except when it comes to parenting," I mutter.

"What? I didn't hear you."

"Nothing, Greg. What do you want?"

"I know I had to cancel our meet up a few weeks back but would like to take Chase this weekend."

"To where?" I only ask because I'm curious.

He clears his throat. "Priscilla's mother is having a party and she's asked that he attend."

I'm surprised with the amount of eye rolling I do at Greg that my eyes haven't gotten stuck. "Let me get this straight . . . your new mother-in-law wants our son at her party?"

"Yes."

"But not you?"

"Bell—"

"Don't 'Bellamy' me, Greg." I talk over him. "He's *your* son. *You* should want to spend time with him."

"I do."

"But it's complicated, right? So, here, let me uncomplicate it for you. No! No, you may not take Chase to your mother-in-law's this weekend because one, it's unfair the way you treat him and how you cast him aside and two, he has a baseball game which I won't make him miss." I'd never even consider asking him to choose between the game and his father.

Greg clears his throat again and I have a good idea of what he's going to say. He wants me to force Chase to come with him, to abide by the custody agreement. "You're being unreasonable. I pay my child support on time and have tried to be there, but the distance—"

"That you agreed to . . . " I point out.

"Yes, but I expected to have some of my weekends free when I did."

"Well, it seems that you have this weekend free if you can go to a party. Maybe you should drive over and watch your son play the game he loves instead."

"About that, do you really think it's in Chase's best interest to play for this bird character? Brett seems to think that there's something shady going on."

I scoff loudly and bellow out, "Ha!"

"Bellamy . . ."

"Listen, the only thing shady is your affection for Brett Larsen. I get that he was in your frat, that you took him under your wing in your fifth year of college when you groomed him to be the president of your disgusting shit hole of a house, but that man is a slime ball." Kind of like you, I want to add. "And this 'bird character' — his name is Hawk Sinclair — and he's giving your son a chance to play baseball when your so called friend wouldn't unless I slept with him." I seethe.

"Regardless of your attraction to Brett, I feel as if this coach isn't right for our son."

"You've got to be kidding me, Greg. Do you even listen to anything I say to you?"

"Of course."

"Right, well then you've heard me loud and clear. Have a good day." I press end just as I pull into my driveway. Hawk's truck is parked in the open space and as my car idles, I stare at it, realizing how much I like seeing it there. I know I could get used to coming home to him every day, even though our relationship is borderline platonic. Karter's voice rings out, reminding me that if I want it to go past that, I'm going to have to be the one to make a move. As much as I hate to admit it, she's right, but time is my enemy. If I don't do it soon, I'm going to miss my chance. After shutting off my car, I gather my things and head into my house.

As soon as I step in, I'm taken aback. Chase is sitting at the dining room table doing homework and Hawk is right next to him. Their heads are bent together and they're going over what looks like math.

"Hey," I say, interrupting them. They both turn and look at me, both smile, and both make my heart race but for different reasons. I lean down and kiss Chase on his forehead and am tempted to do the same for Hawk but can't bring myself to do it. "I didn't expect you until later."

"I was in the neighborhood and met Chase as he got off the bus."

"How was therapy?" I ask as I walk into the kitchen to grab a glass of water. Hawk follows behind me and leans against the counter.

"Good. I can start throwing next week. I have to find a catcher, and asked my therapist for a recommendation."

"Can't Owen or Farmer catch for you?"

He shakes his head. "Farmer's probably too old, but I can ask him. Owen might not be able to catch my fastball."

"Oh, I suppose you throw pretty fast, huh?"

He grins. "About a hundred miles per hour." Hawk places his hands on my waist and pulls me toward him. He's had his sling off for a week now, giving him a bit more freedom with his arm. Still, there are times when I see him grimace or favor his right arm. "How was work? Any news from Longwood?"

I shake my head. "Stubborn old man. This morning he said he wasn't selling, around lunch his son called and said they were. I don't know which way is up with those two."

"Maybe I'll make him an offer, see what he says."

"Couldn't hurt."

He leans toward me and I think this is it; he's going to kiss me. His nose touches mine and my tongue darts out to wet my lips. We're sharing the same air, breathing in and out. He's so close, if I move a quarter of an inch, our lips will press together.

The doorbell rings, we jump apart and Chase yells out that he'll get it. I step away from Hawk, feeling flustered and discouraged. The conversation we had was intimate, in a way a couple would speak to each other at the end of the day, and yet, here I am, pulling boxes of pasta from the cupboard while that bird character chuckles behind me.

TWENTY-ONE
HAWK

WHEN I SIT down to think about my life, I can easily say I'm happy. Despite my shoulder injury, subsequent surgery and being away from my team, I'm doing very well. Not only am I happy, but I'm lucky too. When I look behind me, my thirteen players, their parents, my family, my former coach, David Farmer, my co-coach, Owen, and most importantly Bellamy, are all looking at me with cheerful smiles on their faces. Over on the other side of the room, which has been setup like a courtroom, the expressions of the other parents are disconcerting. A few of the mothers grin, wave and bat their eyes at me. Some of the dads glare, puff out their chests and avoid all eye contact. There's Annie who won't look in my direction next to Matty, who is always smiling and comes to my baseball practices against her father's wishes. And then there are the parents who are downright pissed, not only because I started a team, but that they've been forced to attend this ridiculous hearing which has zero jurisdiction over Little League baseball. Still, Brett Larsen demands his day in court, however futile it may be.

The Richfield town board comes into the room. My chances are good that I walk out of here with my team because like I said, these people really have no say. In fact, I've already pointed out in a strongly worded letter that I hold all the cards, yet they appeased Brett and asked that we have this hearing to set some ground rules, whatever those may be.

As each member takes their seat, my nieces blurt out, "Hi, Grandpa," causing me to chuckle. In Larsen's infinite wisdom, he forgot that one of the members is my sister Avery's father-in-law who, by all accounts, looks rather put out that he's here tonight. I can't say I blame him.

The chairman reads from a script, talking about impartiality and a bunch of horse crap that I don't care about. When he's done, he sets his papers aside, clasps his hands together and says, "The recreation board felt they couldn't make a reasonable determination as to whether the Richfield bylaws have been violated and referred this open matter to us. We'll start with Brett Larsen, Director of Richfield Little League." He nods toward Brett, who stands up.

"Mr. Chairman and Board Members, my first order of business is to ask that Mr. Walker recuse himself due to his conflict of interest with Mr. Sinclair."

The Chairman looks at Avery's father-in-law and back at Brett. "You do realize if Mr. Walker recuses himself, that will only leave four on this panel and if we were to take a vote, it wouldn't be valid."

"Oh," he says, clearing his throat. "Moving on, I ask that the board enforce rule forty of the Richfield Little League bylaws, which states that only the director can establish teams."

I hold that page in my hand and laugh. The very next line says, "unless establishment is approved by the governing body," which my team was. I'm floored by Larsen's attempts to stop my team from playing. I don't know if it's out of spite because of what happened between us in the past or if he's concerned my little team might beat up on his.

"Mr. Sinclair, did you seek permission from . . ." he pauses and looks through his paperwork.

"I did, sir." I hold up a copy of my email, which some man comes and takes from me.

"Mr. Larsen, I fail to see why you're wasting our time with this. Mr. Sinclair has clearly followed your bylaws and sought permission from the governing body."

"He's violated other bylaws as well," Larsen states. "We have a strict policy that uniforms can't be over a certain dollar amount and Mr. Sinclair has exceeded this, using his wealth to outfit his team."

I hold up another sheet of paper, an email from the President of Operations for the Renegades, Ryan Stone. He states that the Renegades organization donated the uniforms and equipment to the Mini Renegades, which isn't a violation of any made up rule Larsen wants to throw at me. I sit there, biding my time while the chairman looks over the email until I finally stand to get their attention.

"If you wouldn't mind, I have something to say," I tell the panel.

"Go ahead, Hawk," Mr. Walker says.

"I grew up in Richfield and the first Little League field was on a small piece of land my father let us play on. When I received my first paycheck, I came back here and established The Sinclair Fields, hoping they'd get used by aspiring softball and baseball players. Every year, I paid the youth center to keep the fields in the best shape possible. It was my mistake for not coming home every year because maybe if I had, I would've seen how the programs using my fields were being run."

"What do you mean?" the chairman asks.

"The Little League system here is broken. Boys and girls are left out, parents squabble and bad-mouth each other and the players — *and their coaches* — demean the players. They don't coach, they yell, and in my opinion are not qualified to coach youth sports. I know you can't do anything to change the atmosphere, but I can."

"Hold on, Mr. Chairman, he can't change anything. He's not even a resident," Larsen blurts out.

I walk toward the table and pass out five copies of the agreement I had drawn up for usage of the fields. "Moving forward," I say to the board and audience, "I will employ the necessary people to run the fields. They will oversee try-outs, appoint coaches and run the day-to-day operations. Coaches will be vetted and required to go through online training, much like the coaching staff from the school. The fields will continue to be free of charge to schools and Little League. However, parents are expected to treat children, as well as others, with respect and allow the coaches to coach and the players to play."

"He can't make these changes," Larsen says.

"I'm afraid he can, Mr. Larsen." The chairman shuffles his papers together. "I suggest you find a way to play nice in the sandbox, Mr. Larsen, otherwise it seems that your team might not have a place to play. This meeting . . .or whatever it was . . .is adjourned."

When I go to the people supporting me, they tell me congratulations, although it's not really a victory. I should've been paying attention to what's been going on a long time ago, but out of sight, out of mind. Avery gives me a hug before she takes the girls to see their grandfather. I have to say that move by them earlier was brilliant and I wish I had thought of it myself. I know it wasn't actually my sister's intent, but I'm glad the twins did it.

After everyone files out, Bellamy and I are the last to leave. I hesitate for a brief moment before I put my hand on her back and guide her to the door. Our relationship — or whatever it is that we have going on here — is at a stalemate. Weeks ago, I was determined to kiss her and now I'm afraid to get attached, although I fear that I already am. My return to Boston is inevitable. It's going to happen, and it seems unkind of me to start something with her that is only going to end in heartache for both us. Yet, the desire to be with her is strong and I don't know how much longer I'm going to be able to hold back.

As soon as we step out of the conference room, we run into Matty, who is standing in the hallway by herself.

"Hey, Matty. Do your parents know you're still here?" Bellamy asks. Matty, whose name I recently found out is Mattingly — I can only assume after Don Mattingly who was one of my favorite players of all time — looks like my nieces with similarly heart shaped faces and blue eyes. The only difference is that Matty's hair is a darker shade of blonde, almost a light brown, and my nieces are blonde.

"Yeah, they're outside." She points to the window and I follow her gesture, stepping forward to look. They're fighting. Arms are flailing about and I can hear muffled yelling. I frown and step back to where Bellamy and Matty are. "I was wondering if you have room on your team for me?"

"Excuse me?" I don't mean to sound harsh, but I'm caught off guard by her question. Bellamy squeezes my hand and I find it calms me almost immediately. "I'm sorry, I don't think I heard you correctly."

"You did," she says. "I'd like to come play for you."

"But your dad . . . " I cock my head slightly toward the window before looking back at Matty. "Matty as much as I'd love to have you—"

"Good, it's settled. Don't worry, I'll tell Brett, you won't have to." The young girl bolts down the stairs and out the door before I can even finish my last thought.

"What just happened?"

"It seems that Matty is going to be a Mini Renegade."

"But why?" I wonder aloud.

"It only makes sense since she's been at every one of your practices."

"I know."

Bellamy steps in front of me and places her hands on my sides. "Maybe this is one of those gift horses you aren't supposed to look in the mouth."

"I've seen Brett's team play. They can make it to the Little League World Series. I won't even be around that long to see this team go that far. As much as I would love to have her, I think it's a mistake."

"Then you should go over there and speak with them, let them know your concerns. Clearly, she wants away from Brett — not that I blame her — but maybe if she knows it's better for her to play with his team, she'll stay." I nod and pull Bellamy in for a kiss on the cheek, again.

On the way to her house, I ask her if she wants to come with me to the Larsens'. She passes, which I expected, but she asks me to stop by on my way back to let her know how things went. All the way over to Brett's, Bellamy's request replays in my mind. Stop by, don't call. She wants me to come over, despite it being late. She's going to tempt me and there's no way I'll be able to say no.

All the lights are on at the Larsens' and their loud voices carry as I walk up the walkway. I don't even want to know what the neighbors must think. It's fear of the unknown and remembering the faint bruising on Annie's face when I last saw her that has me pounding on the door. It swings open and Brett's there, angry.

"What the hell do you want?"

"I came to make peace," I tell him. "This animosity between us doesn't need to be here, Brett."

He scoffs. "You think I'm going to forgive you for all of this."

"I didn't do anything."

"You didn't?" he steps toward me, the small step up into the house gives him a height advantage. "First, you steal my girlfriend and then you steal my career, and now you're trying to steal the program I built from bottom up right out from under me."

"I didn't steal Annie, you tossed her aside. As for your career, I didn't force you to punch a wall which resulted in you shattering your hand. As for the program . . . you play favorites, Brett. That's not what youth sports is about. Everyone should get a chance to be on a team and you exclude kids to be spiteful. If you hadn't done that, then I wouldn't have to coach."

"The only reason you're coaching is because you want to get into Bellamy's pants. Well let me tell you something, it's not worth it."

After he says that, I do the one thing I shouldn't. I punch him. With my right hand. The jarring of my fist hitting his face radiates up my arm and causes my arm to go dead. "You're not worth my energy," I tell him as he clutches his nose.

"I'm going to sue you," he mumbles as I walk away. I flip him the bird and climb into my truck, pulling out my cell phone and calling my manager to tell him what happened. The next call I make has my stomach in knots.

"Ryan Stone," he says into the phone.

"Mr. Stone, it's Hawk Sinclair. There's something I need to tell you."

TWENTY-TWO

BELLAMY

I FIND MYSELF PACING, walking back and forth in front of my large picture window, waiting for the glare of headlights to shine into my living room. Every few seconds, I pause because I think I hear a door slam or the screech of tires, but it's my mind playing tricks on me. After Hawk dropped me off, I filled my mother in on everything that happened tonight and how the town officials really didn't give Brett's case any credence, which they shouldn't. I never knew youth sports could be so political and downright cutthroat. People who I considered friends sat across the aisle from me — glaring. I don't get it. All I want is for my son to play baseball, for all the children to feel like they belong. Hawk and Owen want that as well.

Making my way into the kitchen, I open the refrigerator and pull out the corked bottle of wine sitting on the shelf in front of me. I'm not much of a drinker, but tonight calls for some liquid resolve. That's what I'm calling it . . . *resolve*. I don't need courage. I need peaceful resolution to everything going on. I want to live in harmony among my friends.

After pouring the Pinot Grigio, I'm back in front of my window, staring out at my neighborhood. The streetlights cast an eerie glow along the paved road and most of the houses that I can see have their porch lights on. Across the street lives Brady, or B Mac, as he likes to be called. I thought for sure when I moved in, he and Chase would be fast friends. Hell, I thought my son would be friends with all the kids in the subdivision, it's why I chose the area, but I was wrong. B Mac is a bully. He's the kid that is sweet to your face but the second you turn your back, he's ruthless. I never wanted to see him as anything other than a ten or eleven-year-old boy, until now. In the past, Chase has said Brady's mean, but I brushed it off. However, sitting across from him and his father tonight, I saw it firsthand. The menacing look in his eyes matched that of the adult sitting next him. It's sad, the way he thinks it's okay to be like this.

Finally, headlights shine into my driveway. I set my glass of wine down, go to the door, open it and wait for Hawk to come up the walk. When he does, he's holding his right hand and I instantly fear the worse.

"What's wrong?" I ask as I step out of the house and onto my porch. I reach for his hand and he gives it to me freely. His knuckles are swollen, red and he hisses when I touch them. "Hawk?" I motion for him to come into the house, but he stands firm where he's at.

"I need to ask you a question."

"Go ahead." I don't like his tone or the fear I feel right now.

"Did you sleep with Brett Larsen?"

My mouth drops open as the question tumbles out of his mouth. He's so matter-of-fact that I know he's serious. I take a step back, needing a little breathing room. Hawk takes this as a sign . . . of what, I don't know, but by the look on his face, I'm pretty sure he thinks I'd sleep with a married man. I start to shake my head and despite my determination to stop them, tears start to well in my eyes.

"Why?" he asks.

"I didn't. I would never."

He shakes his head and his lips tighten. "He said——"

"He's a liar. He told me if Chase wanted to sit on his bench, I would have to sleep with him in order for that to happen. I'm desperate to help my son fit in but I would *never* sleep with someone to make that happen."

He reaches for me, but I shy away.

"I can't believe you would ask me this."

"He told me you did, and I punched him, so I had to know for sure that I was right and you're worth the risk of me losing my career."

"You punched him? For me?"

He nods. "And he's going to sue. There isn't a doubt in my mind that he's going to do everything he can to ruin me."

"But why? Why is he like this?"

He steps forward and places his left hand on my hip. "I'm sorry for the way I asked. Deep down, I knew you didn't, or I wouldn't have punched him the first place but his words — telling me that you're not worth it — they kept playing over and over in my head and I had to ask."

"I'm not worth it?" I repeat the damaging words into the night air.

"You're worth it to me," he says as his lips finally come crashing down on my mine. There's nothing sweet and sensual about this first kiss. It's angry, frantic, and tantalizing. My hands are on his shoulders, and then one is cupping his check, keeping him close to me because there's no way I'm letting him go. My other hand moves under his shirt, eager to feel the warmth of his skin against my chilled hand. My fingers skim the top of his pants and he smiles against my lips.

The moment he pulls away, I reach for him, trying to keep this make out session going. He cups my cheeks and looks deep into my eyes. "Seriously, may I come in?"

I nod and start to turn, but he holds me there.

"Bellamy," he says my name softly. I take his hand from

my cheek and intertwine his fingers with mine. After he steps through the doorway, I shut and bolt the front door. With renewed confidence brought on by his kiss, I pull him behind me down the hall and into my bedroom, where I twist the tiny lever, locking us in from the outside world.

"Are you sure?" he asks as I start to undress.

I've never been surer of anything before. I know he's leaving and that's going to break my heart, but right now, I don't care because I want to be with the man standing in front of me.

Hawk and I lay in bed with my head resting on his chest. Every so often, I hug him tighter, keeping him as close to my body as I can but it's really an excuse to run my hand over his sexy abs. Sure, I've seen ads like the Calvin Klein ones, with these men and their insane abdominal muscles but I have never experienced them in real life. My former husband was fit, but not like Hawk.

His fingers draw lazily along my forearm. It tickles, but I don't mind. I'm happy and content right here with him . . .sated, exhausted, and ready to be with him again because once will never be enough.

"I should've never gone over to Brett's." His arm squeezes me closer and I snuggle deeper into him.

"I always play the 'what if' game. What if I didn't move back to Montana? What if Greg didn't cheat? What if I didn't hire Priscilla to work for us?" Hawk and I adjust so we're facing each other. I pull the sheet up to cover myself but he hooks his finger over the top and pulls the fabric down to expose my breasts.

"You're beautiful."

"You're just saying that because we had sex. It's like the obligatory response or something."

He frowns. "I say it because it's true. I'm insanely attracted to you and have been since the morning we met. That night, when we were at the pizza parlor, all I could think about was kissing you, not to mention every day since."

"Why did you wait so long?"

He cups my cheek and pulls me close until our lips meet. "Out of fear."

"Of what?" I whisper.

"Of hurting you when I leave. Of hurting Chase."

I don't know what to say, so I remain quiet. We lay there, staring at each other, with me wishing things could be different, but also thankful that they're not. I love that he's a baseball player, that he's here doing what's right for our community, but also hate that he has responsibilities elsewhere that will take him across country.

Finally, when the silence is too much, I say, "We'll figure it out." Because if this is a relationship that is going to go somewhere, it'll to be worth it to do so. "Tell me about Brett."

He sighs. "He's always been volatile. One minute everything is fine and the next he's flying off the handle and destroying things. His father was the same way when we were growing up."

"But you were his friend?"

"I was because deep down, he's a really great guy who would do anything for his friends. As we got older, our relationship shifted. I became a standout player for our baseball team. Scouts from all over would come to the games, the media would be there, and it didn't matter if I was pitching or if it was Brett, they were there to see me and he hated me for that. After a while I started feeling sorry for him and would bring him along to the interviews or bring up his name to the scouts, but they weren't interested.

"He started partying, drinking, doing some drugs. He cheated on Annie a lot. There were rumors that he got some girl from another town pregnant, but he never copped to it and when I asked, he told me to mind my own business. So I did. I pushed myself harder, worked out, and worked with a pitching coach so I could have an arsenal of pitches. Our senior year, I was unhittable and the only losses we had were when Brett pitched. That didn't go unnoticed by anyone. The town, his father, the scouts, everyone knew I was the better of the two.

"And then Annie wised up and dumped him. She asked me to take her to prom and I did because I felt bad for her. We had always been friends, although it was honestly more like me being the third wheel in their relationship. Sometimes I'd have girlfriends, but I knew I couldn't trust Brett around them and thought being single was better anyway. I could do whatever I wanted without having to worry if I was upsetting someone. After prom, Annie and I became a little closer and right before I left for college, I slept with her. It was a mistake, but it happened. By that point, Brett had an offer to play ball at some low-level Division Two school and things should've been good. Except, he and Annie got back together and she told him that we slept together. He found me cleaning out my gym locker at school, days before we left for college and took a swing at me. I ducked and his hand punched the concrete wall, shattering every bone in his throwing hand, effectively ending whatever chance he had at a baseball career."

"Wow," is pretty much all I can say.

Hawk shrugs. "He's the main reason I stayed away for as long as I did. Sure, I'd come home during breaks, but my parents ranch is pretty isolated so no one never knew if I were home and my sisters would never say anything because they were afraid their girlfriends would all come over to see me. After I signed my deal with the Renegades, I came back and bought the land the fields are on, and had the complex built. I didn't even return for the ribbon ceremony because I had a game that night, so my parents did the honors."

"I remember that," I tell him. "Of course, in the back of my mind I always knew you existed. I just didn't know you."

He laughs and tucks my hair behind my ear. "You hurt my ego."

"Good." I laugh right along with him, but his eyes turn from happy to sad. "What's wrong?"

"Tonight, I let my temper get the best of me. I did exactly what he tried to do years ago and punched him. I'm pretty sure I broke his nose, which means he's probably going to press charges."

"Oh, shit, Hawk. I'm so sorry."

"Don't be, he deserved it."

"But still."

"Thing is, I don't even care if he sues me. I had to call my manager and the boss tonight to tell them before Brett goes to the media or cops."

"Are you in trouble?"

He nods. "If he presses charges, I'll be suspended."

"But you're already missing so much time."

He sighs, leans forward and kisses the tip of my nose before moving to my lips. "I never believed in love at first sight until I met you, Bellamy Patrick."

I lay there, stunned, as a million thoughts go through my mind. Until this moment, I would've never thought that love would find me again. "Hawk . . ."

"It's okay if you're not there yet. I'll show you that I'm worth it."

I cup his cheek. "I'm there and I know you are."

He smiles and kisses me deeply. I'm about to climb on top of him, to show him just how much he means to me when he stops me.

"I have something else to tell you. A few weeks ago, Annie asked me to meet her out by her grandparent's farm. Do you know it?"

I nod and swallow hard. If he says he slept with her . . . I don't know what I'll do. "I'll never forget it. My mom called me while I was in college to tell me everything. It was so sad what happened to the Millers. What did she want?" My voice squeaks.

"She asked me to leave town and to never come back."

"Why?"

He inhales and exhales slowly. "At first, I thought it was because of Brett and this deep seated jealously. I know he blames me for ruining his career and now he thinks I'm trying to take over this Little League stuff, but there's something else. Annie was adamant that I go and now I think I know why."

"Are you going to keep me in suspense?"

He shakes his head. "I think Matty is my daughter."

TWENTY-THREE

HAWK

BELLAMY STANDS AT THE STOVE, fixing the three of us breakfast, while Chase and I sit at their dining room table waiting. It's a small table compared to the one my mother has, but again, Bellamy is feeding two to three people at a time where my mother could have a whole platoon come through for any of the meals she offers. Still, for as small as it feels here, Bellamy has been a trooper when it's come to getting the Mini Renegades off the ground. She's hosted every meeting, pasta party and gathering we've had and hasn't batted an eyelash about it.

I had every intention of being gone before Chase woke up, not because I'm trying to keep my feelings for his mom a secret, but mostly because the dude is ten years old and doesn't need to see some guy coming out of his mom's room. Except, that's exactly what happened. At five a.m. I opened the door to do the proverbial walk of shame and he was standing in the hallway. Seems he had to go to the bathroom, heard a noise in his mother's room and was about to knock on the door. Surprise! Thankfully, Bellamy knew what to do and ushered Chase back to his bedroom while I stood there, completely dumbfounded. Afterward, Bellamy and I talked about it and decided I would stay for breakfast. I think she wanted this, so she wasn't the only one answering all of Chase's questions. Now, almost two hours later, I'm being securitized and stared down by a fifth grader.

Every time I pick up my mug, he eyes me. Prior to now, I considered us friends, but I may end up leaving the Patrick house an enemy today. The awkward silence is killing me. I don't know what to say to Chase. It's not like I planned for this to happen, nor have I ever been in this situation before. Yet, here I am with all these fumbling thoughts running through my head. Avoidance is easy though. I take my phone out and click the icon to bring up yesterday's sports scores. I purposely avoid the Renegades. I know I shouldn't, but seeing their highlights really plays with my psyche. They brought in two more pitchers, as they should've, but after last night I can't help but feel replaced. Even after I return, I still have a mountain to climb until I'm back to throwing one hundred pitches consecutively.

A video pops up of one of the league's mascots doing something funny. I laugh through the whole thing and by the end, I feel the chair next to me slide away from the table and the small body of Chase pushing against my arm. I know better than to make this a big deal, so I turn slightly and show him my phone.

"Do you have a favorite mascot?" I ask him.

"The one for the Astros is pretty funny." Of course, he would like a Renegade rival. Not that I can blame him, they're a hot, young team, and they're doing very well. Many have picked them to be the American League Champions. If I hadn't liked our prospects going into the year, I'd say the BoRe's would definitely give them a run for their money. Their starting lineup, both defensively and offensively is hard to compete with.

"Yeah, Orbit is fun. He likes to tease my friend, Travis."

"Why?"

Because Travis deserves it. "I think because Travis is easy to pick on. He's a funny guy so the mascots like to play jokes on him."

"Do they ever tease you?" he asks.

"Sometimes, once I'm out of the game, but pitchers aren't normally the target."

"We need a mascot," he says and all I can imagine is a tiny piglet running around the field. The thought makes me laugh.

"That would be fun, but not sure where I'd find a piglet."

"He could wear a baseball jersey." Chase laughs.

"Who could wear what?" Bellamy carries over three plates and sets them down on the table. "What are you boys talking about?"

I like the way she lumps Chase and I together. I lean back in my chair and look at the kid, who for a long while this morning, I thought hated me. "Eh, we're discussing business."

"Well," she says with her hands on her hips. "If it's base-ball business, you might as well tell me since everything ends up in my house anyway." She motions toward her living room where boxes of equipment, clothing and uniforms are stacked. Ideally, the boxes should be at my parents' place or the youth center, but due to current circumstances the center is off limits and the delivery driver couldn't make it up my parents' driveway, which left me no choice but to beg Bellamy to store them. The boxes should've gone to the garage, but the driver started carrying them inside and I haven't had a moment to move them.

"I'll take care of them today," I tell her as I right myself. She nods and slides two plates in my direction with one being for Chase.

"Be right back, I need the ketchup," he says as he excuses himself. I reach my hand across the table to hold Bellamy's for a second.

"Thank you for breakfast and not freaking out about this morning."

"I think you did enough of that for the both of us."

"I don't want to pretend I understand what Chase is going through. I know he's angry with his father, but that doesn't mean he wants to see me with his mother either."

Bellamy smiles softly. "Chase adores you, Hawk. We'll be fine, I promise."

Chase walks back in with the bottle of ketchup and container of orange juice. "Good call on the OJ, bud," Bellamy says to Chase. Secretly. I'm happy he went and snagged the ketchup because that's a staple for me and my breakfast. After he uses it, I pick up the bottle and squirt it over my eggs and hash browns, and then mix them together. Before I take my first bite, I look up and find mother and son staring at me.

"What?" I ask, suspecting they're going to find my food habits rather odd.

"Nothing," she says, giving a wink. I don't know if it's directed toward me or Chase, but my mouth drops open when she picks up the bottle and does the same thing. In fact, Chase mixes his food together too. I hold up my hand, waiting for each of them to give me a high-five.

After Bellamy and I drop Chase off at school, we decide to take a drive. This wasn't planned, but after last night, between everything that happened and the bombshell I dropped, I need to get away, and she is eager to do the same.

We're on a back road, nestled in the mountains, when I decide to pull over at one of the scenic spots. We get out the truck and reach for each other's hands as we walk toward the rock wall. Below, the deep valley is a death trap, waiting for its next victim. Between the trees, where the pointy sharp rocks are ready to maim you, live the bears. The hungry, ready to eat any time, black and grizzly bears are biding their time. A bear attack is rare, but they happen.

Growing up, we were always on high alert. My dad and his buddies had a network of people who would share information. The last thing my father wanted was to lose cattle or horses to a bear attack. If that happened, and the bear got a way, they were likely to bring their friends back the next day for more.

Standing at the rock wall, I look over the majestic beauty of this state. The lush green of the trees standing out over the snow-covered ground is a sight to behold. I love it here, but I also love Boston and many of the other cities I've visited over the years.

Bellamy's next to me with her camera poised. She's taking photo after photo and I tell her to send them to me. When she sits, I take the spot next to her and sigh. Her hand rubs down my leg as she gives me a sweet smile. I know she's trying to calm my nerves, but they're frayed.

"What do you want to do?" she asks. I know exactly what she's talking about but am tempted to feign stupidity.

"What if I'm wrong?"

"What if you're right?" she fires back.

"I don't know. I'm torn."

"The way I see it, you have a few choices."

"And each one has consequences?" I look at her for confirmation even though I know the answer.

"If you don't say something now and this comes to light years from now, Matty may have some animosity toward you. Or maybe want nothing to do with you at all . . . "

"And if I say something and I'm wrong, I start World War five."

"What happened to three and four?" she asks.

I chuckle even though this situation is nothing to laugh

about. "Three happened in high school and four is currently going on."

"Eh, mere conflicts," she says. We both laugh and fall into a comfortable silence, although the voices in my head are screaming. I pull Bellamy into my arms and press my cheek to the top of her head. I'm comfortable like this, with her, showing affection, and want to figure out a way to make things last, even though everything is so new with us. One night together shouldn't have me jumping into the puddle with both feet.

"I think he hits Annie."

Bellamy pulls herself away and looks at me. "If he does, that means Matty isn't safe."

I nod. "She wants to play ball for me, and I keep asking why. Is it because Brett's mean to her? Is he hitting her too? It can't be about who I am because right now I'm a broken pitcher who spends three days a week in rehab and the rest of my free time courting the local real estate agent. Other than a team, I really have nothing to offer her."

"You have you." She places her hand on my heart. "People see the goodness you're doing."

"They also see me as an enemy."

"Only Brett's cronies. They're used to kissing his ass and being told their kid is the best — or at least thinking it — when in actuality, their child is mediocre but because of their friendship with him, they're treated differently. It's the same mentality my ex has. He thought if I were more accommodating to Brett, Chase would be on his team."

"I want to go back and punch him again for what he said to you." He needs his ass kicked for being a slime ball. "I still have to contend with that situation too." I take a deep breath and let it out slowly. "I don't know if I'm coming or going right now."

She clasps her hand with mine. "Well no matter which way you're going, Chase and I will be by your side."

"Promise?"

"Of course." Bellamy grins. "Whatever you decide, I'll support you. If you want to talk to Annie, you can invite her over to my house if you're not comfortable taking her to your parents'. My door is always open, and if you want to have Matty there, so be it. Whatever you want, Hawk. It's yours."

The woman next to me is amazing. For almost a month I fought my attraction to her because I didn't think it would be fair to put her through the heartache of saying goodbye. Of course, that was all dependent on her actually liking me, which she does. Still, what we have going on here is going to be worth it. I'll find a way to make things work, even if that means flying her back and forth to Boston and spending my off-season in Montana.

"Would you like to meet my parents?"

Her eyes go wide at my question.

"I know it's early in this . . ." I motion back and forth between us. "But I'd really like to introduce you to my mom and dad before tomorrow at the game. They'll be there to cheer on the team."

"I'd love to, Hawk."

"Perfect."

We leave the mountain turn-off and head back to town and toward my parents' house. I still don't know what I'm going to do about Matty. Ignoring my feelings on the matter seems like the right thing to do, but for who? Matty? Me? I don't know. If I'm her father, I want to know. I want to give her the opportunity to have a relationship with me, if that's what she wants. I'd leave it all up to her. Even if she only wants to be friends, I'd do it. Still, the thought lingering in the back of my mind is that if I say something, am I opening pandora's box? What if she's not mine and I cause a ripple in their family infrastructure?

I don't know what to do.

TWENTY-FOUR

BELLAMY

WHEN I MET Greg's parents, I wasn't nervous, not like I am now. It was after about two or maybe three months of dating when he forced me to talk to his mom on the phone. She called every Sunday at seven p.m. like clockwork. If we were studying, we had to be back in his dorm and near the phone so he wouldn't miss her call. One time, we went to Canada to go skiing. He insisted on driving his own car because there was no way he could miss the weekly call from mom. When parents' weekend finally came in the spring, it was like I already knew Greg's mother. Meeting her officially was easy.

I try to imagine what Hawk's family is like as we drive to the ranch. I went to school with his sister, Elizabeth, but we weren't in the same friend group, which is odd for such a small town. She was part of 4H and those kids normally stuck together, often spending weekends traveling to different shows. I don't know what group I was part of in school. All I know is I was trying to survive, get good grades, and get the hell out of dodge . . . only to return with my own child years later.

Hawk turns onto the long, somewhat windy driveway. On either side, we're surrounded by fields blocked off by white rail fencing and on my side, there are also a half dozen horses or so. "How many horses does the ranch have?"

"Normally a dozen, but those are wild ones my sister picked up the other day in Wyoming."

"What does she do with them?"

"Well," he says, as he reaches the top of the driveway and puts his truck into park. Minus the two-story home sitting in front of me, the view of the vast land abutting the mountains is breathtaking. "This is it."

"You grew up here?"

"I did. The mountains seem closer than they appear, but yeah, this is the Sinclair Ranch." He gets out of the truck and walks over to the passenger side and opens it. "The land extends for many miles in all directions."

"And you'd buy Longwoods for what?" I ask as he helps me out of the truck.

"I don't know. Mostly to protect my father's land from Larsen and his company. Maybe to build a new recreation center with a place for my sister to train her students. She does it here, that's her paying job. The horse wrangling she does because she thinks it's fun. Come on, let's go see who's home."

Wait, he didn't call first to make sure? "What if no one's home or they're busy?"

Hawk laughs and pulls me along behind him, up the wide plank stairs, onto the porch and down the side of the house. When we get to the backside, huge barns block some of the view, but it's all the people I see that has me in awe. They're everywhere. Cowboys and cowgirls on horses, pulling horses by their reins, some are moving cattle into trailers, others are riding horses around barrels.

"Whoa."

"Yeah, you would've never guessed this is going on from the front of the house."

"Not in a million years."

"My great-grandma set it up this way. Said she wanted peace and tranquility in the front and chaos could exist out back."

"Sort of like a mullet," I blurt out before catching myself. Hawk laughs so hard he has to bend over to catch his breath. I know my joke wasn't that funny, but I'm laughing right along with him. When he finally stands tall, he pulls me into his arms and kisses me deeply.

"Ahem." The clearing of a voice breaks us apart.

"Hey, Dad," Hawk says to the man coming up the steps. Instantly, my cheeks heat up and as subtly as possible, I try to wipe my lips clean.

"Son, who do we have here?"

"Dad, I'd like you to meet Bellamy Patrick."

We shake hands. "Oh yes, I've heard a lot about you and your son from Hawk and Nolan. It's nice to meet you."

"You too, Mr. Sinclair."

He waves me off. "Name's John. None of this 'Mister' crap. I'm far too young for that." The three of us chuckle. "Come on, Ma's got something brewing inside."

Hawk motions for me to follow his dad inside. Once I step in, I'm enveloped in warmth and basking in the smell of homemade bread. This kitchen is straight out of a magazine with its farmhouse table, wrought iron light fixtures, farmhouse sink and eight-burner stove. The cupboards are white and gray, and the floors are wide plank, stained to look rustic and old. I am in love with this kitchen and probably the rest of the house if I get to see it.

"Ma, I'd like you to meet Bellamy."

The woman at the stove turns around, wipes her hands on her apron and comes toward me. She's short, maybe five foot. She places both hands on my shoulders and looks into my eyes.

"Okay, I see it," she says.

"See what?" I look at Hawk for an answer, but he doesn't give one.

"My son is in love with you, young lady. I knew it the moment he came home and started talking about this beautiful woman he met. I'm Rhonda, but you can call me Ma, Mom, whatever you like."

"You have a beautiful kitchen," I tell her, but my eyes are on Hawk, who winks at me.

"Thank you, this was my anniversary present from John a few years ago. It's functional and my daughters tell me it's also very stylish."

"They're right."

"Yes, well . . . go sit down, the chili is done. I'll make your plates."

Hawk directs me to the table and as soon as I sit down, the door opens and a string of people come walking in. Hawk tells me that they're the ranch hands. They live and work full-time at the ranch, and some are even second and third generation employees of the Sinclairs'.

Rhonda brings over a tray with four bowls and places one in front of me. My stomach growls, even though I would've said I wasn't hungry if asked. The chili smells amazing, but it's the bread bowl that the chili is in that has my mouth watering.

"Did you make the bread bowl?" I ask Rhonda.

"Of course, everything is homemade here."

"I think I've died and gone to heaven," I say after taking the first bite.

Hawk and I end up spending the rest of the day at the ranch. I spend the day visiting with his mom, giving her my life story, and gushing about the rest of her house.

He makes sure I'm home when Chase gets off the bus, but he's the one to wait for him. I think Hawk is a bit excited about tomorrow, with it being their first game. When Chase and Hawk come into the house, they're talking strategy. Not about tomorrow's game, but how they're going to get me to agree to going out for pizza.

As if I could ever say no to these two.

By the time we arrive at the Sinclair Fields, the parking lot is full of cars, the fields are busy with games, kids of all ages are running around in their baseball gear — some not — and my stomach is growling over the smell of popcorn and hotdogs. Once Hawk finds a parking spot, Chase and I get out of the truck and start lifting the equipment out of the back of the truck. Hawk protests, saying he can get it, but after a long talk with his mom yesterday, I learned that Hawk isn't supposed to lift anything, and he's not allowed to throw a ball any farther than ten yards. I glared at him when she said those things and told him no more. He needs to get better so he can go back to Boston, not that I want him to, but I know he misses his team and the game.

As soon as we see Owen, I pass the bag of bats to him, adjust my mini Renegades shirt and head to the concession stand. I don't think I'm in line for a minute before the gossip starts.

"You know," the woman behind me says into my ear. "He has a girlfriend back in Boston and once he leaves here, he's never going to call you again."

How does one even respond to a statement like this with dignity? I turn around and stand as tall as I can. "I know, we're thinking about having a three-some later." I shrug, smile and turn back around, trying with everything I have in me to stay calm even though I'm anything but. I'm raging. I'm sad. Why are women so nasty to one another? Why can't whoever it is behind me just be happy for her 'sister from another mister'? No, instead she wants to bring me down to her level of pettiness.

When I get to the counter, I place my order for a couple of hotdogs, a few drinks, a bag of popcorn and some candy. Might as well go all out for my son's first game. I hand the lady behind the counter a twenty, but she shakes her head. "Is it more?"

"No, Mr. Sinclair gave us strict instructions not to charge you for anything."

"Oh, is that normal?"

"I'm not sure, he's never been here for a game before."

"All right." I toss my twenty into the tip jar, collect my tray of goodies and head toward the stands. Hawk is easy to spot among everyone. He's the guy surrounded by every little kid not playing baseball and some adults, all clamoring for his attention, while all his attention is on Chase. They're watching a game and Hawk is pointing things out to him.

I stand there, taking it all in, and hating how the woman in the concession line acted toward me. Jealously is an ugly trait to carry around. To me, Hawk's a normal guy who I happen to be falling deeply in love with, and so is my son. It sucks that his job is going to take him away from us, and I'm not naïve enough to think we'll continue our relationship once he's back in Boston either. But until then, I'm going to ride this wave, so to speak.

"What is Chase doing? He should be getting ready." I look to my left to find Greg standing next to me. I continue to glance around, waiting to spot Priscilla, but thankfully I don't see her.

"What are you doing here?" My voice is cold, detached.

"Chase has a game."

I glance back at my son, sitting there with Hawk, and wonder how Chase is going to react to the presence of his father. Not well, I imagine. I start walking toward them, knowing Greg is hot on my heels. I want him to go away, to let us continue living in the bubble we've created for ourselves, but he won't. And honestly, he shouldn't. He should want to be with his son every chance he gets.

Chase smiles when he sees me coming. I return the sentiment and then watch as his grin disappears. "Hey, bud," I say as I come to stand next to him. Hawk glances at me and I give him a look, hoping he understands what is about to happen. I wait for a minute for Greg to say hi to this son and when he doesn't, I make introductions.

"Greg, this is Hawk Sinclair, Chase's baseball coach."

"And mom's boyfriend," Chase adds. Secretly, I want to kiss him for saying this to his father, but right now I'm mortified because he said it rather loudly and others are looking.

Greg starts to say something but closes his mouth. "It's nice to meet you, I'm Gregory Patrick," he says to Hawk while I roll my eyes, before turning his attention to Chase.

"What do you say we go sit down and talk?"

"No thanks," Chase says. "I'm watching this game with Hawk." Chase steps closer to Hawk, who isn't paying any attention to Greg. He's focused solely on Chase and me.

"Bell, may I speak with you in private?"

I spread my arms out. "Where exactly would that be, Greg? Just say what you have to say."

He adjusts his collar and smiles at Chase. "It can wait until after the game." Greg mock punches Chase in the shoulder, "Go get 'em tiger."

Who even says that anymore?

BOSTON RENEGADES

The Renegades finally put together a win streak of five games before dropping a game in the middle of their Twins series. Our bats have been okay, but we've lost some heartbreakers late in the game by one run or two, and we're currently sitting in third place behind the Yankees and Rays.

President of Baseball Operations, Ryan Stone, caught up with us after the last game and told us the second half the year will be better, which leads us to believe Hawk Sinclair will be back after the All-Star break. More on him below.

Branch Singleton, designated hitter extraordinaire, has hit for the cycle and has twenty home runs under his belt so far. Is it too early to start the MVP chant? I think not!

GOSSIP WIRE

We thought we'd bring an update on Hawk Sinclair's Little League team. He's kept us fully abreast to how the team is doing, which is made up of both boys and girls. Hawk tells us that his ace pitcher and clean-up hitter are "young women who will change the face of baseball."

The Mini Renegades are off to a slow start, but Coach Sinclair isn't worried. "Youth baseball should be fun. The kids should laugh, make mistakes, and learn," according to Hawk.

We reached out to Wes Wilson, who shared the same sentiments as his ace pitcher, stating, "The Renegades fully support Hawk's decision to coach. We're looking forward to catching a practice or a game, but more so to having Hawk back in the dugout."

TWENTY-FIVE

HAWK

THE SOUND of the baseball hitting the catcher's mitt echoes through the empty fieldhouse. It's my favorite sound in the world and each time I hear it, I smile. He drops the ball and readies himself to catch another one of my sliders. The catcher, Javier Viernes, was sent to Montana by the Renegades to aid in my rehab. He was injured earlier in the season and sent too AA to recoup, but the organization figured he'd benefit by helping me. I'm thankful for him because I'm not sure there's anyone in town who can catch my fastball. Not to mention, he's been a tremendous help with my Little League team.

Those little Renegades, or Mini's, as we've taken to calling them, are the highlight of my day. They're eager to learn, they hustle, they ask questions, and they grin from ear-to-ear whether they win or lose. I knew going in I had an uphill battle, with Brett being the biggest mountain to climb. Never, in my life, have I met someone *so* determined to stand in the way of kids playing baseball. It's like he's throwing a temper tantrum just because he can. Everywhere I turn, look, or go, someone is commenting. Granted, most of the things being said are positive, but there's still too much negativity out there, especially from the parents who follow Brett's every move. I get it. I left and became an outsider despite the fact I've funded the fields. It's an out of sight, out of mind society. To them, I'm the guy on television every four days trying to win a game. The famous baseball player that the local paper writes about but never sees because he doesn't come back in the off-season. It all makes sense, except it doesn't. What Brett and his cronies are doing, I'll never understand. Nor will I understand why Greg — or *Gregory Patrick*, as he likes to be called — is still in Montana.

I take that back. I do understand and want to believe it's because of his son and how much time he's missed, but I'm not entirely sure that's the case. Chase wants nothing to do with his father, which is understandable considering his dad has pushed him aside a few too many times. I've seen it all unravel firsthand at our games and practices. There's "Game Greg" who sits in the bleachers next to Bellamy, cheering on their son while his ex-wife ignores him. And then there's "Practice Greg" who stands at the fence and yells at his son to do things a certain way while Brett stands next to him and eggs him on. From the beginning, I asked the parents to let Owen, myself and, now, Javier coach the kids, and they all agreed. All except for Greg. After his first outburst, I asked him kindly to refrain from yelling at Chase, going as far to explain to him, while looking at Brett, that effective coaching does not include yelling. This is Brett's way of coaching and one of the reasons I believe his daughter asked to play for me. I let her and I know it has ruined his plans to make a run for Williamsport. Matty understands this but tells me she'd rather play for a team who wants to learn than a team that wants to win. Also, the more time I spend with her, the more I believe she's my daughter, and every time I go to talk to Annie about it, she dodges me. I know there are tests that can be done, but short of speaking to a lawyer, I don't know what I can legally do about it.

I'm trying extremely hard not to come between Chase and his father. I want to believe that Greg means well, but I have yet to see where he's actually helping his son instead of hindering him. The nagging, belittling and yelling isn't how you reach a ten-year-old. I've asked Greg to stop the coaching from the sidelines, only for my request to be honored for about five minutes. He apologizes but starts up again. After one practice I asked him which professional team he played for. Chase laughed, Greg scowled, Brett told me I was finished in Richfield, and Bellamy let me ravish her body all night. Still, the damage was done to Chase.

I have yet to raise to my voice at these kids. Neither has Owen or Javier. Every mistake is a teaching moment. No one is doing anything wrong and every day I see this team, I remind them that we're out there to have fun. We're there because we enjoy the game of baseball. Everyone agrees except for my clean-up hitter, Alexis. She's there to win. She's tiny and powerful, knocking a homerun in every game so far and racking up the RBI's. I almost laugh each time she comes up to bat when there's a runner on there because I know they're crossing the plate.

I also never thought I'd coach girls, but damn it if they're not hungry to play baseball. Who am I to deny them? Up until now the only girl in Richfield Little League was Matty, but once word spread that I was starting a team, three girls asked if they could play. I thought the boys would mind but then I remembered they had been denied a chance to play so they understood and weren't about to stand in their way. Of my twelve-person roster, four are girls, and three of them are the better players on the team.

"Ten more," Javier hollers to me. He's crouched down and his glove is ready. My arm cocks back as I start my motion and hurl the ball toward him. He catches the ball and sets it down beside him as I reach into the bucket marked sixty and grab another baseball.

Last week, I threw fifty. The Renegades staff is working in conjunction with the University of Bozeman's training staff to help get me on track. I should've gone back to Boston to start training but asked that I stay in Montana until it's absolutely necessary. Truth is, I'm not ready to leave Richfield. The thought of being thousands of miles away from Bellamy doesn't sit well with me at all. From the second I met her, I was falling for her and I didn't even try to stop myself. By the time I kissed her for the first time, I was already in love with her. It's crazy to think that because I had never fallen in love before but that's how I knew. The way I feel around her . . . it's unlike anything I've ever experienced. I liken it to starting a game. The rush of emotions, the anticipation, the goose-bumps that take up a permanent residence on my arms. Every day is like that with her. From the first time we spent the night together, we haven't been apart. We're playing house, with me being the dutiful boyfriend. On the nights we don't practice, I help cook dinner, Chase and I play catch in the backyard, and I sit at the table with Chase while he does his homework. I mow the yard, put out the garbage and watch Bellamy's car in the driveway. Since I've met her, I've become domesticated, and my teammates give me crap about it at every opportunity. I'll take it though. I'd rather have these moments with her and Chase, instead of wondering what they're doing all the time.

After I throw my last pitch, Javier stands up and comes toward me as one of the school's work study kids picks up the net and walks under it to start picking up the balls. "How's the shoulder?"

I rotate my arm around a few times and nod. "Feels good, actually." I've measured the tenderness in my arm by the number of pitches I've thrown. When I started with thirty, I was sore. I needed an ice bath after every session and requested more physical therapy. When I hit forty, I wasn't sore until the end of the week and at fifty, I seemed okay. The goal, of course, is a hundred pitches, mixed between my fast-balls, curves, and sliders. I rarely throw a knuckle ball during a game so we're less focused on making sure I'm ready for that pitch. Overall, my rehab is going a bit slower than antici-pated. Twelve weeks is what the doctor said, and of course I had a minor setback after I punched Brett in the nose, for which I'm pleasantly surprised he hasn't filed charges against me yet. I'm still waiting for the lawsuit, which I'll take over a criminal record. Still, I should be heading back to Boston in the next couple of weeks, but it looks like I'll be out until at least mid-July.

Javier pats me on the back as we walk toward the training room and when we get there, we find just what the doctor ordered — ice baths. They hurt, but *damn* they feel good too. We both strip down to our boxers and climb into the tub. I holler while Javier cusses in Spanish, until we're both submerged. The trainer starts the timer for us. No more than six to eight minutes is the recommendation.

"How's the hand?" I ask Javier. He pulls his left hand out of the water and flexes it. Six weeks ago, he slid into home and the catcher stepped on his hand, breaking it. It was a freak accident, but one that put him on the injured list. He was sent from our AAA team down to double to rehab, until I said I needed a catcher.

"Better, but tender. I like the trainer here, she's nice."

Thinking back to my first day with her makes me laugh. "I think I referred to her as "the spawn of Satan", or some-thing like that, when I started working with her, but she knows her job well and knows how to work those muscles. I swear I had aches in places I didn't know existed until I started with her."

"Man, don't tell Stone. He'll fire our current staff and bring her in."

Wouldn't be a bad thing, I think to myself, and maybe it's something I should hint around about before I leave, although maybe she's happy working in a rehab facility and working with college athletes.

For the longest time I wanted to quit on her because of the pain. It didn't matter that I knew I needed her, everything she did, everything she put my arm through, was agonizing. She had a job to do, and that was to get me back on the field. So far, she's done exactly what's been asked of her and I've been right on track with the exception of my minor mishap in using Brett as a punching bag. Even after my run in with Larsen's face, I made sure everyone who mattered knew it was my fault I was behind schedule, not hers. The last thing I wanted was for her to lose her job.

The timer goes off and Javier and I get out of the tub. We wrap ourselves in the towels provided and head toward the locker room where we both slip into the BoRe gear of sweatpants, long sleeved shirts and pullover jackets. It's still fairly chilly in Montana, hovering in the high sixties/low seventies, which is cold to Javier and me who are used to it being around eighty right about now.

Since his arrival, he's been staying at my parents in the room I vacated when I sort of moved in with Bellamy. I get the feeling my mom is upset with me for leaving and I don't expect her to understand, but being at home is awkward, especially when Warner is hounding me about the ranch — not to mention the side comments from my sisters. Besides, staying with Bellamy is showing me everything that I'm missing in life, like a partner and, dare I say . . . a kid. I love Chase. I think he's an amazing boy and I can't, for the life of me, understand how his father can treat him the way he does.

After an hour drive, during which Javier reads all the stats from last night's game even though we watched it, we're finally back in town. I take us to Main Street, park the truck and head into the deli for lunch. It's busy, with the line almost to the door, but fully worth the wait.

"Who knew small town America was like this?" Javier

asks. I look around, trying to see what he sees and how it differs from where he lives. He did a minor stint with the BoRe's last year, caught a few games for me while Cashman was injured, and then went back to Pawtucket and now he's in Portland, Maine until he goes back to Rhode Island. Not exactly metropolises and more like places I'd consider small towns, especially in New England. Every town I have visited is quaint with picturesque Main Streets.

"Do you like it here?" I ask him.

He shrugs. "I like the east coast, the ocean. Makes me feel like I'm home."

"Minus the weather."

He laughs. "Going back to the DR during the off-season is the best medicine."

We finally place our order and decide to take it to go. As I drive toward the baseball fields, I spot Bellamy escorting a couple toward a house. I honk, Javier sticks his head out the window and yells her name as I wave. I think she's smiling, at least I'm hoping she is, but I admit, we were a little obnoxious.

"How long have you been together?" Javier asks.

"Not long," I tell him. "We met a few days after I got here, and I've seen her every day since."

"And you're leaving soon."

I'm silent for a minute before I answer him. "I'm going to be the ultimate dick and ask her to come with me. I expect her to say no, though, because she has a good job and her mom is here."

"What about her son?"

"I want him too." And I do. I want Chase and Bellamy to be in Boston with me, but I'm not sure how to make that work, especially with Greg somewhat back in the picture.

TWENTY-SIX

BELLAMY

MY CHEEKS FLUSH when Javier yells my name and Hawk starts honking, although I'm thrilled that he happened to drive by. He left so early this morning that I really didn't get a chance to tell him goodbye. Normally, we wake, he makes breakfast for Chase while I shower, and we share our morning together before I'm off to my first showing or he's heading to his parents. On the days he has therapy or training, he's gone before the sun is up and does his best not to wake me. Those mornings are lonely and tend to remind me that my time with Hawk is getting shorter and shorter by the day. He doesn't know this, but I'm keeping track of the pitches he's thrown because I've heard him tell Chase that on average, he throws one hundred a game and something tells me that's the magic number that sends him back to Boston.

After Greg moved out of our home, it took me months to fall asleep. Depression took over. I felt inadequate as a wife, a woman. I couldn't even sleep in my own bed because I saw visions of my husband with another woman in there, even though he swore he never brought her into our home. It hadn't mattered if he did; in my mind, my world was violated by them. I quit my job because *she* was there, and I'd have to work with *him* as well. Where does one escape when your world is falling apart around you? Your home is supposed to be your sanctuary . . . mine became hell. Sure, I still had Chase so I pasted the biggest, brightest smile on my face until he got on the bus every morning. Then for seven hours, I'd wallow, wondering out loud to the walls that were closing in what I did wrong. Nothing. That's what. In the end, I realized Greg would've cheated no matter what.

When Hawk spent the first night at my house, I didn't want him to leave but I could never come out and ask him to stay. I don't want him to think I'm clingy, even though I want to be. Just call me plastic wrap. Every night he's stayed I wake up in the morning with a smile on my face because I know he's there. Life with Hawk is easy. We move around each other easily. He helps when I don't expect him to by doing the dishes, sitting down with Chase to go over homework, showing up on Field Day at Chase's school, making sure my son is occupied during the day, cooking dinner, mowing my lawn . . . my *God* the list of things this man has done for my son and me can go on and on. The worst part — he's leaving. I can't even ask him to stay because I know the answer is no. Who, in their right mind, would give up a baseball career to play lover to a single mom? No one I know, that's for sure.

One day, after Hawk had left for therapy, I asked Chase on our way to school if Hawk was good at his job. My son scoffed and rattled off stats that made no sense to me. When I looked at him with nothing but pure confusion on my face, Chase simply said, "He's one of the best, Mom." Of course he is and now he's doing everything he can to get back to his job.

Despite the fact I'm embarrassed, I'm also happy Hawk drove by. I know it was purely happenstance but it feels different, almost like he knew I'd be on this street at this time, walking toward the house. I'm not sure if I believe in fate or kismet, or even love at first sight like he does, but I believe in him and what we have going on. However, I'm not stupid enough to think we'll last with the distance between us. The fairytale is going to end soon, and it saddens me. When I think about talking to him about a future, my stomach twists in knots and the idea makes me ill. The talk has to happen, but I don't want to be the one to bring it up.

"Think you could get me his autograph?" Mr. Pearl asks as I turn back toward him and his wife.

Mrs. Pearl slaps her husband. "Don't be rude."

"What?" he asks, shrugging. "It's a valid question."

Rude or not, he's right, the question is valid. "Hawk is signing autographs this Saturday at the fields. He has a few teammates coming to town. It's mostly for kids, but I have a feeling I can get him to make an exception for you."

Mr. Pearl smiles brightly, that is until I look at his wife and say, "And for you, I'll make sure he and his buddies take a picture with you. Word on the street is the other players coming are . . ." I pull out my cell phone to read Karter's comments verbatim, "...hotter than hot, delicious and lick-able." My cheeks flare up again as Mrs. Pearl fans herself.

"I'll be there," she says, much to her husband's dismay.

I motion for them to walk toward the door. I put my code into the lockbox, wait for it to open and pull the key out. After I open the front door, they step inside.

"I'll take it," Mrs. Pearl says immediately. Oh, how I wish selling houses was this easy. She looks at her husband. "I want this house."

"You barely stepped inside," he points out.

"I don't care, I've seen all the pictures."

"I'm going to be in the kitchen. Go ahead and look around. If you need me, just holler." I leave them in the entryway to duke it out. I met them last year when they sold their home, bought a motorhome and set off into the sunset. Mrs. Pearl called a few months back saying she was tired of living on wheels and wanted a house again. I don't know why they came back to Richfield when their children are spread out across the country, but they had and asked me to find them a home. This is the first one we've looked at with four more on our list for the day, and I have a feeling she's going to want all five of them.

I'm going through paperwork when my phone vibrates against the granite countertop. I look down and smile at Hawk's name.

Hawk: I'm so happy I saw you. You look so hot in that skirt.

Everything he says or does makes me blush. I send him back the emoji showing my red cheeks.

Hawk: I love that I make you blush.

Love . . . that four letter word that lingers between us. It sits on the tip of my tongue. There are times when I want to blurt it out in the middle of a conversation, like when he's sitting next to me on the couch and we're watching a movie. He'll look over at me and move a stray piece of hair away from my face. I want to tell him then. Or when I stand in the doorway of Chase's bedroom, spying on him while he reads some baseball magazine to my son who is focused on Hawk and not the magazine. I want to tell him right then and there, and I know Chase would echo my sentiment. But making such a profound declaration will muddy the waters. Deep down I think Hawk knows how we feel, but I can't let my emotions ruin everything. For my sake and that of my son's, I have to make these last days count.

I contemplate what to say back. My fingers hover over the predictive text. Right in the center is the word love, and to the left of it is "I", to the right, "you". I could easily press the three and not type a single word but telling him I love him for the first time over text is not how the words should be said. Instead, I keep it normal.

I'm thinking ribs for dinner?

Hawk: Need me to stop at the store before going home?

My day brightens when he calls my house home. Hell, he brightens everything about my day. *That would be great*, I text back.

Hawk: I noticed we are low on dish soap. I'll grab some.

I stand there, starring at the text. In all the years Greg and I lived together, I can't recall a single time he noticed we were out of something and went to the store to buy it. Sure, he'd tell me we were out of toilet paper or that Chase needed diapers, but he never took the initiative to restock. Again, I find myself wanting to tell Hawk that I love him, but in this case it's because he's so aware of what's going on around him.

You're the best, I text back, and I mean it. He really is, and in a few weeks when he leaves, I'm going to be a wreck.

The Pearls finally make their way to the kitchen and I pretend I'm reading an email instead of summarizing my relationship in my head. I grab my things and move to the other room, giving them a chance to look around. This house has an amazing kitchen, everything is brand new and state of the art. Mrs. Pearl loves to cook, which is another reason why I think she wants a home. This house is too big for the two of them, but I imagine she's looking toward the holidays when her children will come back to Montana with their children. I believe she told me she had nine grandchildren with three on the way. Her eyes light up every time she speaks about her family.

"Bellamy?" Mrs. Pearl's voice rings out from the kitchen. I walk in and find Mr. Pearl standing at the sink, looking out over the yard. The previous owner left the custom swing set when they moved, and it would be perfect for the Pearl's grandchildren.

"Mrs. Pearl?"

"I love this house," she says, warmly. "It's big with the four bedrooms we're looking for."

"It is."

"And the basement is perfect for a game room."

"I agree." I'm not sure where she's going with this and Mr. Pearl is doing his best to ignore her. She keeps looking at his back and sighing. "I sense a 'but' coming."

She smiles. "It's the price. It's out of our budget."

I should've expected this. They're retired and living on a fixed income, of course the price is an issue. "If you really want the house, why not make an offer and see what the seller says? The house has been on the market for almost six months; they might be ready to get rid of it."

Now Mr. Pearl turns around. "Do you think they'd be willing to sell for less than the asking price?"

I shrug. "I don't know. We aren't the listing agent so the only thing I can do is send over an offer and try to negotiate on your behalf."

Mrs. Pearl smiles at her husband who has walked to her side. "Let's do it." She reaches for his hand and he kisses her softly. I turn away, giving them their moment.

In the dining room, I pull out the contract and put an "X" next to where they need to sign. They come into the room and Mr. Pearl tells me what they want to offer. I mentally calculate the difference and think that it's a fair offer and there really shouldn't be any reason why the seller doesn't accept. As soon as we finish up, I head to the office. I want to get the offer sent to the seller's agent as soon as possible.

When I walk in, our new receptionist greets me, telling me I have flowers waiting for me on my desk. It's nice of her to let me know, but unnecessary since I can see them. As I sit down, I pull the card from the clear plastic stem and prepare to fall more in love with Hawk than I already am.

I saw these and thought of you ~ Hawk

Why is he so perfect? More importantly, why is he leaving? I know the answer to my last question, but it doesn't help make the situation feel any better. I set the card in my purse so I can put it somewhere safe when I get home.

"He's in love with you." Karter's voice startles me. I hold my hand against my heart and glare at her.

"You need a bell or something to announce your arrival."

She laughs, bends slightly at her waist and inhales the fragrant roses. "You're the only one I sneak up on, everyone else hears me coming a mile away. Anyway, when is he leaving?"

I shake my head slightly. "I'm not sure, we really haven't discussed it, nor has he said."

"You don't ask?"

"Not really a conversation I want to have."

"Yeah, I can see that." She sits down on the chair across from my desk. "But you have to."

"Yeah." I do what I can to ignore the elephant in the room. Thinking about Hawk leaving is not high on my priority list. Getting this offer sent in and going home to him and Chase is though. I scan the offer and email it to the other agent, asking him to call me when he's had a chance to speak to his client. There's going to be some back and forth, which is to be expected, but I'm hoping it's all reasonable. I ask her what she knows about this other agent. She says he's objective and easy to work with. I tell her about the Pearl's and how I'd love to close this deal for them, when my phone rings. It's Greg, the last person I want to speak to right now. I send him to voicemail and tell Karter I'll see her in the morning, as I'm calling it a day.

My drive home is quick and when I pull into the driveway, I'm excited to find Hawk's truck there. I'm eager to see him and rush inside, praying that Javier isn't with him, although chances are that he is. I burst through the door and find Hawk walking toward the living room. We both stand there, looking at each other.

"Is Javier here?"

He shakes his head.

"Chase?"

Again, his head moves slowly back and forth. He knows exactly what I'm getting at and moves toward me, except he's too slow. I don't want to wait. I leap toward him and he catches me effortlessly. I try to wrap my legs around him, but my damn skirt prevents me. He senses this and hikes my skirt up over my ass, carrying me toward our bedroom.

TWENTY-SEVEN

HAWK

TODAY'S a big day in the world of Little League baseball in Richfield, Montana. To date, I'm the biggest star to come from this tiny town and since it has been pointed out to me a time or two that I don't actually belong here anymore, I thought I'd do something to show the people of my hometown what they mean to me. And by people, I mean the kids, because when it comes down to it, they're the only ones who haven't shunned me. No, I take that back. For the most part the people have been very welcoming, minus a few who are associated with Brett Larsen. It's fine, I'm not bitter.

I arrive at the fields early, mostly to make sure everything is in place for what's about to happen and to give the guys a chance to check out my complex. I'm proud of it and want to show it off. Travis, Ethan, Branch, Cooper, Kayden and I stay in the confines of my rented SUV. The windows are tinted so the people in the line forming along the fence have no idea that my teammates are with me. But they know someone important is here because they're cheering. I frown as I take in the line. There are more adults than children. It's my hope that with school being out for the summer, more youngsters will show up.

"This place looks awesome," Branch says from behind me.

"I played a lot of ball in complexes like this. My parents loved it because it meant less travel," Ethan adds.

Travis sighs and I look over at him sitting in the passenger seat. "What's your issue?" I ask him.

He shakes his head. "I forgot my lucky pen." Everyone in the car laughs. Leave it to Travis Kidd to have a lucky pen.

"Does this mean you can't sign balls today?" As soon as I say it, I know I'm in for it.

Travis turns, slides his sunglasses to the top of his head and looks me up and down. "The only balls I plan to sign . . ." His head jolts forward, and my eyes catch a hand connecting with the back of his skull.

"Saylor asked me to whack you every time you said something inappropriate," Cooper says, and we all laugh.

"I hadn't even said it yet." Travis rubs the back of his head and mutters a string of cuss words.

As soon as the guys landed, they filled me in on everything, which only made me miss my team more than ever. I'm excited to go back but dreading the day I leave Richfield. Each day is getting harder and harder when it comes to Bellamy and Chase. I want to tell her I love her and ask her to move to Boston but am afraid of what she might say. My ma says the only way to know, is if I put myself out there. I countered with, "Sometimes it's best not to know." It isn't, of course, but that's what I keep telling myself.

The group of us get out of the car. I'm sure to outsiders, the SUV resembles one of those clown cars in the circus. Big guys keep exiting, one by one. All I can say is, thank god for third row seating. And for the BoRe organization. When Ethan and Travis said they were going to come visit for a few days, it was Bellamy who suggested we hold an autograph session. She called it giving back to the community and said it would be fun. Not that I wasn't already doing so with the Sinclair Fields, but this was a chance to do something fun for the kids. I asked the guys if they were interested, which I knew they would be, but when Travis told me that the others were coming as well, I got a little teary. Then I realized the PR nightmare it could create and called the boss. Mr. Stone assured me the organization was fully behind me. Shock doesn't even begin to describe how I felt when posters, hats, baseballs, and mini bats showed up at my parents' place. My father wasn't impressed but Nolan was. He and Chase got first dibs on whatever they wanted.

As soon as we're spotted, the line erupts in cheers and chants. Our names are yelled, and it feels like spring training all over again. We walk together toward the entrance of the complex where one of the Boston Renegades security details stands, decked out in BoRe gear. He's a big dude, buff and looks menacing. He's not familiar to me, but I pat him on the shoulder as I walk by and he acknowledges me and the other guys. He and a few of his co-workers are here to keep the lines in order and to make sure nothing bad happens.

Inside, Bellamy, her friend Karter, Owen and Javier are putting the finishing touches on the long tables we will sit at. Black tablecloths with the BoRe logo cover the folding tables. There are boxes of felt tipped pens in front of each seat and a security guard standing behind each chair, but it's the display before the tables that really grabs my attention. The merchandise the BoRe's sent is set-up and ready for purchase with the money earned today going back into the fields for maintenance and equipment.

"Hey, can I borrow you for a second?" I rest my hand on Bellamy's hip to get her attention. She turns, smiles and nods. I motion toward the guys who have gathered together not far from where I'm standing. "Where's Chase?"

"Right there." She points toward her son, who is sitting on the bleachers with Nolan and Matty.

"Why's she here?" I ask and quickly realize how my question sounds.

Bellamy shakes her head back and forth slowly. Over the past few weeks, Matty has shown up at Bellamy's after practice or one of our games. She stays for dinner and Bellamy drives her home at night. Matty doesn't talk much about what's going on at home, but I can imagine it isn't pretty. "You need to do something," she whispers.

Doing something means asking the question that's been plaguing me for a while. It's right up there with telling Bellamy I love her and want her and Chase to come to Boston. All three issues weigh heavily on my mind, and all three need to be resolved.

I whistle and beckon all three of the kids over. I crouch down when they're in front of us, looking each of them in the eye. Side-by-side, Nolan and Matty have similar features which increases the ache I feel when it comes to her. What if I ask if she's my daughter and I'm wrong? What does that do to her already fractured home life, which I seem to be contributing to? What if I ask and I'm told she is? I can't leave her behind, knowing how volatile and unhinged Brett is. Matty looks at me expectantly and I break eye contact with her.

"I'm going to take you over and introduce you to my teammates." Chase and Matty light up while Nolan remains reserved. He's been down this road before and isn't as excited. "They'll be having dinner with us later, so you don't need to wait in line for autographs. Same goes for you, Matty. Okay?" All three nod. I stand and place one hand on Chase's shoulder and the other reaches for his mother's hand. When we get to the guys, Travis is cracking some obscene joke.

"Kidd, do you ever stop?" I ask.

He shakes his head. "Nope, just ask Saylor."

"Congratulations, by the way," I tell him. I wish I had been there when he announced to the team that Saylor's pregnant. I remember when he told us he was adopting Lucy. After it was said and done, we threw him our own version of a baby shower. "I'd like for you to meet Bellamy." I look at her when I say her name and when she glances at me, my heart stops for a minute. "This is her son Chase, my ace pitcher, Matty, and you guys know Nolan."

Everyone shakes hands, animatedly, and the kids gush about the players before them until someone yells, "Hey, what do we have to do to get some attention around here?"

We all turn and look. Saylor and Lucy, Ainsley and the twins, and Daisy with her growing mid-section are coming toward us with a chorus of "Daddy!" being yelled.

"You fucking dog," I say to Ethan.

"Only our parents and the wives know, and now whoever sees it on social media after this event."

"Why the secret?" I ask.

"Just want to enjoy her being pregnant before the media starts hounding her."

"I can understand that." I can't, personally, but it makes sense. Ethan made a lot of social media mistakes early in his career, and the press has never let up on him. They're always waiting for him to screw up again.

Hugs are given and introductions are made. Saylor tells us that Ryan asked that she come and make sure there weren't any PR issues, plus Lucy wanted to be with Travis. Cooper holds both his children in his arms. I say hi to them. Janie, who they refer to as JC, is shy and buries her face into her dad's shoulder. Cal, on the other hand, wants to be let down and as soon as Cooper obliges his son, the boy is off and running. I tell the kids that we'll pay them to keep Cal out of trouble.

Saylor tugs my arm, pulling me over to the side, away from our group. "The girl," she says, and I pretend to think she's talking about Bellamy.

"As soon as I saw her, I was smitten. Found her at the top

of a ridgeline one morning, trekking through the snow with a skirt on. Best part is, she had no idea who I was. She doesn't watch baseball and was long gone by the time I got to high school, so she missed all the fanfare of me playing."

"I'm not talking about your lady friend," she says pointedly.

"Oh."

"You see it right?"

I nod slowly. "It's complicated."

"Do you need my help 'uncomplicating' it?"

I shrug, not knowing what I need. "I don't want to ruin her life."

"Hawk, if it gets out that you spent time with her and she *is* your child, it could ruin yours."

"I know."

"What do you need me to do? Is there a story the BoRe's should get in front of?"

I nod. If Matty is mine, I can't imagine Brett is going to welcome the news. I fill Saylor in on everything, from the conflicts with Brett, to Annie asking me to leave town, and how Matty left her dad's team to come play for mine. "I have a feeling Brett is going to explode soon. I know I would if I were in his spot."

"Well, maybe he knows and that's why he hasn't said anything."

"He doesn't seem like the type to keep things to himself."

Saylor sets her hand on my upper arm and smiles. "I'm here for whatever you need."

"Thank you, and congratulations."

She rubs her hand over her growing mid-section. "I never thought I'd travel down this path again but am so thankful for Travis. I'm the luckiest woman in the world."

"Actually," I tell her. "If it weren't for you, Travis would probably be in jail." Saylor looks over at her husband who is carrying their daughter on his shoulders.

"Me too," she says, sighing. She walks toward Travis, leaving me with those lingering words. I follow behind and reach for Bellamy's hand when I get to her side. I lean down and kiss her.

"What's that for?" she asks with a smile. Before I can answer, Karter yells that it's time to get things moving. The guys all take a seat along the table. Cooper holds onto Janie, while Lucy half stands, half sits, on Travis's lap. I glance behind me at the field to find Nolan, Chase and Matty corralling Cal. The wives have all found something to do, with Daisy working the merchandise booth, Saylor standing behind the table babysitting us, and Ainsley and Bellamy are in the concession stand.

"I like her," Travis says.

"I like her too," Lucy adds.

"Thanks, Luce. Do you want to go play with the other kids?"

She shakes her head. "Nope, staying with my Daddy." Travis kisses her on the cheek. I remember how when he first came into her life, she had a little possessive streak. Travis and Saylor had hoped she'd grow out of it, but that doesn't seem to be the case.

The people who waited in line file in. Some stop at the merchandise stand, while others get in line to have us sign their items. After a few minutes, my clan returns. Chase is by my side and Nolan is with my parents who have showed up in support. But it's the hand resting on my shoulder that gets my attention the most. I look and find Matty standing next to me. We look at each other deeply and for the first time, I see her as my daughter, and I think she sees me as her dad. I vow to myself — this is the day I find out. I can't wait any longer.

TWENTY-EIGHT

BELLAMY

HAWK STANDS and holds up his glass. "I want to thank everyone who came out today and supported us. We raised a nice bit of change for the fields, which will go to buying new equipment and helping the youth who need a little extra. A special thanks to my teammates. You went above and beyond today, especially Kayden and Branch, who took to the field and played with the kids. I can say with absolute certainty that they'll never forget today."

"Here, here," Branch says as he lifts his glass.

"You inspire me to do the same in my hometown," Kayden adds.

"Me too," Travis says.

The whole group of us is at The Depot enjoying the finer things in life . . . pizza and arcade games to keep the kids occupied. We're sitting in the back corner, away from everyone else, and for anyone who thinks they can come talk to us, the BoRe's security guards are at a table in front of us, ready to turn people away.

Aside from Hawk's teammates — along with their wives and children — Hawk's family is here, as is my mother, Karter, and Owen. As I look around the table, I marvel at the people here who all love Hawk in one way or the other. His mother beams with pride each time her son speaks, his father is a bit harder to read. His sisters and brothers-in-law seem to be enjoying themselves, but they're at the end of the table, sort of in their own world. Hawk has mentioned a few times there some animosity between them, and more so now that Nolan wants to play baseball. But for the most part, he brushes it under the rug and will nonchalantly say, "Everything will return to normal when I leave."

What he doesn't understand is that I don't want everything to return to normal because normal for me isn't good. Normal means Chase is sad and doesn't have friends, whereas now, he's surrounded and he's happy. Normal means lonely nights and an empty bed. As much as I told myself not to get attached, I am. It means Brett is back to making my life difficult, not that he's ever really stopped. He's doing everything he can to prevent Hawk and his family from buying the land next to his building. I fear, once Hawk leaves, it will become Brett's because I'm guessing Hawk's brothers-in-law might be friends with Brett. I can't prove it, but Brett always seems to be one step ahead of me. Of course, it could come from the seller's family as well, but they've assured me they want nothing to do with Larsen. Normal also means Greg is back to harassing me about the way I parent and how I need to give into Brett to makes things easier for Chase. I don't want normal, not one bit.

Greg was here for about ten or fifteen days, off and on, until Priscilla gave him an ultimatum. I realized then that no matter what goes on in our son's life, he will always choose her and that's fine. He's made his choice and Chase has been very clear that even at the young age of ten, he doesn't want his father around. I worry this all changes when Hawk leaves.

Hawk's hand squeezes my thigh, bringing my attention back to the table. "Are you okay?" he whispers in my ear. I look into his eyes and tell myself tonight's the night. I'm going to tell him how I feel. I'm putting all my cards on the table because if I don't, I may not get another chance.

"I'm good," I say, hoping to reassure him. I'm not sure I've done the job because he asks if I'm sure and all I can do his nod. From this point, he does his best to include me in the conversations floating around, but most of what is being talked about is his life in Boston, their hectic schedule and whether he knows his plans once he gets back.

"Wilson said something about relief."

"No AAA?" Ethan asks.

"Nope." Hawk shakes his head. "I thought for sure I'd finish the season in Pawtucket."

"What's Pawtucket?" I ask.

"It's where the BoRe's have their AAA team," Daisy interjects. "I'll take you there when you come visit."

"Oh yes, we'll go shopping. Providence has the best mall around," Ainsley adds.

"The one in Burlington is nice," Saylor says. "Plus, less taxes."

I slink back into my chair. Hawk and I haven't discussed me visiting him in Boston and here the wives are, talking about including me in their shopping trip, as if it's a done deal. Hell, maybe he's just assuming it'll happen since we've practically been living together, with him already playing a parental role to Chase. Except, nothing is ever said about future plans, whether we have one together or not, other than what time Chase has practice or a game. Suddenly, I feel like an outsider even though I know that isn't Hawk or anyone at this table's intention. I don't know what to say, so I smile and thank them for including me.

When the little kids start to get fussy, we call it a night. Thankfully, the wives who surprised their husbands today rented a car, and Hawk happily hands the keys over to his borrowed SUV so everyone else could go back to their hotel. The plan is for everyone to meet at the field in the morning for the mini BoRe's baseball game. Although, I don't know how the kids will do, knowing there's professional baseball players in the stands watching them.

As soon as we're home, I tell Chase it's time for bed. As usual, he requests Hawk read to him and even though going over stats isn't exactly education, I don't try to stop them. They've bonded and I'm not about to come between them.

Afterward, Hawk enters my bedroom, shutting and locking the door behind him. We don't expect Chase to burst in but we're still cautious. As upset as I am over the impending situation, I can't help but smile at the man as he comes toward the bed. He's stripping, taking off each article of clothing with each step he takes. Only, he's fumbling and laughing his way to nakedness.

"Are you naked under that comforter?"

I shake my head and pull the blankets back to show him I have his t-shirt on.

"Panties on?"

"Yep."

"Ugh," he groans as he crawls into bed. "You gonna make me work for it tonight?" he asks, placing his hand under the shirt. His touch is cold and I shiver.

"I thought we could talk."

Normally, this would push a guy away but not Hawk. He keeps his hand where it is and props himself up with his other. "Yeah."

"You're leaving soon, aren't you?"

He nods and moves his hand from my hip to my cheek, brushing his thumb back and forth. "I've been trying to find a way to tell you, to bring it up, but there never seems to be an appropriate time to say the words."

"It's okay, I understand." I don't but I also don't want him to feel bad. I knew this day was coming.

"How can you understand when I don't?"

"What do you mean?" I ask him.

He adjusts slightly, pulling me closer. We lay on our respective pillows with our hands clasped in the middle. "For weeks I've been trying to come up with the words, things I need to say to you and Chase. In my head we have this amazing conversation, and everything goes the way I want it to, but then reality slaps me in the face and reminds me that not everything is about me. So, here we are and the things I've been wanting to say to you still need to be said. Earlier, I saw the way you were looking at everyone, and could see something in your eyes."

"For a guy, you're pretty perceptive."

"I grew up between two sisters; my mother raised me to be sensitive to others and my father taught me to always listen to my gut. Sure, he was talking about animals and ranching, but the thought still applies now."

"If you say so." I try not to laugh but a giggle still escapes.

He leans forward and kisses me softly. "I'm in love with you, Bellamy. I asked you from the beginning if you believed in love at first sight because I hadn't until I met you. That day, up on the top of that hill, as soon as I laid my eyes on you, I knew I had to know you. And now that I do, I don't want to let you go." He brings our conjoined hands to his mouth and kisses mine.

"Hawk," I say his name quietly into the stillness of the room.

"I'd ask you to marry me if I didn't think you'd run. So, I'm going to ask you the next impossible thing . . . will you considering giving up the life you have here to move to Boston to be with me? I know it's a lot to ask, leaving your job and Chase switching schools, but I see a future with you, and I've tried to picture how it would work with me there and the both of you in Montana. I'd only see you in the off-season and summer vacations if you came to Boston. I love you and I love Chase and I understand if this is moving too fast for you. We can try the long-distance thing, but I can already tell you that you'll hate it. When I go on road trips, it'll be early morning or late-night calls. On nights we travel, it'll be quick texts before I jump on a plane and if I lose a game, I won't want to talk."

"And if you lose a game and come home to us, what's the difference?"

Hawk smiles. "Because you'll be there to comfort me, and Chase will tell me everything I did wrong because that's the kind of player he's going to be — constructive and supportive. I want to raise your son, Bellamy. I want watch that boy grow into a man, guide him, and be someone he can look up to."

"You want all of this after only a few months of knowing us?"

"Minutes, hours, days, weeks and months of knowing you. Time has stood still here for me since I met you, measured only by my time in rehab. Part of me wishes I was still hurt so I could stay longer, but the other part of me wants to get back to Boston and do my job because every game I'm away, I'm letting my team down. I know that may not make much sense to you, but to me, they're my family."

He trails off and in our dimly lit room, I see him searching my eyes for an answer. It would be so easy to say yes, to tell him we'll pack up and move tomorrow, but it's not that easy.

"You're in love with me?"

He nods. "From the first day."

"I'm in love with you as well," I say, and then smile. "Not exactly on the first day, but shortly thereafter."

Hawk grins. "I'll take it." He leans in to kiss me, but I place my hand on his chest to stop him. "What is it?"

"I have to talk to Chase and my mom. She's one of the reasons we moved back, and I want to speak with her before I decide. I think I know what Chase wants, but I'd like his input. His opinion is important to me and while I think he's going to say yes, I think he should wait until his baseball season is over."

"I agree," he says.

"And if we do this, where will we live? I'm assuming we'd live together?"

"Of course," he says, smiling. "Right now, I have a two-bedroom apartment. Not conducive to a ten-year-old though. I figure we can pick a neighborhood and buy a house together, something that fits a family."

A family. "Hawk," I draw out his name and sigh. "Do you want children? I only ask because . . . well I'm not exactly a spring chicken anymore."

His hand is back to caressing my cheek. "If we were to have a baby, I'd be ecstatic, but I have Chase and he's more than I could ever ask for, Bellamy."

I want to tell him he has Matty too because while he may be in denial, I'm not. The more time we spend with her, the more I'm convinced he's her father.

I pull Hawk toward me, urging him lay on top of me. I love the way his weight settles over me, as if he's trying to keep me safe. My fingers brush against his hair; it's become shaggy over the past few months and I know he'll cut it before going back to Boston. He's made many comments about the long-haired ball players and how it's a distraction.

"I love you," I tell him before reaching up to press my lips to his. Earlier this evening, and days leading up to now, I fretted about what life was going to be like with him gone, and now I know . . .

He wants me.

He wants Chase.

And he wants us in Boston.

TWENTY-NINE

HAWK

IT'S like the weight of the world has been lifted off me now that I've told Bellamy how I feel. Last night, the time was finally right. Earlier, during dinner, I sensed there was something wrong, even though she assured me she was fine. She was quiet and sort of disengaged from what was happening around us. At first, I thought she wasn't connecting with the other wives, but I saw the way she lit up when they spoke to her . . . until Pawtucket was mentioned. In that moment, her demeanor shifted, and I realized what was going on. In the end, I'm happy it all happened because I don't know if I would've said something last night otherwise. Effectively, all I've been accomplishing by avoiding the subject is putting off the inevitable, but time is drawing near. I'll be returning to Boston shortly.

Today, I'm at the field early and I can't figure out why. Something told me I needed to be here, maybe to oversee the grounds crew. The rec department does a good job making sure the lines are down, and David Farmer is always early to check the lightbulbs in the scoreboards and to post the day's schedule. The concession stand is already cooking hotdogs and even though I've already eaten, my stomach growls. After parking, I walk to the field where our game is today and sit down in the dugout to look out over the field. The grass is short, there's fresh chalk running down the first and third baselines, and the scoreboards are lit up. So why am I here when I could be home with Bellamy and Chase, getting ready for the day? There's no reason. I'm about to leave when I catch something out of my peripheral. I turn and find Matty standing at the entrance of the dugout.

"Hey, Matty. You're here early."

She nods and walks toward me, taking the seat next to me on the metal bench. She's dressed in her uniform and has her mitt on her hand. "I was hoping to find you here."

"Sometimes it feels like I live here."

"Not such a bad place to live," she says. "Especially if you're here, because you don't yell."

And there it is, the opening I've been waiting for. The problem is, I'm not sure if I should take it or call Bellamy and ask her to come talk to Matty about her home life.

"My dad yells a lot," she says, as if she's reading my mind.

I hold my hand up, silently asking her to stop. "I'll happily sit here and listen but want to offer Bellamy as an option as well, being that she's a mom and all. I can call her."

Matty shakes her head. "I want to talk to you."

"Okay, I'm all ears."

"I remember the day you first came to Richfield. My dad came home from work yelling. He started throwing things around the house. He didn't think I was home, but I was. I cracked my bedroom door and listened to everything he said. He kept saying to my mom 'your lover is back' and I didn't understand what he meant for the longest time." She pauses and grips the end of the bench and her legs swing back and forth. I don't want to pretend I know what she's going through, but at her age, her biggest worry should be whether her bike has a flat tire or not.

"The day I met you, I remember I went right up to you

and told you that I watch you on TV. That night, my dad took the television out of my room and canceled our cable. I couldn't understand why he wanted to punish me for watching the sport he desperately wants me to play."

"Do you not want to play baseball?" I ask her.

She shakes her head. "I love it, I do. But I'd also like to do other things like basketball and maybe take a dance class. I'm not allowed to, though, it's about baseball in my house all the time."

"I get that. Kids should try a lot of different things while growing up."

She nods and continues to swing her legs. "Do you know that my dad told me to be mean to Chase, Nolan, and the other kids he didn't take on the team? Said a message had to be sent. Whatever that means."

What? Now I'm gripping the bench and can feel the metal digging into my fingers. What kind of man . . . what kind of father says that about other children?

I clear my throat and struggle to maintain composure. "Why would your dad say something like that?"

She shrugs. Of course she doesn't know, and she shouldn't. "I didn't listen to him unless he was around, but the other kids on the team did and were mean to them at school."

"Thank you for being nice to the boys."

"But I wasn't, not if my dad was there. I'd make faces and roll my eyes at them. I knew it hurt them."

"But you're nice to them now and they seem to like you."

Matty nods and wipes at her face. I lean forward a bit and see that she's crying. I don't know what I'm supposed to do. Do I console her? Put my arm around her? Or stay where I am? I chose to stay because I'm her coach but I don't want anything to be misconstrued. Damn, I wish I had texted Bellamy to come down.

"Matty, I don't really know what I'm supposed to do here."

"I'm not done talking," she says, putting me in my place. "I have a lot of thoughts going on and sometimes can't keep them straight."

"Okay, I'll sit and listen. You tell me when you're done."

She says okay and starts talking again. "My dad kept saying 'your lover this and your lover that' and I tried to ask my mom what my dad meant but all she does is tell me to mind my own business . . . and I'm not good at minding my own business. One day, I decided to pretend I was sick so I could stay home and after my parents left for work, I went into the basement and found their yearbooks. Everyone looked so funny back then. But in the box, I found this."

She hands me a piece of yellowed paper. I unfold it carefully, noticing that it's been folded and refolded many times by the holes in the creases. It says, *Dear Hawk*, followed by the lyrics to Heart's *All I Wanna Do Is Make Love to You*. I don't need to read the rest of the page to know what Annie is saying here. I fold the paper back the way it was. I don't want to read into this, but my mind is spinning. If this girl isn't my daughter, life is playing a cruel trick on me.

"Did you ask your mom about this?" I ask, trying to keep my emotions in check.

"No, I looked the video up online though."

"You should talk to your mom, Matty."

"Did you know about me?" Her voice breaks and now I'm fighting my own emotions.

I clear my throat and tap my feet nervously. "If I did, we wouldn't be having this conversation."

"I think you're my dad," she says, breaking my heart.

I nod. "I think I may be too, but we need to sit down with your mom. Only she knows the answer."

Matty and I agree that we'll speak to Annie after the game. Matty doesn't want to wait and I don't either, especially if things aren't going that well at home. I can't imagine how Brett will react once he finds out I know. Right now, my life feels like a bad soap opera and I don't like it. I need structure, consistency. My life needs to be in order, or I feel out of sorts, and right now it's a huge cluster.

By the time Bellamy arrives, she knows everything. I told Matty I had to use the restroom, but I went and called Bellamy instead, filling her in. Her eyes are wide when she approaches me. Without a word, she pulls me into her arms and assures me that everything's going to be okay. But will it? How can I go back to Boston and not worry about Matty's home life? Worry about Bellamy and Chase? What if Brett decides to do something to one or all three of them? If life in Richfield is weighing heavily on my mind, I won't be focused on the game, and that'll hurt my return.

"I don't know what to do."

"We'll figure it out," she says reassuringly but I'm not sure she even believes her own words. "Right now, you have a game to coach and a team of kids waiting for your words of wisdom."

"Right," I say.

"Oh, and a set of bleachers full of your teammates . . . so you might want to win this one." She winks and gives me a kiss before turning toward the stands. My eyes follow her until she's with my friends. It's fun to see them having a good time being spectators at a baseball game, rather than playing in one. I'm sure the wives are enjoying it as well.

In the dugout, the kids are sitting on the bench, waiting for me to give them a pep talk. I'm about to open my mouth when my eyes land on Matty's. She smiles brightly, which tells me she's ready. I crouch down and motion for the kids to gather around me.

"Don't worry about who is in the stands today, okay? They're just normal people, here to watch you play this game. If you utilize the skills we've been working on, you'll succeed. Matty and Alexis will take care of the plate, while the rest of you watch the ball go into your mitt, know how many outs there are and where the play is. Most importantly, talk. Cheer on your pitcher, catcher and other players. Positive reinforcements and happy thoughts. Everyone in." A dozen plus hands are thrust at me and piled on top of one another. "Family, on three. One, two, FAMILY," is yelled loudly. By the time I stand, the kids are out on the field.

"You never make it to three," Owen points out.

"So, their math skills aren't the best," I say, laughing.

Because we're on defense first, I'm stuck behind the fence of the dugout, trying to encourage Matty. I thought about pulling her, but she assured me she was okay. After she throws her last warm-up pitch, I jog out to the mound and place my hand on her shoulder. "You good?"

She nods. "I can do this."

"Okay, you say the word when it becomes too much. No one can ever fault you for not finishing a game. I've been there many times."

The ump yells, "Play ball!" and that's my cue to get off the field. I give Matty a fist bump and jog back to the dugout, but not before I spot Brett standing at the fence. I wish I could say he was on our side, but he's standing with our opponent, showing Matty exactly where his allegiances lie. I look around for Annie and don't see her which pisses me off even more. She should be here no matter what.

The first boy comes up to bat and points toward the outfield. I want to chuckle, but I used to be that cocky. Now, I can't bat for the life of me.

"Let's go Matty!" I clap my hands and wait for her to deliver the first pitch.

"Strike," the ump calls.

I give Alexis the next sign and she sends it to Matty.

Strike two.

Alexis stands, throws the ball back to Matty and looks at

me for the next sign. I give it to her and watch as she squats down, gives the sign to her pitcher and sets up.

Before I go back to my spot, I find Annie, staring at me. She's at the end of our dugout, far away from everyone. I only look at her for a second before turning my attention back to the game. After Matty strikes out the side and I've praised her, I take a few steps toward Annie.

"We need to talk after the game, Annie."

"Don't have anything to say."

I chuckle. "Please don't make this harder than it has to be." I have no idea what that's supposed to mean, but it felt damn good coming out of my mouth and I'm rather proud of myself. Back in the dugout, Javier is calling out the line-up and Owen is heading toward first.

"Matty and Alexis started us off with a bang, let's finish it!" I say to the team. "Who's up first?"

"Me, Coach," Nolan hollers. My nephew gives me a fist bump as he heads to the plate and I take my spot on third. I give Nolan the sign to hit away. I want to see what he can do after spending more time at practice. He steps in, grinds his back foot into the dirt and waits for his pitch. It comes on pitch five and Nolan sends it deep into right field. By the time the right fielder has the ball, Nolan is rounding second. I wave my left arm in windmill fashion and send him home. It's his teammates who tell him to slide.

"Safe!" the ump yells as he fans his arms out.

Nolan jumps up, claps his hands and heads to the dugout where his team is waiting for him. When he glances at me, I clap my hands, letting him know that I'm happy for him.

By the middle of the sixth inning, we're up by five runs and when the last out is called, the kids all run toward each other. Parents are cheering, my teammates are shouting their praise, but my attention is focused solely on Matty. Her head is spinning around, eyes are wild. She's looking for someone and when she spots that someone . . . *me* . . . she grins from ear-to-ear. I don't know if this is a daughter smiling at her father, a player smiling at her coach, or pitcher smiling at another pitcher. Either way, it feels damn good to be on the receiving end of that grin.

THIRTY

BELLAMY

WE'RE on a high from the win yesterday. It wasn't our first win, but this one felt different. Maybe it's because Hawk's teammates were in the stands or maybe it's because Hawk and I finally told each other how we feel. Those are my reasons. For Hawk, I think it's something else, something deeper. His time is coming to an end with the mini team and he's worried about Owen taking over. It's not that Owen can't do it, but Hawk's afraid of how Brett is going to react or what he might do to the team. There's still a divide . . . us versus them. Adults, who grew up together, and were friends through high school are no longer on speaking terms. Of course, it's not uncommon for people to grow apart, but living in a small town with same aged children, you'd think we'd be close or at least friendly. I'm still the outcast, even more so because Chase is now playing. According to the rumors, and believe me there's a string of them, the only reason Chase has a team is because I'm "banging" — their word, not mine — the coach or it's because I went to David Farmer and complained. The only truth to any of this is the part where I went to Farmer, but I didn't complain, I asked how to help my son. As I sit at the table and think about the catty women and their rumors, I wonder what they would think if they found out Hawk and I actually didn't sleep together until after the Mini Renegades formed. The thought makes me laugh. It also makes me ache inside that people are like this.

One by one, children file into the kitchen. After the game and subsequent pizza party, where we all ended up back at the Depot after saying goodbye to Hawk's teammates, Chase asked if he could have a sleepover. I thought he meant one or two of the boys and because he had never asked before, I told him he could. When the endless string of kids showed up, I stood there holding the door and assuring each parent that everything would be fine; I was able to care for twelve ten-year-olds. What a lie that was. Hawk ran out to the store to grab drinks, snacks and something to make for breakfast, while I wrangled the team into the living room for a movie. About half-way through the show, they were bored, and Hawk had the great idea for flashlight tag, except we only had two flashlights so back out he went. By the time he came back, the movie was over, the kids were anxious, and I was beginning to doubt my parenting abilities. Hawk saved the day. He wore his team out, and while they raided the snack cabinet, he and I set up the living room for the sleepover. By the time Hawk and I went to bed, I was exhausted.

"There's pancakes, French toast, eggs and bacon on the counter for breakfast," I tell them, which is set up like a buffet or assembly line. "Grab a plate, pick your food and juice — choice of apple or orange — don't forget your silverware and napkin, and find a seat." Normally, I don't let anyone eat in the living room but this morning is an exception.

Hawk comes into the kitchen freshly showered and smelling like Old Spice, which is my new favorite. I can't even tell you what Greg wore while we were married, but distinctly remember a change when he started cheating. It's odd what your brain remembers, or your heart becomes fond of. He leans down and gives me a kiss before going into the kitchen.

He's talking to his players, but I'm focused on him and his demeanor. Yesterday was earth shattering for him. His suspicions have almost come to fruition when it comes to Matty. More troubling is the fact that she came to Hawk on her own with the feeling that he's her father. It bothers me so much that her parents have been so flippant about hiding their feelings since Hawk's return. Their petty behavior and childish antics have scarred this little girl.

Last night, she came to me while I was in the kitchen preparing snack bags and worked along the side of me. For the longest time she was quiet. I'd ask her questions about school, like what her favorite subject was and whether she liked her teacher. She gave me mostly one-word answers and the only question she asked was when Hawk would be back. Minutes before he returned, she told me Chase was lucky to have me as a mom. I smiled and bit my tongue from asking adult related questions about her parents. Hawk had already told me everything she said earlier about how her parents fight, the things Brett says, and the yelling. Even when Greg and I were at our worst, we never fought in front of Chase. I had the mindset that suffering in silence was best until Chase went to school. Once Hawk returned and the flashlight game concluded, I found the two of them on the patio talking. He later told me she asked him to stay.

When Annie comes to pick Matty up, Hawk is going to demand answers. He tried yesterday after the game but Annie left the park. Avoidance. It's a clear sign that Hawk's feelings are being validated. If he *is* Matty's father, that would definitely explain Brett's hatred of Hawk. From everything Hawk has said, they were close through high school, the best of friends. And while he admits to sleeping with Annie, he insists she was single, and they had been seeing each other all summer. Besides, according to Hawk, Brett had moved on. In his opinion, he didn't violate a bro code or anything like that. As far as he knew, they were finished. It was only after Brett tried to punch him that he realized Annie spilled the beans.

Hawk stands in the kitchen and eats his breakfast. From where I sit, I can see his eyes are focusing on the floor. He's thinking, he's in his own head, likely playing out how the conversation is going to go. I startle when his phone rings, he answers and seems excited to speak to the other person. Still, I watch him closely, looking for any sign that may alert me to how he's feeling. When he hangs up, he sighs.

"That was Wes."

"Your coach, right?"

He nods. "I'm clear."

A lump forms in my throat and I swallow it down. He's leaving. I knew this day was coming but to hear him say he's clear . . . I honestly never wanted it to happen. It's selfish of me to think this way, I know. Still, I smile and try to convey how happy I am. He's returning to work. His job just also happens to be his biggest passion and I would never begrudge him that.

He walks to the table and pulls the chair out next to me. He places one hand on my back and the other pulls my chin toward him. "I know I just asked you the other night about moving and figure you haven't given it much thought," he pauses and inhales.

I place my hand on his cheek. "I've thought about it. It's all I've been doing. I haven't made a decision yet, but I will. I promise." If I only had myself to consider, I'd pack up and follow him, but there's Chase to think about and his opinion is the only one that matters. I want to think he'll be on board, but I don't know.

Before we can dig deeper, the doorbell chimes. None of the kids yell that they'll get it, but they all groan, thinking it's their parents coming to get them. I stand and head toward the front room when I hear Matty's voice ask, "What are you doing here?"

"I'm here to see Hawk." Her mother's response is stiff and cold.

My heart drops. There's such a disconnect between Annie and Matty, my heart breaks for them. I don't even want to imagine what's going on in the Larsen house as of late, especially considering that on top of all of this, Brett's having an affair. I take a deep breath and paste a smile on my face as I round the corner and come face-to-face with Annie.

"Annie, come in. Hawk's in the kitchen." As soon as she steps by me, I close the door and watch Matty retreat into the living room. She sits down next to Alexis and starts talking to her in hushed tones. Alexis puts her arm around her friend and holds her. Life at ten shouldn't be this hard.

When I come back into the kitchen, Hawk is ushering Annie outside. He makes eye contact with me and beckons me forward. "Are you coming?" he asks.

"Shouldn't this be a private conversation between you two?"

He shakes his head. "Not if you're planning to be a part of my life."

I take a small step back and let his words wash over me. Hawk could come away from today with a daughter, one that would become part of our lives if we stay together. I look over my shoulder at Matty, Chase, and the room full of kids and move forward. As soon as I step outside, Hawk slides the patio door closed.

"Mind if I smoke?" Annie asks, showing us a pack of cigarettes.

I shake my head slightly.

She pulls out a cigarette and lights it. She inhales deeply, exhales, and repeats the process a couple of times before turning toward us. "My kid is nosey."

"She's inquisitive," Hawk corrects her.

Annie flicks her ashes onto my concrete patio and chuckles. "You're a lot alike, the two of you. I ask you to leave, you don't listen. I tell her to mind her own business, she doesn't listen."

"I had no reason to leave, Annie. My family is here. My home is here."

"Except you left for years and never came back. Then all these years later you show up here, acting like your shit doesn't stink. Mr. Machoman throwing around his money around and questioning my husband about how he runs his baseball team, making him feel inferior once again."

Hawk says nothing.

"All you had to do was leave, Hawk. But you couldn't. You just had to stay and keep jabbing the knife in Brett's heart."

"Annie, I've done no such thing. I may disagree with him on how he runs the program, but let me remind you, those kids have a place to play because of me. I built those fields. Yeah, I've been absent, but that'll change. What Brett's been doing in town, bullying people — parents and *children* — that's not okay."

"You're trying to ruin him."

"All I did was create a team to give twelve kids who had been cut by Brett an opportunity to play baseball. Nothing more."

"You stole Matty."

He shakes his head. "She came to me asking if I'd take her on my team."

"You don't get it," she says, pointing with her cigarette between her fingers as him as she walks toward us. "You stole her from the get-go."

Hawk takes a deep, shuddering breath. "Are you saying she's mine?"

Annie scoffs but says nothing.

"Why didn't you tell me?"

"Would you have come back? Married me?"

I look at Hawk instantly, waiting for his answer. "No, but I would've taken care of my daughter."

Annie shrugs. "Brett was there. He took care of us. And all I had to do was never bring your name up again."

"All while keeping my daughter from me."

"It was better for her, a full-time dad who loved her, nurtured her. I didn't want her growing up and seeing you on TV, wondering when you were going to come visit her."

"You know that's not how things would've been, Annie. She has family here. Grandparents, aunts and uncles, and cousins. I would've been here for her."

"But not for me?" she asks.

Hawk sighs and I reach for his hand. He's hurt, angry, frustrated and barely hanging on at the seams. This whole thing with Matty has been weighing heavily on him since he started putting the pieces together.

"Annie, for as long as I've known you, you've been in love with Brett. The two of you have the worst kind of relationship. He's verbally abusive, a cheater, and yet you stay. For what, I have no idea. It can't be for Matty because you've had years to pick up the phone and tell me, my parents, or my sisters. Had you knocked on their door, they would've opened it and welcomed you in."

"You say that now."

He shakes his head. "You know it's the truth. My father tried to help your grandfather get out of trouble. You know this. My parents are good people, they wouldn't turn their backs on anyone, especially their own flesh and blood."

"Why's she here?" Annie nods toward me.

Hawk's grip on my hand tightens. "Because she's part of my life and that means she will be part of Matty's as well."

The thought is terrifying and welcoming all in one.

Annie scoffs again. "She slept with my husband! You think I'm going to let her raise my daughter?"

Hawks jaw clenches. "First off, she didn't sleep with Brett and you know this. Second, she's *our* daughter."

"You're not on her birth certificate, Hawk. You have no say."

I see red. I want to ask this woman what her problem is, but before I can find the words, Hawk steps closer to her. I try to hang onto his hand, but it's extremely awkward so I let it go and cross my arms over my chest.

"I know all about the fights, Annie. Matty has told me everything. And if you think I'm going to allow for her to live in fear, or that I'm not going to fight for my rights as her father, you have another think coming."

"Brett will bury you."

This time, it's Hawk who scoffs.

THIRTY-ONE

HAWK

THE TERM, "get your affairs in order" is so broad, I've never really considered what it meant until now. My "affairs" currently consist of saying goodbye to my family and securing travel arrangements for Bellamy, Chase and Matty to come to the All-Star game. Even though I'm not playing, I think the experience will be fun for the kids. I also need to upload my work-out schedule for the BoRe's to my calendar, highlight my projected return with my business manager . . . oh . . . and sue the *shit* out of Annie and Brett Larsen for custody of my daughter.

The latter, which is my focus, is a mountain I'm willing to climb. Is it the smartest thing to do, uprooting Matty from the only family she knows to move her across country and potentially have a nanny take care of her? Is growing up in a dugout the right thing for her? Maybe not, but it's also not the safest situation for her to be living in that house with everything she's told me.

Since the Sunday morning revelation, Matty has been with me twenty-four-seven. Annie didn't even try to take her home once she left here. Bellamy and I thought Annie would come back, because no mother would leave their child behind. Matty tried not to let the hurt show, but I saw her watching out the window, waiting for her mom to pull into the driveway. I called Annie, but each time it went right to voicemail. This woman wasn't even concerned about her daughter's well-being and when Bellamy handed me a journal, I looked at her oddly until she said, "Document everything."

All day, I paced with my phone to my ear, waiting for Annie to pick up. Bellamy gave me Brett's number and it, too, went straight to voicemail. Maybe they were off trying to fix their marriage, which would be great, but not without some sort of notice or word to Matty. They're her parents, they're all she knows.

By the time dinner rolled around, we had made plans with my parents. Bellamy and I spoke earlier, and I told her I need my parents to know about Matty now, because there's a possibility she may need to stay with them if things go south with Annie and Brett. Plus, they're her grandparents and the three of them deserve to know each other. Telling my parents was the hardest thing I've ever had to do. My mom cried and my father, in his typical fashion, sat there in silence. I thought he was going to get up and head outside, but when I saw him shed a tear, I started crying too. My mom held me, assured me everything would be okay. Would it? Would everything be fine once I return to Boston? How am I supposed to build a relationship with my daughter when she's here and I'm there? We've already lost so much time. Time we will never get back. I will never understand how Annie could keep Matty from me. To not even give me a chance to be her father. I would've been home in the off-season, had her with me in Boston during the summer, and would've been her biggest cheerleader for whatever she was doing in her life. But no, I was dismissed before I was even given a chance.

After my parents, I went over to the Larsen's. No one was home. No lights on. No cars in the driveway or in the garage.

Nothing. I couldn't believe it. When I returned to Bellamy's, I found her and Matty wrapped in a blanket, watching what they referred to as "girly movies" and I was told to go hang out with Chase and play video games. He, too, said his mom and Matty were being girly, that they had even done each other's nails earlier and he needed a man break. I was happy to oblige, but my focus was on my phone, waiting for someone . . . *anyone* . . . to call me back.

That night, we had dinner for the first time as a family with my parents and Bellamy's mom. My parents didn't make a big scene but brought Matty gifts and made sure she knew she could call them for anything. I fully expected the night to be awkward, but Chase somehow knew we need some humor. Along with Matty, the two of them kept us laughing with tales from school, the baseball field and the previous night's game of flashlight tag.

As the night wore on, there was still no word from Annie or Brett. I couldn't very well take her back to an empty house, so she stayed at Bellamy's. I took the couch and laid there all night, wondering what my next move was going to be. I had no idea that I'd wake up to the next day, ready to fight for a girl who I barely knew, yet shared my DNA.

The man behind the mahogany desk is a friend of Bellamy's. His father handles a lot of the real estate transactions and this guy is fresh out of law school by about two years. He specializes in divorce cases and while he didn't handle Bellamy's, she's had to consult him a few times when it comes to Gregory.

"How do I file for custody?" I ask the second I sit down, forgetting my manners. Thankfully, he smiles and greets me, making me feel about two feet tall for my rudeness. We finally shake hands and make the necessary introductions.

Peter Smith straightens his tie and pulls himself closer to his desk. "Our first step is a DNA test."

"And how do I get one of those?"

"It's a simple cheek swab, and we can have the results back in twenty-four to forty-eight hours. You and Matty can do it at the clinic."

"Okay, and then what?"

"Then you'd file for visitation, custody and to have her birth certificate modified to show you as her father. We'd get a court date and go in front of a judge. I want to caution you though, with your salary, you're looking at paying a fairly large sum of child support."

"I don't care about the money. How long does it take for all of this to happen?"

"Months. You live in Boston, right?"

"I do. I maintain a full-time residence there. My off-season is dependent on a lot of factors but normally from November until the end of January, I can be here."

Smith jots something down on his yellow legal pad. "And your daughter's biological mother lives in Richfield, right? If we can get her into court, we could have a simple agreement in place before you return to Boston. At least establish your paternity. I can represent you until there's a hearing. Have you spoken to your ex about any of this?"

My palms are sweaty, and I rub my hands down the front of my pants. I want to tell him she's not my ex, but it seems so trivial right now. "I haven't spoken to or seen her since Sunday, and she hasn't come to pick Matty up either. She came to Bellamy's, we talked about why she hid Matty from me. I told her that I was going to fight for my rights, and she told me her husband was going to bury me. I expected her to take Matty with her when she left, but she didn't. She hasn't answered any of my calls and every time I go by their house, no one is home."

"Where's your daughter now?"

"She's at school," I tell him. "On Monday, I went out and bought her some new clothes because everything she owns is at her mother's, and she doesn't have a key to get in and get her stuff."

He makes more notes and excuses himself for a minute. My leg bounces and to pass the seconds, I go through the emails on my phone. Most of them are about my return home, my flight, work out plan, team meetings — my career is going to consume me from the moment I touchdown in Boston while my mind is going to be here in Richfield, wondering and agonizing over my daughter and what's going to happen to her.

"Sorry about that," he says when he comes back into the room. He takes a seat behind his desk and shuffles a few papers. "I asked my secretary to schedule you and Matty for the clinic today. She's also asking for an emergency custody hearing with the judge, but I need some more information before I file."

"Okay."

"Has Matty had any contact with her mother?"

I shake my head. "She doesn't have a cell phone and she hasn't said anything to me or Bellamy whether Annie called the school or anything."

"What kind of house do you live in?"

"I have a two-bedroom apartment."

"School district?"

I shake my head. "I don't know. I know there's a school nearby, I've been there a few times for fundraisers. I can find out."

"Do it, it's important. How long is your contract with your current team?"

"Three years, why?"

He scribbles on his notepad. "I want to show stability."

I adjust in my seat, a bit uncomfortable. "I know I'm not a parent now, but many guys in the league have children and they adjust."

Smith puts his pen down and looks at me. "You're

requesting to uproot a ten-year-old who has only known Rich-field as her home, to move across country, to a place she's never been, with a parent she doesn't know. The more I can throw at the judge, the better."

I nod, understanding everything he's saying. "My parents are willing to take her, if need be."

He writes that down.

"And I've asked Bellamy to move with me — she has a son who is friends with Matty."

"What will you do when you have a road trip?"

I don't know. I stare out the window behind his desk. His office is in a residential neighborhood and there's a man walking his dog outside. No traffic. It's calm and peaceful which is a stark contrast to my life. I take a deep breath and let it out slowly. I don't know what I'm doing or what tomorrow brings. All I know is that I'm Matty's father and I have to do whatever it takes to protect her. "Honestly, I'm hoping Bellamy moves. If she does, she will be home with Matty. If not, I can hire someone or there are team wives she can stay with. I believe I have options. She won't be alone."

"Game nights?"

This one is easy. "Games are family affairs. All the kids come, they have reserved seats or can stay in the owner's luxury box. Knowing Matty, she'll want to be where the action is. I'd make arrangements so she's with the other fami-lies. I have friends who will look out for her. She wouldn't be alone in the ballpark. Plus, there's security."

Again, he makes notes. "If we can get a hearing before you leave, can you be there?"

"Yes, but what would it be for?" I ask, feeling completely stupid.

"It's a stretch, but I think we can show abandonment."

"Okay."

"At the very least, we get in front of a judge and get an order for visitation. In the meantime, spend as much time with Matty, without her missing school, and continue to try and reach her parents. Establishing a connection with her is going to be key."

"We have a connection," I tell him. "She's very smart and is the one who figured out I'm her dad."

He looks up and smiles. "The judge will want to speak with her."

I nod and make a mental note to talk to Bellamy. She knows more about this stuff than I do. "If he needs to, I'll tell her."

Peter Smith and I stand and shake hands. He tells me that he'll be in touch in a few hours and not to worry. Easier said than done. He doesn't have a job to get back to, thousands of people depending on him, a girlfriend he's trying to convince to move, and a daughter to protect. Nope, nothing about my life right now is easy, but I'm hoping this lawyer can at least solve a few of my problems before I head home.

THIRTY-TWO

BELLAMY

HAWK LEANS AGAINST THE WALL, dressed in a navy-blue suit with a red tie. Chase laughed this morning when he saw him, saying Hawk was dressed for game day because those were the Renegade colors. I hadn't thought much about it when we went shopping, but it makes sense Hawk would gravitate toward the colors he's familiar with. Matty stands next to him, dressed similar, although in a dress, with her hair curled and pinned back.

Today is odd. We woke up to the sun shining, birds chirping, and still no word from Annie or Brett. Neither of them has been heard from or seen around town. Brett, not since he coached on Saturday and Annie, not since she left my house on Sunday. Vanished, gone, and done so without a word to their daughter. I'm afraid something has happened to both or either of them. One of the worst things I've ever had to do was pump Matty for information about Brett's family. She told me they live in Florida and I rarely sees them and has no other family in town. We finally went to the police station and filed a missing person's report, which was an ordeal unto itself because they're Matty's legal guardians. Hawk had to prove he had a court date seeking custody before the police would let her come home with us.

Court is where we are today to determine if Hawk can gain custody of Matty, even if only temporarily until the police can find her parents. Today will also tell us if Hawk can take Matty to Boston with him or if she must stay in Richfield. If she stays, I've told Hawk that I'll stay too. We don't want her to feel more abandoned than she already is.

Peter Smith held true to his word, not that I expected anything less of him. He's been a real champion for me when it's come to forcing Greg to act like a parent. He promised Hawk a quick turnaround on his and Matty's DNA test and within twenty-four hours, he had confirmation that he was a father. I wanted to give him a party, yell "Congratulations, it's a girl!" but the timing and the situation isn't right. It's not often you see a man cry, but he did. He hugged Matty tightly and they cried together. I have to say, for being ten, she's a strong young lady, especially when people are around. At night, she lays next to me and asks me questions about her mom — things I can't answer — because I don't get it. There isn't a single person or reason that would force me to leave Chase behind. He's my life, and I can already see a similar shift in Hawk — Matty is now his.

Matty mimics the way Hawk stands. They look at each other, smile and start talking. As slyly as I can, I snap a picture, something for me to look back on in the next couple of days when I'm missing him and worried about her. My motherly instinct has kicked in where she's concerned. She's going to need another female she can trust, and someone to count on. With Hawk's schedule, she's going to be alone or with strangers unless I move. It's not that I don't think Hawk can take care of her, I know he can. Because of him, I've seen a difference in Chase. My once shy, reserved son, is now out-going, happy and tells crude boy jokes at the table to embarrass me. The worst part is, I laugh, so I can't really scold him, but I do give him a stern look. When Hawk first asked me to move with him, there wasn't any pressure. Stay until the end of summer, once Chase finished baseball, and consider it. Now, I feel this weight on my shoulders even though he's told me to make the best decision for myself. I've asked Chase, who wants to move, and then Greg . . . he agreed, saying he's going to do what's best for our son. I think that was a veiled threat, but who knows with him.

Hawk looks up and catches me taking pictures of him and Matty. He smiles, looks at Matty and points to the camera. They move closer to each other and he puts his arm around her. It's uncanny how much they look alike, minus their hair color.

"Did you get a good one?" he asks as he pushes off the wall and comes toward me with Matty following. I hold my phone out and he swipes through, pressing the heart icon on the ones he likes. He leans down and kisses me. "Thank you," he whispers against my lips.

"You're welcome." Although, I'm not sure exactly what he's thanking me for. I took the pictures for myself, to give me something to look at later when they're gone.

Hawk's name is called, and we turn and find his parents and sisters scurrying down the hallway. "Are we late?" his mom asks.

"No, we're still waiting for our names to be called." He kisses his mom on the cheek and hugs his sisters and father. One of us is leaving the courtroom today as temporary guardian. I hope beyond hope, it's Hawk. If not, his parents or myself. We'll all step up to keep her out of foster care.

Owen is the next to arrive. He's another character witness on behalf of Hawk, and probably the best one out of all us. We're biased, Owen isn't. He has nothing to gain or lose in this matter. When I suggested him, Hawk scoffed, saying

Owen doesn't know him. I countered with, "He does. He's seen you coach for the past few months. He knows your character around children better than anyone else right now." Peter agreed and put him down as a character witness.

Peter steps out of the courtroom and joins our growing crowd. "Are we ready?"

I look at everyone, trying to decipher the feelings of our group. It's Matty that I pay the most attention to. She's quiet, somber and her eyes are downcast. I go to her and clasp her hand in mine. She says nothing as she looks at me, and that's okay. I have a good feeling I know what she's thinking right now, "Where's my mom?" Over this past week, I've waited for a sighting, a phone call from Annie, Brett or the police. Anyone, who could tell us something.

Peter tells us it's time and we follow him into the courtroom. Hawk, Matty and I are last to enter. Matty and I take a seat in the front row while Hawk follows Pete through the swinging half door. The courthouse and subsequent courtrooms are old, dating back into the twenties or thirties. Truth be told, we don't have a lot of crime here, mostly speeding tickets and the occasional rancher squabble. Richfield and its surrounding towns keep a laid-back lifestyle, and the only reason we come to the courthouse is to file documents, get a marriage license or file for divorce.

The judge enters the courtroom, we stand and then sit once we're instructed to do so. Peter told us earlier the judge is Jan Mash. He assured us this is a good thing, saying she's fair and a single mom. How he knew about her life outside the courtroom is a mystery, but if his knowledge works in Hawk's favor, I'll take it. Jan sits behind her massive desk and looks out over the galley. I'm curious as to what she sees. Does she see a man desperately trying to protect a little girl who he just found out was his daughter or does she see the state of Montana and a social worker trying to do what they think is right for a girl they know nothing about. The social worker came to my house, sat with Matty for a half-hour and left. How someone can determine a child's fate after such little time is beyond me.

"It seems we have a temporary guardianship on the table. Mr. Smith, you're up."

Peter stands and gives a detailed summation of Hawk, Matty, their lives and the situation they're in. He's eloquent, poised and passionate. The whole time he's speaking, Matty's hand is clutching mine. She knows her fate lies within his words and the judge's decision. When Peter finishes, Judge Mash instructs the state to present their case.

The lawyer for the state, Ms. Harold, stands and speaks. She focuses on how Hawk and Matty met only months ago, how his schedule isn't conducive to raising a child, how she'd be shuttled from sitter to sitter, and kept out late on school nights due to his games. Each word she says is a hole in Hawk's case. She's painting him as an absentee father, when he hasn't even had a chance to prove otherwise. When she sits down, she looks smug, almost as if she knows she's succeeded in putting a child into foster care and that's a good thing.

"I see that the young woman in question is in the courtroom?"

Peter stands and says, "Yes, your honor."

"Please have her come forward."

I let go of Matty's hand and whisper for her to go sit by the judge. We talked about this last night and went over some of the questions that Peter thought the judge might ask. Matty stands tall, looks at her dad as she walks to the front of the courtroom and takes a seat.

"How are you today, Mattingly?" The judge asks.

"I'm good," she says.

"Do you like to be called Mattingly or Matty?"

"Matty, please," she replies softly.

"Okay. I know this is difficult. You're going through a lot of stuff right now, but can you tell me why you want to live with Hawk?"

She nods and turns her head in Hawk's direction. "He's my dad," she states proudly.

"You've only known him for a short period of time."

"I know." Her voice is quiet. "But his job is in Boston and if he leaves without me, how will I get to know him better?" She looks at Judge Mash for an answer. There isn't one given. "Hawk has taught me so much since I met him. We're a family with Bellamy and Chase."

Now I have tears falling from my eyes.

"When my mom left me at Bellamy's, they could've sent me away but they didn't. They made it seem like I've always been there. Chase and I have chores, a bedtime, they sit with us while we do our homework, and then my dad takes us to baseball practice."

"Are you prepared to move away from your friends?"

She nods.

"Okay, you can step down." Judge Mash watches and Matty rushes back to my side. I pull her close and kiss the top of her head. "Mr. Sinclair, the State of Montana has concerns that your daughter will be shuffled back and forth, that you can't create a stable environment for her."

I don't know what possesses me, but I stand up and blurt out, "My son and I are also moving to Boston, Your Honor. I'll be taking care of Matty while Mr. Sinclair travels for his games."

Hawk turns and looks at me while the judge slams her gavel down. I slink back in my chair, completely aware that I may have ruined any chance he has at gaining custody.

"Your Honor," Peters says as he stands. "It's just come to my attention that Bellamy Patrick is intending to relocate to Boston as well. In your paperwork, she is also listed as a potential temporary guardian in this case, in the event custody isn't awarded to Mr. Sinclair."

"I do not like outbursts in my courtroom, Mr. Smith."

"I apologize. Emotions are high right now."

As she's looking over the papers, her side door opens and the police chief walks in. My heartbeat increases as he leans down and says something in her ear. "Mr. Smith, Mr. Sinclair, and Ms. Harold, in my chambers, now." Hawk and I exchange looks as he follows Peter into the other room.

"What's going on?" Matty asks.

I shake my head slowly. "I don't know, sweetie. Your dad will tell us when he comes back."

Hawk's family is on edge, as am I. We're watching the door, waiting for it to open, and when it finally does, Hawk's face is white. Peter and the attorney for the State, Mr. Harold, are expressionless.

Judge Mash sits back down and says, "I have come to the decision, in light of new information, that it is in the best interest of the child to remain in the temporary custody of her biological father, Hawk Sinclair, for a period of one year after which we will reconvene to determine permanent custody of the minor child. The State of Montana will work with the State of Massachusetts to set up a home study and to periodically check on the minor child. Mr. Sinclair, you are free to take your daughter out of state, but if you need to leave the country, you'll need permission from this court." She slams her gavel down, stands and exits.

I'm stunned, although I shouldn't be. Hawk is the better choice, especially over foster care, but I want to know what the hell just happened. Matty leaves my side and rushes to Hawk. He picks her up and twirls her around before setting her back down. They hold hands as they walk toward us, but he still says nothing except that it feels good to win.

It's later that night, when we're alone in the living room

and the kids are fast asleep that he starts talking. "Did you mean it?"

"I did. Chase and I want to be in Boston with you. We'll leave after he finishes the season. I think it's important for him to stay. Matty can stay as well."

He shakes his head. "I'm taking her with me."

"Okay."

Hawk goes quiet for a minute before turning to look at me. "They found Annie and Brett."

"Where?"

"In Bozeman, off the slide of a cliff. Preliminary reports show Annie was intoxicated. She was driving and neither were wearing a seatbelt. Their bodies were found on Monday, but the car was registered to some rental company and neither of them had any identification on them. Once we filed the missing person's report, the medical examiner got the alert and called it in." He pauses and looks away from me for a few seconds before continuing. "I have to tell Matty. I'm not sure how, but in the morning, we're going over to her house to get her things. The police are meeting us there, so I have to talk to her beforehand. She's ten and has to make a decision on where to put her parents' belongings."

"No, she doesn't," I say. "We'll put them in storage until she's ready. No child should have to make this type of decision. I'll organize everything, hire packers, and you focus on getting back to Boston and getting Matty acclimated. It may be a good idea to get her started in some type of therapy or support group because I think she's going to need to talk to someone who isn't us."

"You'd do that for her?"

I nod and pull him close. "Without a doubt. We're going to be a family. It's what family does for one another."

"You know what this means, right?"

I look at him oddly. "No . . . "

"Well, first it means the three of you need shirts with my

name on the back, and second, it means that I'm going to have to ask Chase if I can marry his mom."

"Hawk . . . " My breath catches.

He smiles and brings my hand to his lips to kiss it. "Once things slow down and we're in a routine that works for us, I'm going to ask you to marry me. You can count on it."

Have you recovered from the thrilling All-Star game? We certainly haven't because our Renegades are hot, hot, hot and about to get hotter with the return of Hawk Sinclair. We first reported he would only be out until the All-Star break, but he had a minor set-back and recovery took a bit longer. However, we're happy to say, actually scream, HE'S BACK!!! Now before you get all excited about the starting rotation, Sinclair is going to do some relief work first before sliding back into his starting spot.

Right now, our Renegades are dropping bats at the plate and running those bases. We're well above 500 and sitting comfy in second place, behind those Astros. With the return of Sinclair, we have a full roster and they're all healthy!

GOSSIP WIRE

It was a nice surprise to hear about Travis Kidd, Ethan Davenport, Branch Singleton, Kayden Cross, Cooper Bailey, and their respective families flying out to support Sinclair and his Little League team. It's rumored that the autograph session lasted four hours and raised over $3000 for the Sinclair Fields.

But . . . that's not what you want to hear!

The biggest surprise of all and one we've been kept in the dark about is . . . Daisy Davenport is pregnant!

Now, we're not talking a little pregnant. From what witnesses are saying, she's ready to pop any day now. Our question here is, how did we not know?

One of our reporters ran into Shea, famed niece of our third basemen, and asked for her thoughts. Here's what she had to say, "Oh, I think it's great, but I'm not babysitting."

So, there you have it. New Renegades will be here soon thanks to Saylor Blackwell-Kidd and Daisy Davenport.

And you know, as I write this . . . we haven't seen Hadley Carter around lately either. Hmm . . . makes you wonder why she's hiding as well.

———————————————

THIRTY-THREE

HAWK

BEHIND MY BLACKOUT CURTAINS, I know the sun is up and blazing over the city. The heatwave blanketing New England has been relentless the past few days, with temperatures hovering close to a hundred and the more inland you are, the hotter it is. I can hear the television and from what I can gather, it's a talk show, likely Sports Center or something similar. Chances are, Matty isn't even watching whatever is airing. She's mostly likely out on the balcony, with the sliding glass door open and letting the air conditioner cool off my neighborhood, reading last night's game recap or watching the traffic down below.

Boston is a cultural shock for her. Each day, it's a new adventure. Places and activities I've taken for granted, like twenty-four hour grocery stores, food delivery, and the harbor, are all new and fun things to explore. If we're not at the ballpark, we're walking, taking the train or driving somewhere she's found on the map. Every place we go is a "must see" and the urgency to get there is like no other.

Not gonna lie, being an instant father is hard, especially in our situation. My parentage started off with telling her that her parents passed away, followed by having her pack her stuff because we had a flight to catch, and then welcoming her to her new home, all in one day. The timing couldn't have been worse. I'm grateful for my friends more than ever through all of this. Ethan's niece, Shea, has been visiting and she's close in age to Matty. At Lowery Stadium, Shea wasted no time showing Matty where everything is, who they can sweet talk for free merchandise, and who to stay away from. Apparently, there's a guard who Shea doesn't like and insists on tormenting him whenever she's in town. Saylor has also stepped in to help, despite being pregnant. She's taken Matty shopping, to get her haircut and helped her pick out a comforter for her bedroom. Matty asked about painting, but I told her we weren't staying here once Bellamy and Chase arrived, which happens to be today. The Mini Renegades finished their season and while they didn't make the playoffs, not that we expected them to, it came down to a last inning base hit and the winning run scored. Still, I'm so proud of that team.

Of course, the thought of moving to a new place gave Matty something to do and once I gave her permission to log into the computer, she started house hunting and sending links to Bellamy to set up appointments. We're currently scheduled to see an enormous house in Marblehead. It's eight bedrooms, and nine and half baths. I asked Matty why we need something so big when it's only the four of us and she said, "Because it has a pool and is on the ocean." I'm still trying to figure out why we she thinks we need something so big, but I'm appeasing her, and we'll drive the hour plus away from the city to look at it. Truth is, we really don't need something huge. A five or six bedroom house will work. It gives us space to expand our family if we decide, there would be space for Bellamy to have an office if she chooses to go back to work, and it won't be so large that we'll feel lost or separated.

Call me crazy, but I want to hear the kids screaming and making noise. I want our home to feel alive and vibrant. I don't want something where the four of us can retreat into our own corner of the house and forget about each other.

My body screams that it's time to get up. I stretch, rotate my shoulder and pop my hips before climbing out of bed and slipping into the silky pajama pants Bellamy insisted I buy. She said it's one thing for Chase to see me in my boxers, but a whole other thing for Matty to see me in them. After I use the bathroom and wash the sleep away from my eyes, I make my way to the living room where everything I assumed earlier is taking place.

"Hey," I say as I stand with one hand on the sliding glass door casing and the other on the wall.

"Morning, Hawk."

Most of the time, I'm Hawk and I'm okay with it. I get why she does it and I plan to never ask her to change. Her entire life she's known Brett as her dad, and as much as it pains me, it is what it is. When we're in public though, she calls me dad or refers to me as such, and I cherish those moments.

"What did I say about leaving this door open with the air conditioner on?" I hate my tone the second the words come out of my mouth, but I have to be strict sometimes according to the therapist we're seeing. Matty and I go together every other week, for nothing more than finding an even ground to co-exist on, and she goes alone, once a week to talk about her loss, the transition of moving, and living with someone who could be considered a complete stranger.

"You said to keep it shut, but I have a good reason."

"Which is?"

"I wanted to make sure I heard the doorbell in case Bellamy arrived."

I laugh and shake my head. "Nice try, kid. You know

we're picking them up from the airport. Keep the door shut, okay?"

She nods and follows me into the house, thankfully sliding the door shut behind her.

"Are you hungry?" I ask as I look into the refrigerator. Like most of the guys on the team, I have a housekeeper who also does my shopping. Sometimes, she'll even cook dinner and leave it for us to heat up when we get home from a game.

"No, I had toast."

"Okay." I pull out the carton of eggs, the box of pre-cooked bacon and the jug of orange juice. "What time is our appointment?"

"At three. Bellamy and Chase arrive in an hour and half. You better get ready."

"We live fifteen minutes from the airport. We'll leave right before the plane touches down." I pull the bacon out of the box and set one of the sleeves in the microwave, and then crack my eggs over the frying pan.

"Won't we be late?"

"No, by the time they get off the plane and make their way through the airport to get their luggage, we'll be there."

"Is your sign ready?" She asks. A few nights ago, Matty and I had arts and crafts night after we had watched one too many welcome home videos on the internet. It was her idea to make signs. One for Bellamy and one for Chase so they both felt welcomed. Matty made Chase's.

"Yes, is yours?" I counter.

She nods and comes to where I'm standing. "Can I make your eggs?"

"Sure." I'm not the best cook so trying to teach her how to cook is a challenge. Still, she wants to learn so I'm educating her on everything she asks. Of course, once my breakfast is ready, she declares she's hungry and ends up taking my plate. "Next time, I'm making extra."

"Technically, I made this." Touché, kid.

After breakfast, I head into the shower. I opt not to shave, letting the two-day growth stay, at least until game day which is two days away. After I dress, I make my way into Matty's room. There are baseball posters everywhere and a new twin bed on the other side of her room. Bellamy and I discussed the sleeping arrangements and while not ideal, Chase and Matty will share until we've purchased a house which is our top priority. I suspect by the end of next week, we'll have a place to call home and if we don't, a new apartment it is.

"Hey, you still okay with sharing a room with Chase?" I lean against the doorjamb, waiting for her to reply.

"Yeah, it'll be fun."

"If you say so." I remember sharing with my sister while my parents renovated our upstairs and I hated every minute of it. "You ready?"

She nods, climbs off her bed and follows me out and to the elevators. Today must be our lucky day; normally we run into our neighbors who like to talk about everything and anything. We ride down to the basement and Matty runs to my SUV. She yells, "shotgun" even though she's the only one riding in the car. I can thank Travis for teaching her this.

Like I told her, we make it to the airport in fifteen minutes, thanks to my ability to weave in and out traffic. I will never understand why someone goes under the speed limit in the fast lane and then has the nerve to flip you off when you speed past after tailgating them a mile.

Matty and I hold hands as we walk through the airport. At first, I thought this was strange, a ten-year-old wanting to hold my hand, but then I realized it's not strange, it's life. I'm her protector and she's in a big scary city. That doesn't preclude her from running off when we get into Macy's or some other department store. Right now, I seem to be losing more battles than winning in this parent game.

We stand in baggage claim at the end of the escalator with our signs poised, waiting for the rest of our family.

People ooh and ahh as they walk by and a few even proposition us. Every few seconds Matty looks at mine and giggles. I do the same for hers. We were creative with our jars of glitter and glue, highlights and markers. I'm sure my housekeeper didn't think so because she had to scrape tiny shards plastic off the island when we were done.

I see Chase before Bellamy and when she comes into view, it hits me how much I've missed her. I don't care that I've only known her since late spring, I'm madly in love with her. When she spots me, I hold my sign up high so she can see it as she rides down the escalator. Her hand covers her mouth and nods. As soon as she reaches the bottom, she's in a dead sprint to get to me. With the sign in one hand, I catch her as flings herself toward me and bury my face in her shoulder.

"I've missed you so much," I tell her. Video chats and speaking on the phone every day did nothing but make me fall more and more in love with her. I set her down and as I do, I drop down to one knee and pull the black velvet box from my pocket.

"Bellamy Patrick will do me and our children the honor of becoming my wife?"

"If she doesn't, I will," someone says as they walk by.

Bellamy laughs through the tears streaming down her face. "Yes, I'd be so honored to be your wife" she says. Everyone around us cheers as I stand and kiss her.

"Thank you," I whisper against her lips.

"I can't believe you did this at the airport."

"I know, but I told you I was going to do it when it felt right."

"It does feel right, doesn't it?"

"It does." We kiss again before she goes to Matty and I go to Chase. Chase and I grab a trolley and he shows me the many bags they came with. The rest of their belongings will arrive in a few weeks from the moving company.

The women in my life catch up to us as Chase and I load

the last bag. Matty is filling Bellamy in on everything that Boston has to offer, even though they speak on the phone daily. After we have the SUV loaded, I ask them what the first thing they want to do as a family is.

"Go home," all three say in unison.

"Home it is."

EPILOGUE
HAWK

THE MUSIC IS loud as I walk back to the mound. I glance at the scoreboard, even though I know we're up three to zero, there are two outs and the bases are loaded. Three isn't a cushion, not in baseball, not when I'm about to face one of the best players of this generation . . . and definitely not when one hit could be a game changer. I survey the outfield, looking at each one of my teammates. They've done their job and I've done mine until now. The first two outs were easy, a blooper right to Davenport and the second, a strike out, giving me nine for the day. Then everything went to shit. A base hit, a walk, followed by another. I thought after I walked the first guy and then the second, Wilson would pull me. He came out to the mound and asked me about my shoulder. "It feels good," I tell him, which isn't a lie. I've learned my lesson when it comes to my body and injuries. "Can you finish this game?" I thought about his words and nodded. There's a lot on the line, mostly a spot in the history books for pitching a shut-out. I've done it before, but it won't make this one any less special. In fact, this one would be a milestone, especially after surgery and rehab.

I continue to look at the field, eyeing each Angel standing

on their respective bases in their gray travel uniforms, us in our whites. The guy coming out of the dugout, the one destined to change the outcome of this game, is none other than Mike Trout. He is likely the American League MVP, although there's a few guys on my team who are giving him a run for his money. I turn in time to watch him saunter to the plate, wondering if he's thinking the same thing I am — *home run*. I would if I were him. He has three guys waiting to come home, eager to step across that dusty diamond and have four runs added to the ancient scoreboard. All during my rehab, I lamented about the pressure I felt to return, to be with my team, but none of it compares to what I feel now. The weight on my shoulders is heavy . . . agonizing. One wrong pitch from me and this game is over. I need to keep my pitch high and fast, nothing down and inside. That's his sweet spot.

As soon as Trout steps up to the plate, the music dies and the only noise is the crowd. The fans are on their feet, their rally caps on. Some chant my name, and others pick up on it. After I made my return, Matty asked me how I felt when people chanted my name and I told her I tuned them out and that sometimes I didn't even hear the fans. She told me I should listen sometimes.

I'm listening now and the melody of their voice is soothing yet energizing at the same time. My skin buzzes with anticipation of what's to come. They call me Hawk instead of Sinclair, and when thousands of people say my name all at once, it sounds like a bird is soaring overhead.

Before I place my foot on the rubber, I look to where my family sits. Bellamy, Chase and my daughter Matty, all behind the dugout, all staring at me intently. It's Matty I seek out the most though. While we waited for Bellamy and Chase to arrive, she came to practice with me. She's become my biggest cheerleader when I've vowed to become hers, and now I look to her for some sort of signal that I can do this. Her hands cup the sides of her mouth and I imagine she's yelling, "You got this, Dad!" Maybe I do and maybe I don't, but I'm sure as hell going to try.

I step onto the rubber and Trout steps up the plate while Michael Cashman crouches down. His head angles toward Trout's feet and his hand goes between his thighs to give me the sign. High, outside, curve. I nod, put my hand and the ball inside my glove, shield it as best as I can from the base runners and adjust my fingers. My world goes quiet as I block everyone and everything out. It's only Cashman and me, playing catch. I cock back and deliver the pitch, loving the way my arm feels as I follow through.

The umpire rises slightly from his crouched stance, raises his right hand, turning it into a fist as he punches the air and yells out, "Hike," or some other guttural sound that's meant to sound like strike. Back in high school, I took an umpire class so I could better understand the game and was taught to never say "strike" because it took too long to say.

Cashman tosses the ball back to me and everything is repeated. Trout steps in, points his bat toward me or the wall behind me, Cashman squats and the umpire crouches. I block everything out and play catch with my teammate. The call is for a slider. I go through the motions, sending the pitch hurling toward the plate. Trout takes a step and his bat projects forward. The crack is loud, and the ballpark is suddenly the quietest I've ever heard it. I don't watch the ball; I keep my eyes on Trout. He's hopping up and down, with a big smile on his face.

Perfect. Game over.

Out of my peripheral, I see the guy on third trot home, and I stand there, waiting for Cashman to throw me a new ball . . . except it doesn't come. He does instead. He bulrushes toward the mound and I brace myself. The next thing I know, I'm up in the air and Cashman has his arms braced under my ass. Easton Bennett, Kayden Cross, Ethan Davenport and Bryce Mackenzie are jumping up and down, yelling congratulations and calling me a motherfucker. Through all the jostling, I spot Trout, heading to the dugout. He throws his helmet and stomps down the steps, and that's when it hits me. It was an out, caught by whom, I don't know.

"Who caught the fucking ball?" I scream.

"I did," Travis Kidd says as he throws the white and red seamed rock at me. "You're welcome!" he yells.

Cashman finally sets me down and I go over to Travis and hug him. It's a long one, filled with emotion. "Thanks, man."

"Just doing my job," he replies. His job or not, he's cemented my return with this victory.

After I've had my press conference and showered, I step out into the hallway to find my family standing there. Matty and Chase rush to me, each taking a side to hug, while Bellamy steps to my middle and gives me a kiss.

"You had us worried."

"Nah," I say, as if pitching a shut-out is something I do often.

She laughs. "Nice game, Hawk."

"Just doing my job."

"Come on," she says. "There's someplace we have to be." She winks and I squat down so Matty can climb onto my back. I hurt, my body is sore, but she likes to be carried out like this.

By the time we're to the players' parking garage, most of the guys are gone. Normally, we'd hit a bar or plan to grab dinner somewhere, but today, we're doing things a bit differently. There's a party we must get to.

My family piles in and I slide into the driver's seat of my SUV. With its heavily tinted windows, none of the fans waiting outside know who we are, that is, until Chase rolls down his window and starts waving at everyone, causing my name to be chanted once again.

"Hear that, Dad?" Matty asks. "They love you."

And I love you I want to say, but instead I look at her in my rearview and wink. The drive over to the Davenport's newly acquired home in Beverly takes a little over an hour. In the backseat, the kids are giving Bellamy and me a recap of the game, right down to the last inning, as if I'd ever forget the stress I put myself under. I'm thankful for their enthusiasm though.

I pull along the curb of the residential neighborhood of the who's who in New England sports. When Ethan gave us the run-down of who would be at his party, he had everyone from the NFL, MLS, NBA, NHL and of course MLB, on his list.

"Hey, look," Bellamy says as she stands next to the car. "That house is for sale."

I nod and dread what's coming next. We've been searching for a house, but since the kids have already started school, I've suggested we wait until summer. However she wants to move and get settled before our wedding. I can't say that I blame her.

"Get the number and we'll call tomorrow," I tell her. She walks over and pulls the listing sheet from the box. Honestly, I wouldn't mind living near a teammate, it would make carpooling so much easier.

The four of us walk to the front door, which is open, and enter. The house is decorated in pink — streamers, balloons and a banner saying, "Welcome Baby Girl Davenport."

"Everyone's out back," someone tells us and that's where we head with gift in hand. Sure enough, the backyard is full of adults and children. Laughter rings out, the sound of splashing from the pool echoes and the kids ask if they can change into their swimsuits to go swim. We tell them yes and watch as they run off, Matty seeking Shea out immediately.

It's easy to spot Ethan and Daisy, they're in the corner, under the shade tree. Daisy is beaming as she holds her daughter and Ethan is hovering over the women in his life.

"Congratulations," I say to Daisy as I lean down and kiss

her cheek. The newest Davenport arrived three days ago, early in the morning and on game day, Ethan sent us all a message saying she was in labor and that we'd have to do without him for our game. When he showed up, we wanted to know what the hell he was doing there. "We have a game," he said. Every one of us yelled until he showed us a picture of Daisy holding their daughter. We tried to encourage him to go back to the hospital, but he assured us this was where Daisy wanted him, saying his mom, sister and Shea were with his wife and newborn daughter. That night, he hit a homerun.

Bellamy coos and gushes over the baby and looks at me. I nod, letting her know that if she wants one, I'll happily do my best to make it happen. We've discussed it and know time is not on our side, so it needs to happen sooner rather than later.

Daisy excuses herself and Ethan follows. They stand in their backyard together as a family, and Ethan calls for everyone's attention.

"We'd like to introduce you to, Posey Davenport," Ethan says as he looks down at his daughter.

Everyone around us claps. I put my arm around Bellamy and ask her, "Do you want one of those again?" even though I know she does.

"Yeah," she says. "We'll have our own in about seven months."

My mouth drops open, almost as if I can't believe her. She takes my hand and places it on her stomach. Her eyes glisten as she says, "We're going to have a baby."

As much as I want to announce it to everyone, I can't. It's Ethan and Daisy's moment, and ours will come later. I lean down and kiss Bellamy. "I love you."

"I love you," she says, cupping my cheek.

There's so much more to say, but this isn't the time nor the place. When we get home and we're in bed, I'm going to thank her for taking a chance on me and jumping feet first into my hectic life. Until then, I say to her, "I guess I better get you down the aisle, huh?"

"Something like that."

Yeah, definitely something like that.

If someone would've asked me at the beginning of the season how I saw my year going, I would've simply said I saw it heading toward the playoffs. Never in a million years would I have guessed I'd have surgery, miss half my season, meet the woman of my dreams, and become a father all in a matter of months. Yet, here I am, at the prime of my life and career with two ten-year-olds, a fiancée who has been my rock and is growing the child we created inside of her, and I'm happier than I ever thought I could be.

Of course, if the Renegades could win the pennant . . .

Yeah, that's for a whole other story.

BOSTON RENEGADES

As the season comes to an end, we sadly say goodbye for another year. Be safe, good people of Boston, and be sure to say hello to the guys when you see them out and about. They love hearing from their fans.

We will, of course, update you when we have news of contract extensions and off-season trades and acquisitions.

Until then . . .

GOSSIP WIRE

We're excited to announce that Saylor Blackwell-Kidd has delivered a healthy baby boy. No word on his name yet, but the happy father of two had this to say, "Saylor and I are over the moon with the arrival of our son. My wife and son are happily resting at home, while my daughter insists on pancake delivery for her new brother."

Not to be the only baby making the news, Posey Davenport made her first public appearance at the BoRe's last home game, instantly stealing the show on the JumboTron.

And for those who don't believe in insta-love, Hawk is a testament to the fact it exists. He will wed his fiancée in November. These two love birds are proof that you don't need years to make a decision about love. We wish them many years of happiness.

***

Want to talk about books, movies, and have meme wars? Join us on Facebook in The Beaumont Daily
Or on Goodreads in Heidi's Hangout

ABOUT HEIDI MCLAUGHLIN

Heidi McLaughlin is a New York Times, Wall Street Journal, and USA Today Bestselling author of The Beaumont Series, The Boys of Summer, and The Archers.

Originally, from the Pacific Northwest, she now lives in picturesque Vermont, with her husband, two daughters, and their three dogs.

In 2012, Heidi turned her passion for reading into a full-fledged literary career, writing over twenty novels, including the acclaimed Forever My Girl.

When writing isn't occupying her time, you can find her sitting courtside at either of her daughters' basketball games.

Heidi's first novel, Forever My Girl, has been adapted into a motion picture with LD Entertainment and Roadside Attractions, starring Alex Roe and Jessica Rothe, and opened in theaters on January 19, 2018.

Don't miss more books by Heidi McLaughlin! Sign up for her news-letter, or join the fun in her fan group!

Connect with Heidi!
www.heidimclaughlin.com

ALSO BY HEIDI MCLAUGHLIN

THE BEAUMONT SERIES

Forever My Girl – Beaumont Series #1

My Everything – Beaumont Series #1.5

My Unexpected Forever – Beaumont Series #2

Finding My Forever – Beaumont Series #3

Finding My Way – Beaumont Series #4

12 Days of Forever – Beaumont Series #4.5

My Kind of Forever – Beaumont Series #5

Forever Our Boys - Beaumont Series #5.5

The Beaumont Boxed Set - #1

THE BEAUMONT SERIES: NEXT GENERATION

Holding Onto Forever

My Unexpected Love

Chasing My Forever

Peyton & Noah

Fighting For Our Forever

CAPE HARBOR SERIES

After All - March, 2o2o

THE ARCHER BROTHERS

Here with Me

Choose Me

Save Me